I0734816

CALLING

BOOK TWO of *THE STARLIGHT CHRONICLES*

C. S. Johnson

THE STARLIGHT CHRONICLES

As always, this is for Sam.

But also this is for a new friend, Satori, who helped me see this with a renewed vision.

To Get *Awakening* (A Special Christmas Episode of The *Starlight Chronicles*) as a bonus for picking up this book,

Download It At:
https://www.csjohnson.me/awakening

THE STARLIGHT CHRONICLES

☼1☼

Awkward Games

"He's more awkward than a vegetarian in a meat factory!"

"He's more awkward than a democrat lowering taxes!"

"He's more awkward than a lactose-intolerant ice cream driver!"

"He's more awkward than a sumo wrestler trying to ice skate!"

"He's more awkward than Tim Ryder trying out for the football team!"

I put my fingers to my chin thoughtfully, striving to look pensive. As I pretended to think over my decision, my friends began arguing about whose answer was the best.

"Come on, Dinger, mine's perfect!"

"No way, Poncey! Can you just imagine how hard it would be to be allergic to what you're selling?"

"Jason, being lactose-intolerant isn't the same as being allergic. Gosh, you are just dumb sometimes … "

Finally I spoke up. (The moment of truth …) "All right, guys. Simon, sadly, has a valid point. I'm going to go with his answer."

As the rest of my friends let out the last of their chuckles and/or groans, I smirked in satisfy action. "Good one, Simon!" I reached out a fist bump, and my humble sap of a friend vied for it like Olympic gold. "It's a great description for Apollo City's new mayor."

It was more than appropriate, too. Mayor Stefano Mills had taken office only a few days before and already he'd been hailed as a "Politician's Politician" by already going back on his campaign promises and seeking a lot of bipartisan agreements—or "settlements," depending on which news network I happened to be overhearing.

I felt sorry for Mayor Mills more than anything else, to be honest. Our last mayor, under increasing pressure, had resigned and no one really wanted to take his place. The town council had instated Mills after a lengthy debate followed by a quick election.

"I knew you'd like mine, Dinger," Simon grinned knowingly.

"Yeah, you probably spent all week thinking of it," my sidekick, Evan von Ponce (more affectionately known as "Poncey" to us), spoke up, the teasing evident in his tone.

"Come on, mine was much better," my friend Drew McGill harped. "Can't you just see a sumo wrestler slapping the ice over and over … "

Aw. Jealousy can be so cute.

I sighed happily to myself. "Come on guys, let's start a new round. Simon's the judge this time."

While Simon tried to think of a topic for the next round of the Awkward Game, I surveyed the room much like I imagined the president did when he walked into the Oval Office. After all, it was all because of me more or less that people were here, at Gwen Kessler's surprise Sweet Sixteen.

True, my best friend Mikey Salyards had volunteered his house, since his grandma and mother were out of town for the weekend, and all my friends had invited pretty much anyone who was even decently popular. But *I'd* been the one who had thought of having the party in the first place.

The familiar faces of my friends and frenemies were paired around poor Mikey's house, looking like some sort of bizarre clique collection, laid out in no particular order. With the mountains of pizza boxes, the music of our favorite video games, TV shows, and movies, and the rush of getting together outside of school hours, it was like being in a second sort of home. A home I didn't have to worry about cleaning after everyone left.

Yes, I decided. It had been *much* too long since our last blowout.

There were good reasons for that, surprisingly none of which involved my parents. The sad lack of parties was mostly due to the last time I was at a party, when my life had inexplicably and irrevocably changed for the worst.

But I wasn't really going to think of *that* while I was at this party—I had much more pressing concerns, as usual. I was focusing all my brainpower, all my available skills, on winning the next round of the Awkward Game.

The Awkward Game is where a bunch of friends get together and make fun of people or ideas in a more intelligent way than just saying they're stupid, dumb, or ugly.

Here's how it works: One person is the judge, and the judge will call out a familiar topic. And you can pretty much call out whatever you want, whether it's the drama nerd you wish you'd never met last fall, the latest bill passed or passed over by Congress, or the latest celebrity who'd walked out of their house "accidentally" wearing leeches. Then everyone goes around and makes an awkward comparison. For example, if you pick your school librarian, you could say she is more awkward than a fruit bat sucking blood or a bald man trying to get a haircut. Finally, after everyone puts in their answers, the judge makes the decision on who has given the best response. After so many rounds, you tally up who has the most wins and that person is the winner.

I won the game a lot, needless to say. But I also relished being the judge.

Simon looked thoughtful for a moment. "Okay! I got one!" he cheered. "How awkward is Wingdinger?"

The rest of the guys laughed as I felt the fun flerb out of me. I faked a grin as the guys all began to snigger at the mention of Apollo City's "superhero."

Of course *he'd go with Wingdinger. And* of course, *I have to sit here and take it. Nothing is going to save me from this unless by some miracle—*

Splintering pain slipped around my right arm like a shackle.

Ah, there it is. Supernatural calling. I grimaced.

"Hey guys," I spoke up. "I'm gonna duck out this round. Gwen's over there and I want to give her my present." A round of "Oohs" and "Awws" and "Go HD!" and other unintelligible comments ensued.

Oh, what I would've given to be telling the truth.

I headed out of Mikey's house as quickly as I could. I didn't have a lot of time before Gwen headed home, and I hadn't actually had a chance to give her my present.

But my other problem, still winding its way up my right arm, had more serious potential consequences at the moment.

Keeping this at the forefront of my mind, I slipped around corner of the stairs and tiptoed towards the front door.

Why did I, the great Hamilton Dinger, the pride of Apollo City Central High, suddenly have to leave? What reason called me to sneak out away from the only bright spot of my life since winter vacation ended, jumble my way through the backstreets of the city, and head off in the direction of certain unpleasantness?

The same reason I didn't like to think of Wingdinger as awkward.

For one thing, he's me.

For another, I had a monster of some demonic nature to battle.

And then there was—

"Hammy?" There was a hand on my shoulder.

I turned around to see none other than Gwen Kessler staring at me, looking so pretty it just made the ugliness of my situation even more awful. "Gwen!" My voice went up at least an octave pitch, as if I'd swallowed Mickey Mouse and he suddenly wanted to pop up and say hi. I cleared my throat hastily. "Gwen. There you are. I was just … "

Gwen's honey brown eyes warmed and I felt part of me melt. "Looking for me?" she ventured a lure, and I grabbed onto it.

"Yes! I was just looking for you," I agreed. "I have to … " *I have to distract her.* "You look amazing tonight," I said.

She giggled. "Thanks."

I laughed easily, trying to force my body to relax. *Get a grip, Dinger!*

"I was just going out … side. For a moment. It's warm in here. Don't you think it's warm in here?"

Gwen's eyes lost their sparkle. "Are you going home already, Hammy?"

I wish. "Oh. No, I just forgot to bring your present, and I wanted to go get it really quick," I assured her.

"But you're not going home? Where is it then?" Gwen looked charmingly confused.

I was getting there myself, frankly. "Oh, uh, it's at Rachel's Café," I lied. "I was there this afternoon, and I must've left my backpack there, and that's where I put your present earlier."

Gwen's brow wrinkled. "Are you doing okay, Ham? You've been acting weird lately."

"Weird? Huh. Doesn't sound like me."

"Really?" Gwen held up her hand and began counting off on her fingers. "First, you miss meeting me at Christmas, and call up the next day with some strange excuse of getting lost. Second, at New Year's, you and Mikey come over on your way to Jason's, and you leave me and Mikey hanging as you suddenly have to run home for your homework?" She giggled a bit. "I heard you've been sick during swim practice a lot too, to the point where even Coach Uzziah is getting on your back. And then, you're just so forgetful lately, it's almost like you've been avoiding me."

"Um … " I guess Gwen had noticed my rather poor run of excuses.

Ugh. I mentally slumped over in some kind of defeat. If it had been possible for time to stop for several moments, I would've spent all of it complaining about how irritating it was to be running constantly from battle to battle. 'Wingdinger' might have been needed on the interdimensional frontlines, but 'Hamilton' had a string of present obligations to fulfill. And I could only get so sick, forget so many things, or have my grandmother die so many times before people caught on.

Pain bit through my arm again, like a shackle shrinking around my wrist. I looked down to see the familiar mark on my wrist glowing. Trouble was brewing. I had to go. A cringing shudder went through me. I had to go, and that meant I had to leave Gwen.

"I'm sorry, Gwen, I just have to go. Sorry," I stammered. "I'll be right back soon!" Dreading the thought of the accusing look on her face, I intentionally turned away from her as I scooted out the door, nearly tripped down the porch stairs, cursed Mikey's grandmother for needing so many safety railings, and ran away as fast as I could.

As I approached the end of the driveway, I looked to see Gwen being pulled back into the party by her best friend, Laura Nelson. The music blared out one last time, seeming to give me an extra push as I hurried away. The comforting lights of the fun-filled house diminished with distance, as did any control over my burning anger.

Awkward games indeed, I thought bitterly to myself.

☼<u>2</u>☼
Problems

The evening streets of Apollo City were minimally populated, I noticed. The small city sitting on the edge of Lake Erie seemed dark, as though encouraging its inhabitants to indulge in a night in. That was good, I decided. I didn't need people tripping me up.

After a moment of quick reconnaissance, I headed off for a nearby community sports field. I smirked as a slight, deadly-colored aura surrounded the area; not only was it (thankfully) close by, I was getting better at finding the battlefields. (The first time I'd seen the deadly shadows of supernatural trouble, I thought I'd needed to go to the eye doctor. Now that I knew what it was, it was the first thing I looked for as I barreled into action.)

"Kid!" the deep, familiar voice resounded through the treetops as I scuttled through the darkened alleyway leading to the recently renovated Central City baseball field.

I sighed. I'd recognize Elysian anywhere; then again, how many talking dragons could one person possibly know? Especially one as irritating as Elysian. It had been the right move, as hard as it was, to leave the party, I thought. Recalling the various times he'd come close to being discovered, I had little doubt my self-proclaimed "mentor" would have had the common sense to stay out of Gwen's party.

Elysian swooshed down beside me, his long, scaly, fully-transformed body gliding effortlessly through the air. "Transform," he ordered, his voice deep and rough. "We are getting close."

"I know," I bit back. Glancing down, I saw the black, four-pointed star on my seething wrist peeking out from under my sports wristband. This mark, seared into my skin as much as the power it symbolized branded my life, was key to my power. Pressing it released a surge of energy, scattering lightning across my blood, changing my clothes, sprouting my distinctive wingdings out of my head. Despite the interruption to my life, I grinned. "You know, I'm not stupid. I know how to do this by now."

Elysian rolled his glowing, yellow-green eyes at me. "You could still speed it up a bit," he muttered. "Our enemies don't—"

The park ground suddenly began tunneling underneath me. "Run!" I ordered Elysian, momentarily forgetting that in his full dragon form, Elysian could fly.

No sooner had I yelled when the dirt and grass twisted away from my feet. The ground caved away from itself, as though a giant underground blender had suddenly sucked it through a vacuum. I would've sent me spiraling into the earth if it hadn't been for Elysian's quick-clenching jaws.

A quick scream flew out of me as I felt the world drop from underneath me. (Hopefully no one heard me.)

"Itz zunderground!" Elysian barked with me between his closed bite.

"No kidding," I muttered. Elysian underestimated my ability to think clearly quite frequently. Which was a big part of the reason I thought he was annoying. He also thought he was in charge; that did him no favors in gaining my favor, let me tell you.

Elysian dropped me onto a tree branch nearby, and then proceeded to breathe his celestial flames at the ground. When the ground only caught fire, I groaned; not only was that going to make it hard to see the monster, the park rangers were going to be sending a bill to the mayor's office—*again.*

"Watch the collateral damage, Ely!" I screeched the stern instruction, anger on my flame-lit face. If, by some unlucky instance, the government did manage to find out my identity, I would get stuck working off more than two lifetimes of debt.

Elysian shrugged, and I rolled my eyes. I would've called him on his stupidity if I didn't need to think of something quickly to stop the demon monster.

"Okay," I muttered to myself. "I need a plan."

Watching the former baseball field burn, I felt ready to give up. I slumped against the trunk on the tree, my wings bristling at some of the wayward branches.

Life had certainly changed drastically for the citizens of Apollo City last fall, I surmised, thinking for the hundredth time just how galling it was to find myself where I was.

When a meteorite had struck the town last October, I had no idea it would've brought so much trouble along with it. In addition to causing general city-wide panic, some broken buildings, and even earning me a trip to the hospital, a number of what could only be termed as supernatural creatures had appeared: *eelas, bakreels,* even some *tenwaleisks.* Demonic monsters, seeking power by stealing the souls of humans, suddenly rampaged through the city streets under the charge of the Seven Deadly Sinisters and their supposed caretaker, Orpheus.

You can see where it gets complicated to follow along. If I hadn't happened to have some kind of superhero type powers—apparently, I was some kind of "fallen Star," some kind of warrior for "good,"—you can be sure I wouldn't have believed any of it. Just even saying it like that makes me cringe.

But there was no doubt it was all true, much to my displeasure. And when Elysian had shown up, there was much more displeasure to be had. His instruction, while it had given me the basics of defeating each type of demon, and limited insight into what he called the Celestial Kingdom, or the Immortal Realm, it did nothing to comfort me on the loss of my normal, teenage life.

My less-than-critical thinking was interrupted as the monster finally broke free from its muddy sheath.

"*Grum!*" A ring of endless teeth eclipsed my line of vision. It was the framework of a mouth ten feet wide, which was followed by a burbling body of a monstrous mutant worm. I sighed. Another *bakreel*—a spirit demon. That made three just this week, I thought, annoyed again.

The only bright side I could think of to this was that at least they weren't the worst to deal with. In fact, spirit demons were the lowest on the rating of demons for me to kill. They were simple monsters who'd taken up a vengeful residence in some of the silliest places, although there have been a few exceptions. They didn't seem very bright to me. After all, what could a *bakreel* really hope to do in the form of worm?

True, this one was an enormous, evil, flop-happy worm with a huge set of chompers, but still, I'd dissected one of its smaller counterparts in Biology last year. I wasn't afraid of it, even as giant and mutated as it was.

I smirked as I called forth my own stream of energy. A warmth sparked from my heart and poured out into my palms. "You won't worm your way out of this!" I cried. (I could hear the familiar *whirr* of a news helicopter coming in from behind me, and for showmanship's sake, it was the only real pun I could think of.)

My punch's power, like cackling energy, latched around its neck and tightened, trapping it; Elysian let out another burst of celestial flames as we held it down.

"Yes!" I cheered as I saw the monster struggling to scurry back underground. I'd learned if it tries to retreat, it usually means it's been weakened enough for me to go in for the kill.

And that was when, all of a sudden, my cell phone, tucked in a shoulder pocket of my armor, vibrated and let out a loud ring.

Unable to help myself, I swiped it up to see Mikey Salyards, my best friend, was calling. Right as I was trying to polish off the gardener's work (He just *had* to call *right then*, didn't he?)

I groaned to myself; no doubt, Mikey had noticed I was no longer at the party (Let's face it, without me, there really *was* no party.) I glanced over at the situation behind me briefly before answering the phone. I would have to think on my feet for this one, but it was best if I didn't ignore it.

I launched myself behind a nearby bush, squirming at the prickly leaves. "Yeah?" I couldn't ignore it, but I had to make it quick.

"Hey, Dinger, where'd you go?"

"Ugh … Cheryl called me and wanted me to come home." I instantly smacked my forehead. Not one of my better excuses, that's for sure.

"Since when are you listening to your parents?"

"Ugh … It's nothing. So, what're you guys up to?" I asked. Changing the subject was imperative for me during the dark days of my dual life. I was thinking of telling people I had ADD or something so they wouldn't bother me about it; maybe they would even feel sorry for me after hearing the excuse so many times.

"We're all watching the news."

"Really? Since when is the news cool enough to watch, Mike?"

"I know, right? I would agree but Wingdinger's back in action!"

"Oh really?" I rolled my eyes before glancing around for the news helicopter again.

"Yeah, it's awesome! Some huge caterpillar is leeching around and humping the old baseball grounds near Main Street."

"What's he doing now?" At this point, having asked a pointless question, I turned on speaker phone and stepped out of the brush to finish off the beast.

"*Grum!*" It howled and huffed in an awkward rhythm. I was unpleasantly surprised to see it was still just wriggling around, flopping on the topside, like a goldfish chucked out of its bowl.

"He's standing around doing nothing while Starry Knight just stabbed it straight between the eyes! Or at least, what I think are the eyes. You should see it man, her power is beyond anything I've ever seen … "

Mikey's answer was slowly silenced to my ears as I felt a growl gurgle up inside of me. So Starry Knight had arrived.

I muted the phone and leaped into action.

Calling forth another power beam, I aimed for the heart of the beast, knowing it would be a point of weakness for the spirit monster. "Augh! Take that!"

A burst of light and a moment later, a gloomy cloud of dust hurricaned around the park grounds and a whimpering "*Grum*" settled into the ground.

The monster was gone.

And I was left in a whirlwind of gray snow, staring into the violet eyes of my so-called co-defender.

She was spotlessly graceful, not a hair out of place. Just as always. In the months we've fought and fought with the Sinisters, I've never quite felt as solid nor as strong as she looked. She seemed to me to be more ghost than real, but I knew from experience the extent of her power as a Starlight Warrior.

"Starry Knight," I muttered in greeting.

"Wingdinger," she nodded back. A moment passed before her eyebrow arched and she remarked, "I don't suppose you're ready to give up on this charade?"

It was her big thing, ever since we started fighting against the Sinisters and all their minions, for her to convince me to quit. "There's no charade here, unless you count your masquerade as 'help,'" I retorted back. "I can do this just fine on my own. Why don't *you* just give up? Relax a little bit?"

She frowned. "I'm not the one who thinks this is some kind of social club," she bit back. "You've hardly improved at all since you started this. Your power is still weak and unpredictable, and your focus is off while your attitude is as flippant as a child's."

"What if that's what I wanted?" I shot back. I couldn't let her have the last word.

"Please. It's clear you just love the attention you're getting from all this," she waved off. "It's all about you and your image."

Duh. What else would I fight for, if not myself? Sure, truth and justice were important. But I didn't really need this cutting into my social life. Or the huge damage bill I was racking up.

Before I could make my next amazing retort, my cell phone rang again; I'd knocked Mikey off the line. Groaning to myself, I hurriedly turned it off before determinedly turning back to face my co-defender foe.

She suddenly whipped out her bow again. I was taken aback; Starry Knight and I had never gotten along (understatement of the century) but we had never physically fought each other. She usually just harangued me long enough to feel good about herself before flying off.

But all of a sudden, she was flying through the air at me, her bow between us. I felt myself pushed back, hard, and I flew back through the air. I finally landed against something hard and scaly. Elysian.

His tail wrapped securely around me before I could counterattack. "Hey! What are you doing!?" I screamed as he jolted quickly away, my body tugged awkwardly behind him as we shot out of there. "Hey! What are you doing? She attacked me! Let me at her!"

Elysian looked back at me curiously; before he could say anything, a huge fiery explosion blasted behind us.

The boom was deafening, and the fire was fierce; I looked around to see the news helicopter had just fallen from the sky. A couple of parachutes in the distance skyline hovered precariously. Starry Knight had taken to the skies, guiding them away from the flames and melted metal now stuck in the ground behind us.

Her wings fluttered; I saw her as she looked back at me. "Don't expect a thank you," I huffed bitterly. She seemed to expect that, because a moment later, I looked back over to see she'd flittered off. A flicker of light whistled against the horizon as she flew out of sight.

Anger surged inside of me. This wasn't the first time she'd saved my life. And it wasn't the first time I was going to deny it.

"Elysian!" I scowled over at my dragon mentor, who was sniffing the tunnels from which the giant worm had come out. "Elysian, you're supposed to be helping me! Why can't you keep tabs on Starry Knight and warn me about stuff like that?" I jabbed my thumb in the direction at the tangled metal mess, which would probably be in the mayor's next propaganda campaign as a future site for a playground ("Help Helicopters give Hope," I could hear the cheesy slogan already.) "And why don't you ever just scare her off when we're in the middle of an argument like before?"

Elysian snorted. "She's usually got a point. And I don't think she minds arguing with you. She even seems to like it."

It had always bothered me that Elysian seemed to like Starry Knight more than he liked me. It also bothered me when he took her side, and that he didn't really interact with her like it was a chore, or bother her any more than he felt he had to. What I wouldn't have given for a life like that.

Anger suddenly seethed at me, burning my bones, much like the helicopter crash flaming wildly behind me. "Do you want me to quit this?" I asked through gritted teeth.

"No. But it's clear you're not really trying, either."

"What!?" I was flabbergasted. "What do you mean, I don't even try? Of course I do! Do you know what I could be doing instead of this?"

"Kid," Elysian said, "Listen to me. There is a difference between knowledge and wisdom. There's also a difference between accepting the truth and believing it."

"I know."

"Are you listening to me? Or just hearing me?"

"Yes. Both—I'm doing both!" I put my head in my hands. "Just stop it, all right? I'm going to try to be nicer towards people and watch what I say. I'm sure it'll make me stronger, so you can just shut up!"

Elysian rolled his eyes. "Great way to get started, kid. Some restraint on your mouth would help, I'll give you that. If for no other reason than to get you to be quieter. But I bet anything it'll be two minutes before you fall back into your usual habits."

THE STARLIGHT CHRONICLES

"You know, Elysian," I grumbled, "Ever since you came into my life, all I am anymore is angry!"

The dragon laughed. "That's a lie. You were angry before. One creature like me won't change a hardheaded spitfire like you."

Our conversation was proof that not only was Elysian terrible to deal with, but I was perpetually unrewarded for my good deeds and my sacrifices. (I was never going to get back the moments I missed from the party!)

Elysian sighed as he slimmed down to his smaller size. As a changeling dragon, he had the ability to change his form; I liked it when he was in his usual, smaller form, because his voice was more hilarious and less terrifying when he was angry.

"Come on. You don't really try to find out about our enemies, you get all huffy when I try to correct you, and you just don't care about anyone else, except where your reputation in concerned. You try harder only *after* the cameras arrive." He paused for a moment, as though weighing his options, and then added, "Or when you're trying to beat Starry Knight."

"Did it ever occur to you I don't really know why I am doing any of this?" I asked. "Why can't the Prince of Stars just come down here and take care of it himself?"

Elysian sighed. "There are always questions which we will not be able to answer, and even if we were given the answers, we wouldn't understand them."

"That's stupid."

"No, it's not. It's just that good judgment requires a broad perspective," Elysian rolled his eyes. "One you clearly don't have, since it's hard for you to even look past yourself."

I turned on my heel and stormed away. There was no need to deal with this.

"Where are you going now, Hamilton?" Elysian heaved out an irritated breath, surprising me by calling me by my first name for once.

"Back to my party," I huffed. "And don't even think about following me. You're not invited!"

I thought I heard him sigh before he began muttering under his breath about how irresponsible I was and how disappointing I was and how I was too selfish and how I was never going to be a better fighter and how I should just be stripped of my powers and let go with some kind of *Astroneshama*—Starlight Warrior—pink slip.

I felt better knowing he was not happy; it was enough to even make me smile briefly, before I caught sight of the Apollo City Time Tower.

It was hard to tell whether I was more frustrated, angry, or disappointed to see how much time had passed. My palms grew warm with rage as I hurried through the nighttime streets. I still had to give Gwen her present.

☼3☼
Reprieve

When I arrived back at Mikey's house several long moments later, the party was still going somewhat, although I was going to have some difficulties rounding up another round of the Awkward Game.

I was torn between climbing in through the bathroom window and just heading home when Gwen came out the door, carrying bags full of her presents.

"Bye! Thank you guys!" Gwen called out, waving with her free hand as she headed out.

A couple of them called out their goodbyes, a few jokes, and she laughingly replied. All as I just stared.

My pulse had dulled since the end of the battle, and my body even felt like the world was slumping over. But Gwen's presence was enough to convince me to perk up.

"Hey Gwen, want some help carrying those home?" I asked, stepping out from the shadows as she finally made it to the sidewalk.

"Hey Hammy," she greeted with a hint of surprise in her voice. "I wasn't sure if you were going to come back or not."

"Sorry I'm so late. Um, Cheryl called and wanted me to come home. But then I realized I didn't get a chance to really talk to you or wish you a happy birthday, so I came back." It was cheesy, but it was all I could think of at the moment.

She smiled, the smile I knew crinkled warmly into the corners of her eyes. "Well, you certainly picked out a great gift. I loved the sweater." She indicated the small bag in her one hand. "I guess you didn't forget it at Rachel's restaurant after all."

"Oh, good," I said, reaching out and taking some of the other bags in her hands. I wanted *my* present to be the only one she carried. "I'm glad." Really glad, I added to myself. The cashmere sweater had been her Christmas gift, but thanks to a last-minute Christmas Eve superhero run, it had been drenched in chai. I'd needed to get it replaced. That meant waiting for the Christmas return season to catch up, and I'd only just gotten its replacement in the mail three days ago. "I think the green will look great with your hair."

"Thanks," Gwen flushed. "I think it will, too. Are you sure you're able to walk me home?"

I'd fought supernatural demons. I could handle another lecture from Cheryl about curfew. "Sure." I grinned.

"Great," Gwen agreed.

We talked for a bit—well, I did, as I told her all about the trouble I'd gone to getting the sweater, which involved my mother's reluctant personal shopper and an edited version of the Christmas debacle—before I ran out of the story details to share and we lapsed into silence.

It was not an awkward silence—or at least, I didn't think so.

Gwen finally spoke up. "My house is right up here."

THE STARLIGHT CHRONICLES

"I remember," I assured her.

"Thanks for helping me."

"No problem."

"I hope your mom doesn't get mad at you for being out so late."

"Why would Cheryl get mad?" I asked, before abruptly reminding myself that is what I'd told her I was doing when I left the party. "Oh, I mean … Cheryl will understand. 'Cause it's you, you know?"

Gwen cocked her eyebrow at me. "I thought you were starting to listen to your parents."

"Gotta draw the line somewhere, right?" I laughed. "Besides, we both know I can't hold a candle to you in that regard, no matter how much I try, Ms. Gwen Goody Two-Shoes." I gave her a teasing smile, but the frown I received back tells me I've stepped over some line.

I rolled my eyes, not sure if I was irritated at her or myself as the silence resumed. She was probably thinking I had been referring to the whole Tim Ryder incident. And if so, she was right. But I'd been hoping she'd gotten over it by now.

Gwen's parents had finally gotten to meet Tim Ryder, a geek from school who had passionately declared his love for Gwen just as I'd been planning to ask Gwen out. Gwen had invited Tim over to her house to meet them over the Christmas/New Year's break. I have to admit, it was the best gift I received. Some of the details were so deliciously awkward, *I* even almost felt sorry for him. But then, you can't expect a man like John Kessler, a prime candidate for the county's next school board president, to appreciate a gawky boy teenager's dreams of starring on Broadway, no matter how well he constructs a replica of the Globe Theatre with his mashed potatoes and peas.

We came up to the darkened house and I was just about to ask Gwen if she had her key when the lights blazed on.

"Gwen, is that you? Who's that with you? It's not that pansy Shakespeare boy again, is it? I swear, if he's bothering us again after I told him there's no way in hell I'd let him date you, I'll get him expelled!"

I had the hardest time keeping in my snickers.

"Dad!" Gwen was mortified. I could tell by her tone, but I was suddenly able to see it on her face, as the lights glared on. "Stop it! This is Hamilton Dinger, not Tim, so you can relax."

"Hamilton?" John's face looked funny, with the dumbfounded look on it. I couldn't see much, but I knew I would be bursting with laughter while recounting this story to the guys later.

"Yeah, you'll remember Hamilton," Gwen huffed, the bitterness in her voice not escaping me.

"How are you, Mr. Kessler?" I asked. "Uh, just helping Gwen carry her presents home from her party."

"Oh. Well, Hamilton, it's nice to see you again." John smiled, coming over. He plucked the bags out of my hands

THE STARLIGHT CHRONICLES

and nodded his greeting. "Sorry about that. Can't be too careful these days, you know."

"Oh, understandable," I assured him. I smiled. "Especially with someone as pretty as Gwen here."

Gwen frowned some more, before abruptly turning toward the door. "Thank you for your help, Ham, but we're here and it's late. I'll see you in class on Monday, okay?"

"Gwen, let me get these bags," John insisted. "You can say your good-byes to Hamilton properly."

Gwen bit her lip as she watched him head back toward the door.

"He means well," I said. Which was more than I could say for my parents.

"Maybe."

There was nothing else to be done. "Speaking of your best interests, Gwen, would you like to go out on a date with me?"

Gwen blinked in surprise. "How is that in my best interests?" she asked, with something like suspicion laced in her response.

I shoved my hands in my pockets. "Well, your parents like me, so it's a start." She glared at me, so I knew I'd best keep talking. "And there is the matter of how if you agree to go out with me now, I won't have to keep asking you several times over the next few weeks."

She laughed a bit at that, so I allowed myself to breathe correctly.

"You have Tuesday night free," John called out from the door.

"Dad! Gosh, you are terrible!" Gwen hollered back as she flushed a shade above purple. "Go away!"

I laughed as John went back inside the house. "Well, I was going to suggest Tuesday anyway, if that makes you feel better."

She sighed. "Well … I don't know."

"What?" I asked, pretending to be offended. "What do you mean, 'I don't know,' Gwen?"

"You just seem really preoccupied lately," Gwen told me. "Remember? You're always busy or forgetting something or running off."

The teasing quality had obviously been lost on her. "Well, that's not—"

"And then there's still the swim season, too. Aren't you worried about how much you'll have to do?"

"No," I lied, reaching out and take her hand.

Her fingers curled inside of her hands gently. "I'm just worried you won't have the time to spend with me."

I laughed. "Geez, Gwen, I'm just asking for a date." I took her hand in both of mine and held them up, pulling her closer to me. "Please? Just go out with me once. You won't regret it. You'll see."

There was a long moment of silence before Gwen sighed. "All right. Tuesday's fine."

A thousand little bursts of fireworks went off inside of me, happiness dashing across all my senses. After months of carefully playing chase, I had caught my quarry with a rush of satisfaction.

Of course, there was no way I would ever tell her that. So I played it cool. "Okay, sounds great." Deciding to play Prince Charming, I brought her hand up to my lips and kissed it gallantly.

The contact of her skin on mine, at that moment, had a right to make me happily unnerved. And it did.

Though not the way I had been thinking it would.

Little wisps of an aura flickered around her fingers, and for a moment I stared. For no discernable reason, I suddenly felt an array of uncertainty and hesitation, resignation and slight irritation. I flinched and dropped her hand.

Gwen's eyes widened just a bit, and I am pretty sure my mouth dropped open in the worst stupidly surprised look possible.

"Ugh … sorry, was that my phone?" I recovered as quickly as I could, and dove for my phone (which was still off from the battle), pretending to see if I had any text messages. "Uh, yeah. Cheryl just texted me. Got to head home now."

Gwen looked dubious, but said nothing. "Okay. Well, I'll just meet you after school on Tuesday, okay?"

"Sure. Sounds great. Can't wait."

Gwen laughed. "You're not trying to sound like a poet, are you?"

Ha. That was a laugh right there. But I smiled, knowing girls like that kind of fluffy feel-goodness, and said, "Yeah, you're an inspiration to me, Gwen." And with that, because I knew I could get away with it, I leaned in and kissed her cheek.

The same spurt of aura lights—the trepidation, annoyance, and slight bitterness—leaped at me again while I touched her skin.

Were they Gwen's emotions? I wondered instinctively. Intuitively, that sounded about right. But it didn't make me feel any better myself. "Happy birthday, Gwen," I murmured, confused and angry at the same time. Why did the thing that made me different have to make me unable to enjoy something like this, now?

She flustered again. "Thank you, Hammy," she said. "So … see you next week in class."

I waved as I headed back down her driveway. "You bet," I called back.

And as I watched her head into her home, and the outside lights click off, I allowed myself a brief moment of self-celebration, a brief moment of reprieve from worrying about the rest of the world. Happiness bubbled up inside of me, and I rode the crest of its wave as I headed home.

Even if there were awkward games to deal with, there was no preventing me from gaining my prize. Everything was going to be great. I had a blissful feeling that, come next week, my life would change forever.

☼4☼
Insights

I hardly classified myself as a superhero. There were some who would. There were also people who were staunchly convinced Wingdinger was just a super nuisance, including my own mother. I would just say I was super annoyed. There were a lot of downsides to my line of work.

I've already mentioned a few. Another one was that I was constantly in a state of insanity. Not the kind that gets treated with happy sleepy drugs or special attention. No, my kind was much worse.

Flashes of another place in space or time. Dreams from another realm. Nightmares. I had learned to deal with them, tried not to let them bother me, and when I could, ignored them completely.

After close to four months or so of it, and getting nowhere close to letting myself go see a counselor, I was getting more numb. I felt less fear, less confusion. Elysian told me the visions, these sometimes premonitions, were good, since I would be able to see more attacks coming.

These were the type of things he said to make me hate him. And he made sure he said them at the most inappropriate times so I hated him even more.

Like when I woke up gasping in the middle of the night.

It's always after the defeat of a minion the visions became most clear. I could see every hair on the heads of my foes— whether it was meticulously pulled back like Asteropy, who I

35

would call the lead Sinister, or mussed all over the place, like Maia, who never seemed to quite willing to take her job seriously.

Starry Knight told me once a long time ago, when we first started fighting with each other as well as fighting our enemies, that I didn't know much about our enemies. I supposed she had a point—not that I would admit it.

From what the Sinisters have told me while they were busy monologuing, along with whatever Elysian *says* he's told me, I figured they were some kind of aliens from another world— Elysian called it the Realm of Immortality—and they'd basically come to Earth to destroy humanity and take their Soulfire, their *neshamasifa*, to use to fight off their old leader, I suppose.

I wouldn't believe any of this, normally. And I still didn't like to even consider its truth. But I'd met the old leader, the Prince of Stars, in person. He was the one responsible for giving me my power. I couldn't explain everything, but I'll tell you one thing: After meeting him, there was no question about whether or not all of this was true or not. And there was no hope of ignoring it, either.

And because of that, I got stuck with dreams from another world.

It's nearly always the same cast of characters—Orpheus and his sweaty rainbow of charges. Sometimes I even think I could smell the sweaty sulfur and burnt smoke.

I watched in my dream, transfixed. I can't seem to ever get out of them early or control them.

In this one, Orpheus definitely was giving off some steam.

"What do you mean, another one of your minions has been destroyed!?" he yelled.

I'd quickly come to think of Orpheus as the babysitter of the Seven Deadly Sinisters, for more than one reason. Every time I'd see him—whether it was in real life or just in my mind—he always seemed to be yelling at them.

This time, his fists were clenching spastically in anger, turning from a normal grayish color to an unpleasant shade of violet.

Taygetay, the red-toned one, shrugged. "It wasn't like I planned it," she informed him. "I just found out myself."

"And you don't care at all Grum is gone?" Orpheus asked, seething. The vessels over his missing eye—a result of the first battle between Starry Knight and himself—contracted and expanded at an alarming rate. I would've laughed if I felt I could. These situations had a way of suffocating me.

The sharp, dark crimson eyes gazed up uninterestedly at him. "Not really; he was quite irritating … not unlike some others I could mention."

I knew these girls were my enemies. But I had to admire their spunk. I'd known them long enough to know each of them had their own little quirk; some of them were funny, while others were just irritating.

Taygetay's keen on plotting revenge. Maia was the epitome of lazy. Alcyonë wanted to make the world jealous of her.

Asteropy was my least favorite; she believed no one could ever do anything better than her and she was the greatest person(?) in the world. At that point, I'd never fought her, personally, but I knew I would immensely enjoy putting her in her place behind me.

The others were more or less unexceptional in my opinion, or at least hardly memorable.

"Come on, Orpheus, lighten up with the whole anger thing," Alcyonë insisted. "Really, this is not the first time we've been defeated before we could get anything for our trouble."

"Yeah," Maia agreed as she yawned. "We're bound to make some mistakes."

Asteropy stood up, her yellowish skin flaring. "Some of us who aren't always taking a nap, *Maia*."

"Hey, I went the first two times, and I'm sleepy! It's not my turn again yet. You haven't done much either, Asteropy!"

"Would you guys just relax and have some of this cake here?" Celaena insisted as she engorged herself with the chocolate fudge cake she had in her hands. Celaena was hilarious; she's always eating and making really awkward remarks about how she always needed more of everything. She's like a fat, spoiled, purple baby.

"You might think you have room for mistakes, but you haven't had any recent successes, either, if I might remind you!" Orpheus hissed.

Maia yawned. "It's not like we're counting, Orpheus." I knew there was way too much effort involved in that for Maia.

"You are to listen to me, remember? If I say we have a problem, we have a problem!"

"I'd say it's you that's the problem at the moment." Taygetay smirked.

"Look, Orpheus, it's clear we need to rethink things a bit," Asteropy stepped forward. "After all, *I* can't have all these failures on my shoulders."

"I have an idea," Taygetay jumped in.

"How could you possibly have anything good to say? You just failed, in case you've forgotten already," Asteropy sneered.

Taygetay ignored her. "We should investigate our enemies; you know, look for weaknesses, downfalls, those sorts of things. And then destroy them."

"I have a *better* idea. We can overshadow a human and cause it to produce more powerful Soulfire!" Alcyonë broke in. "Any addiction or obsession would grow until the human is not only *soully* consumed, but *wholly* consumed."

"'Soully' is not a word," Asteropy huffled, impatient.

"Who asked you?" Alcyonë snorted. "You're just jealous you didn't it realize sooner humans have a destructive tendency to become obsessive, especially over silly things."

"I like this idea," Orpheus muttered softly. "Hmm … yes, humans are so intentional about putting their energy projects and things to give them temporary meaning in their lives."

Alcyonë smirked. "And this way, we could attack humans one at a time; much like you did to revive us, Orpheus, and not draw so much attention to ourselves."

"You think we've been thinking too big?" Orpheus asked.

Was he really asking that? Recalling the huge debt over my head from the building and roads and foliage needing repairs these past months, I would say he'd definitely been thinking too big.

"Not at all," Alcyonë purred. "But subtly has its advantages."

Orpheus' face creepily contorted as I saw him smile. He rubbed his hands together ominously. "Excellent. I like your ideas, Alcyonë. Begin your mission immediately."

Orpheus would've made an excellent video game villain, I sighed ruefully.

"Of course, Orpheus … I shall find the perfect human to be our first puppet."

Taygetay's anger visibly boiled, an interesting look on her ruddy face. "I'm not jealous of your stupidity. Unless you find the weakness of our enemies, you will not be able to get to them."

Alcyonë didn't hear her I guess, because she faded out a moment later. And then I did too, thankfully.

I woke up to find my world buzzed into reality. The stark contrast was immediate, almost startling. But I was glad to be free of sleep's clutches.

I doubted any other teenager had insomnia for the same reason I wanted it.

"Another vision?" Elysian asked eagerly. I got the feeling he had been watching over me with enthusiasm. When I had one of my disturbing dreams, he liked to ask me questions about it and try to decipher it. Or so he said.

I glared at him. Elysian might've called himself my mentor, but I was more inclined to believe he's in the same helpless boat as me. Sometimes, when I told him about the dreams of the Celestial Kingdom, he would get this wistful, confused longing in his eyes.

I guess coming to Earth really screwed up his memory. Or something really horrifying happened to him before he came here. I've never been interested enough to ask him or angry enough to accuse him of anything.

"Go away," I muttered.

"If you don't tell me, I won't be able to help you."

"If I don't tell you, I don't have to be reminded of it for weeks on end." I glared at him, even though the room was dark.

He huffed back; a small stream of fire flared out, and I briefly saw him with his claws crossed and his belly bunched out. "Fine. But I will remember this the next time you run into another demon and Starry Knight has to save you."

I decided not to answer him for once. We bickered for hours last time we'd fought, and I had to go to school in three hours. I tugged on my covers, rolled over, and squeezed my eyes shut, as though by doing so I could squeeze out the memory of my abnormality.

I didn't even know why I was a 'superhero.' I really didn't. Sure, I mean I was a great guy. Anyone would want me to be some heroic warrior for their team. I was strong and fast, thanks to years of sports conditioning, good-looking and I was quick-witted. I was the ideal fighter.

But I mean … I didn't know how I'd gotten this way. Spider-man had been bitten. Batman had lots of money but was too cheap for a grief counselor. The Fantastic Four had solar radiation. The Hulk was genetically engineered by his father. The X-Men were all mutants. Captain America was a government experiment.

There were only some many scenarios a person could run through before hitting a wall. Chosen by some all-powerful starlight overlord and granted some supernatural ability was hardly on my list. Born with it didn't make any sense either, no matter what people thought about Superman.

And those were the only things I could deduce to be true, back at the beginning.

That's the nice thing about the truth. You don't have to believe it if you don't want to.

It's just better to forget it all. Thinking about it only when I had to. Who wanted to live a life for others? I only had one life, and I wanted to just enjoy it. I didn't want to question what my duty was to the rest of the world.

In my opinion, I shouldn't even have had a duty to others. That's fine for people who join the army and marines and such; they at least have some incentive. But why would you do something for others for no reason or reward?

Hours passed, but I remained wide-awake. I could hear Elysian's breathing as his chest rhythmically rose and fell. The soft morning light was slipping through my window, and I knew I was not going to be able to fall back asleep. School was going to be hard today, I thought. Even for me— superstar student Hamilton Dinger, the star of Lake County, Ohio—things couldn't always be easy.

I sighed and sought comfort in the only thing I could: My date with Gwen.

A small smile crept onto my face. It was enough, for now.

☼5☼
More Problems

I slapped my bag down on my desk angrily, just as the first bell rang for the day. I'd just barely made it in time for class to start.

Obviously, the universe was not as apt as I was that it would give me some relief.

One of my best friends, Jason Harbor, looked up from his history book. "What's up, Dinger? You okay?"

"Yeah, just spitting up flowers here," I muttered. Any idiot could see I was frazzled.

"What's wrong?"

"The family institution, for starters."

"For starters, Dinger, we have presentations on yellow journalism, so please wait until lunch to get your rant out."

I smirked as I gazed into the bespectacled eyes of my AP History teacher, Martha Smithe. "Anything for you, of course, Martha."

The fifty-some year old woman I'd come to adore throughout my years in high school gave me her best skeptical look, took a swig of her ever-present coffee, and then turned towards the front of the board, where my assignments were already waiting for me.

I sighed. It had been a long morning.

"Did your mom get a new chef?" This time it was my other friend, Evan von Ponce, who turned around to inquire.

"Yes, she did. Now she's on some kind of sugar-free 'body cleanse,' but that's not why I'm upset," I muttered. "There's another reason Cheryl's infuriating today."

"Did she make you break your date with Gwen?" Jason asked as he tried copying the notes on the board.

"No, thankfully, but she might as well have," I spat. "She needs me to pick up Adam at the daycare this week." So that meant I'd either be grounded for leaving Adam there until I was done with my date, or I'd be dragging my babbling brother along with me when I met with Gwen.

"Ouch, that sucks man," Jason agreed.

"Yeah, she's starting her new job at the District Attorney's office today, and once again, her children are taking a backseat to her career." I rolled my eyes. "And of course Mark is busy going through orientation with the new interns at the hospital."

My parents were definitely made for each other, I thought bitterly as I copied down the notes as sloppily as possible (just keeping up appearances for Martha's sake.) Both of them wanted to be the best in their careers, and they'd sacrificed everything practically to get there. My mother was well-known as a tyrant in the city courts, and my father was a cardiologist; these were the formal titles of perpetual child neglect, I assure you. I had no idea why Mark and Cheryl had even wanted kids. Probably to get some kind of award at work.

"Sucks," Poncey agreed.

"Dinger! Ponce! Do I need to separate you?" Martha's voice crackled out like a shot of lightning.

Lightning it might have been, but it didn't faze me. I smiled brightly up at her. "No, we're good," I assured her. "Just getting all the notes down."

Jason, Poncey, and I retreated to silence as we really did have a lot of notes to copy. Well, they did. I was, of course, just faking.

And it was for the best they had to be sufficiently distracted, as I couldn't tell them the other reason I was upset.

My mother's first case, as the newly appointed District Attorney for the newly instated mayor of the city, was to take on Starry Knight and Wingdinger. Cheryl had blathered on and on and on about it all through breakfast, and for the first time in a long time, it wasn't the food which turned me off from eating. It was the thought of my mother personally taking me through the court system, haranguing me, and relishing in the intellectual, emotional, and legal defeat of her oldest child.

"Okay, class, presentation time," Martha announced. "If you didn't get the notes get them from someone else later. I suggest someone trustworthy." I could tell from her piercing gaze she knew I'd blown off the majority of the assignment. I gave her a charming grin in reply.

"Any volunteers to go first?"

I quickly glanced around; no one was really volunteering (as usual.) I took that as my cue to pull out my Game Pac. It had saved me countless times before from the mighty forces of boredom. And no offense to Martha, but her class would be no exception today.

I hadn't played as much because of winter break from school, but I was anxious to keep my title as Tetris King (a small title with a big ego boost.)

"Harbor? Why don't you go first?" Martha barked, after the awkward silence declared no one would step up willingly.

Jason smiled widely (what a fake.) "I was just about to ask if I could go," he declared.

I snorted back some laughter. Jason was trying to imitate me, no doubt. But to no avail; I would've done it with more feeling and a slight pause, to show I was *really* thinking about it. *Amateur.*

Don't get me wrong; Jason had his strengths, but sucking up was not one of them.

"I brought in a newspaper article," Jason said. "It's about Wingdinger, one of the city's superheroes." He grinned. "It's cool because Wingdinger is a bit of a loser. If I was a superhero, I would have a *much* cooler costume and wouldn't have put the wingdings on my head."

I nearly choked on my sudden outrage. A loser!? *Me?* I'd never been called a loser before in my whole life—unlike Jason! Now I had a new appreciation for running out of the party on Friday.

THE STARLIGHT CHRONICLES

True to the superhero creed, none of my friends knew of my Wingdinger identity. Elysian had warned me (more than necessary, of course) the more people who knew, the more danger I would be in. And knowing some of my friends' loud mouth tendencies (Poncey), I agreed with him. For once.

Although I had thought about telling Gwen more than a few times. If for no other reason than because all the superheroes who tell their girlfriends about their secret identity get to be with them in the end. I looked over at her now, and she had a small smile on her face as Jason presented. It made me feel better. Slightly.

"What do you mean when you say 'wingdings,' Harbor?" Martha asked, distracting me out of my angry stupor. "I've never heard that before."

"Wingdings are the wispy strands of hair at the side of your head. Guys normally have sideburns, let's put it like that," Jason replied. "A woman probably named him."

I was really glad when Poncey started haranguing Jason about his excessive knowledge of hair, because I was having a hard time not going red. I couldn't help the costume! And it *had* been a woman who'd "officially" given me the name (Patricia Rookwood, the local news anchorwoman, held a contest two months ago to name my dual persona. After everything from knockoff pop-culture names like "Fairy Trotter" and "Frequent Flyer" to awkward ones like "Crisp Angel," Chatty Patty declared 'Wingdinger' to be the winning name of choice.)

And I was stuck with it, because if I were to get a lawyer to sue, my mother would find out about my identity (what is the point of being a teenager if you don't keep secrets from your parents?) And Cheryl, since she is now on the opposing side, would make sure I lose (despite her inadequacies as a mother, her lawyer skills were razor sharp.)

Plus I didn't really have any idea what else I could call my superhero self. It's not something I'd ever really had to worry about before a few months ago. So *that* might be a good lesson for teenagers today: Always have a superhero name ready, in case you ever find out you actually are one.

"Do you think you'd like to be a superhero, Jason?" Martha asked, mildly intrigued.

"Yeah, it'd be cool. Especially if I could fly," Jason grinned. "I'd never take the bus and I wouldn't have to pay any money for gas! I'd save billions."

"What about helping people?" Martha asked. "Do you think superheroes are obligated to help people out who need it? Anyone?"

"Well, sure," Poncey spoke up. "But there are more important things like girls, and dating, and money to consider—"

"That's enough. Thank you, Harbor," Mrs. Smithe interrupted. "Why don't you pick someone to go next?"

"Sure," Jason smiled.

I bit back another laugh. Jason could never be like me; he was too ignorant to be good at being a ringleader.

Jason picked Poncey to go next.

When Poncey's first words were, "I got this article from my friend Mikey Salyards," I groaned to myself. I knew what was coming at that point.

Mikey was my best friend; a few months back, he'd even helped me save Gwen from the evil supernatural forces currently inhabiting the city. Mikey was very popular. He was so popular, he used to be known for having a new girlfriend almost every week. I mean "used to" here because Mikey hadn't had a new one in some weeks. But there was a reason as to why.

I paused my game briefly to watch. If I knew Mikey the way I think I do, I'd bet anything he brought Poncey an article about—

"This magazine article from *Trends* features Starry Knight, the other superhero running around town," Poncey grinned, proudly presented the article.

Yes, there it was. I'd been right (of course.) And then I was back to the Tetris game.

"No one's gotten a good picture of her or Wingdinger," I could hear him drone on, "So they attempted to draw Starry Knight based on Mikey's and Gwen's descriptions. But Mikey insists they didn't have it right. She has slightly slanted eyes, and they are more like violets more than grapes."

I pushed the pause button again; a mixture of admiration and disgust rushed through me.

I knew Mikey was obsessed with finding Starry Knight and asking her out; until then, no other girl was for him—including all the cheerleaders. And *I* was even tired of teasing him about it at that point; it didn't work out well for me when I did anyway, because he said I was stuck on Gwen.

That reminded me, I hadn't told him yet she'd agreed to go out on a date with me. A smug look pushed its way onto my face. I decided I'd tell him during English. It wasn't like there was going to be anything important to worry about in that class. And Tim Ryder was going to be there, too, so it would be doubly satisfying.

Let's put it like this: If I was an X-Box, Tim was the toy you would find at the bottom of a cereal box—a box of cheap cereal, at that.

"Mikey insists Starry Knight is the most beautiful woman in the world. Plus she's got the best archery skills," Poncey concluded.

Pathetic. I had a strong feeling Mikey had babbled the entire speech to Poncey about three minutes before class had started.

"Nice to know you've got standards when it comes to girls," Jason called out jokingly.

The class fubbled with laughter. And I felt left out, because as much as I couldn't stand her, Mikey/Poncey had a point. I laughed anyway.

"Okay class, Poncey is entitled to his own opinion," Martha snapped. "Even if it is actually someone else's."

The end of first period came soon after I finished my presentation, which was a respectable tabloid report on some celebrity's arrest and upcoming court date. Other than my presentation, I hadn't taken the slightest break from my Tetris game.

"You guys think these presentations will go on for the rest of the period?" I asked blandly as I aced another row.

"I don't know," Poncey shrugged. "Martha'll probably just make us go back to notes otherwise."

"That's good," I muttered. "I don't really want anything to exciting to happen today."

I glanced over at Gwen, whom I had been ignoring for the most of the morning while I was working off my bad mood. She was busy talking to her friends, Samantha Carter and Brittany Taylor, who in turn were sneaking suspicious looks in my direction every other moment.

Ugh. I decided it would be best to get Gwen some new friends after we were further along in our relationship. Hopefully, I wouldn't have to do any actual work with that, though; it was in my best interest to distract Gwen and allow my friends to overshadow hers, until her friends were lost in some sort of oblivion.

Jason leaned in. "Hey, I hear the swim meet coming up is going to be packed," he said. "I'm getting excited."

"Me, too," I agreed, both with his statement and the change of subject.

The swim season was my real chance to shine, believe it or not. Don't get me wrong—I was a star on the football field as well. But when I hit the water, people were brought to tears with the perfection of my form and the amazement of my speed. Well, close enough to tears, anyway.

And at the next swim meet, college scouts would be present. It's always something to look forward to, when people come hundreds of miles to beg you to sign onto their college—offering full tuition and fees—merely because you can swim better than practically everyone else in the state. Maybe even in the whole country, too.

I'd known for some time already my parents would pay for my college, but I was really one of those people who didn't really want to be a trust-fund baby. Not without my own effort.

Besides, at the rate I was going, I'd be getting money *back* from college.

Still focused on my Game Pac, settled down into my chair, I fiddled away my time as Jason and Poncey talked sports. All the while, my mind was once more helplessly and gloriously sacrificed to the onslaught of mindless and addictive gaming. I grinned as my Tetris pieces started falling faster and faster, almost like shooting stars … I barely noticed the passing time.

"Wonder if Mrs. Smithe is coming back?" Jason asked.

"Don't know? You think she fell in?" Poncey snickered.

"Maybe she's trying to get more coffee?" I suggested, hardly paying any attention at all to them.

I didn't really care where Martha had gone, since it gave me some worry-free time to play my game system in peace. I was still a bit sore at Mrs. Smithe for giving me a detention last semester—not that I held it against her, or anything.

Martha entered the room at last, but I barely noticed. She began talking to the class, while I was so wrapped up in my game—I was closing in on thirty-five thousand, which would set a new record if I passed it—that I only snapped back to attention when I heard my name.

"… So why don't you take the seat behind Dinger there? I'm sure he'll be more than willing to help you feel welcome."

My eyes shot up to see a girl up front with Martha. My first thought was I couldn't believe she was wearing a Rosemont uniform. In Central, of all places.

There was an accompanying stillness in the room at that moment, like an invisible barrier of pure tension. It's only when I heard a small beeping noise I realized I'd lost my Tetris game. In the two seconds I'd been distracted. Short of a new record by only ten points.

I mumble a curse or two under my breath before tapping Jason on the shoulder. "What's going on?"

"Apparently we've got a new student or something," Jason shrugged.

"Looks like she's from Rosemont. Probably a preppy, spoiled brat," I dismissed easily enough.

Meanwhile, Martha turned toward the rest of the class. "Everyone, this is—"

The girl stepped forward. "Please, call me Raiya, Mrs. Smithe," she interrupted gently.

"All right. Class, this is Raiya Cole. She'll be joining our class for the rest of the year. I expect each and every one of you … "

"Raiya Cole?" Jason leaned forward in curiosity, interrupting my attention to Martha. "I wonder if she's—"

"All right boys and girls, you've had your break. We've got a history benchmark coming up soon, and we need to finish our presentations today."

Raiya made her way over to the seat behind me. I looked at her briefly as she passed and sat down. I snorted to myself at the ugly brown and white Rosemont uniform; I hadn't seen one since the school's failed attempt to put on a play last fall, and I could honestly say I had no regrets about that.

Rosemont Academy had been Central's main football rival, but that all stopped (supposedly) when Rosemont had been demolished by the meteor that smashed into the city last October. Since it was a private academy, most kids there were rich and spoiled; there were some 'normal' kids, but they made up only two percent of school's population.

"Psst! Raiya!" I glanced over to see Gwen hanging out of her seat as she waved to the new girl. "Hi!"

Great, Gwen seems to know her, I thought. Maybe Raiya *was* from the play. There *was* a nagging tug on my memory when I looked at her.

She didn't look back as I discreetly scrutinized her. It was weird having someone sitting behind me. I don't think I liked it.

It was probably more out of this concern or maybe it was just boredom that I decided to keep tabs on her throughout the hour. I did want to be sure she didn't do anything weird to me. Like putting chewed gum in my hair. Or putting a curse on me (You can't blame me for thinking this. She *was* from Rosemont, after all.)

Boy, she was not pretty. Her dull, brown hair was pulled back, but a lot of it had fallen free, blocking a lot of her face from clear view. She seemed to be very plain. Very, very ordinary looking.

It was closer to the end of the period when I peeked back at her, and saw her dark eyes snap to mine. "What do you want?" she asked, blasé enough to make me irritated. Like she'd been expecting me to say something.

"Er … hi," I attempted to act normal even as I felt awkward for getting caught gawking.

She said nothing in reply, just staring at me under the cover of her shaggy bangs. It did nothing to help me feel less awkward, to say the least.

I didn't want to be rude, or at least appear rude, even if she was certainly not worried about that. So I tried again. A bracelet on her arm caught my attention. Obviously it's one of a kind, very expensive. "Nice bracelet," I complimented.

Girls love it when guys compliment them. And if they're rich, they love it all the more, because all the rich girls I know are flaky (Via Delorosa, my ex-girlfriend from last year, dashed across my mind's eye.)

So I was surprised when she didn't stop looking at me.

That's odd. I compulsively stared at her for a few more seconds, flustered.

Her eyes narrowed; I could almost feel the *snap!* of her patience as it finally cracked. "What?" she asked a moment later, her voice clearly tired and borderline irritated.

"Nothing," I replied disdainfully, my patience and politics gone. "It's not every day I see someone from Rosemont in this school."

"Well," Raiya finally met my gaze again, this time with a pinch of challenge sparkling in her eyes. "I guess it's not every day I get stared at by someone who looks like a turtle."

Poncey, who apparently was listening in to my conversation without my knowledge, burst out laughing. "That was good," he laughed, holding out his hand to Raiya for a high-five. When she didn't respond, and he noticed my glare, he wisely pulled back (he was already in trouble for eavesdropping, no need to make it worse.) "Sorry, Dinger."

Looks like I've got some adversaries in school as well as out of school.

Oh well. It was nothing new, really. Such was the fate of the popular.

I was about to say something nasty about Rosemont again, just to get her going, when Gwen came up beside us. Apparently the period was over.

Huh? Where did the time go?

"Hi, Raiya!" She smiled. "I haven't seen you in a while. How are you?"

I interrupted here. "Gwen, you know her? She just called me a turtle!"

"No, I said you *looked like* one," Raiya calmly corrected me. "I didn't say you *were* one."

Gwen laughed. "Hmm … you know, she's got a point."

"What!?"

Raiya shrugged. "Is this a friend of yours, Gwen?"

Gwen turned to me. "Why didn't you introduce yourself?" There was a bit of surprise in her voice, which annoyed me; it was like I'd fallen short of her expectations, and I *never* did that.

"I'm Ham Dinger," I sneered out, only for Gwen's sake. "And I was not—"

"I'm sorry, what? Did you say "Humdinger"? You're a humdinger?" Raiya smoothly interrupted me. A little too smoothly …

"That's it!" Poncey practically squealed with delight (What was he doing, eavesdropping again!?) "Humdinger! It's a perfect nickname for you."

"I like it," Jason agreed, turning around with new enthusiasm. "You're a real humdinger, Dinger." He laughed.

I was suddenly torn between beating up my friends for giving me trouble or cursing out the girl who started it all. I was just about to carry out the latter when the bell rang.

"Come with me, Raiya. I'll help you find your way around school," Gwen offered, pulling on Raiya's arm.

Raiya brushed right past me. I wouldn't have thought anything of her ignorance if she hadn't flashed me a small smirk as she walked out the door. Sharp heat flashed through me as my rage boiled.

She might have won this round, but there's no way she would ever get the best of me again, I thought. I marched up to Mrs. Smithe's desk, ready to face the challenge directly. "Mrs. Smithe, would you move that girl from behind me, please?"

"Why? She's perfectly fine where she is. Besides, I didn't see her distracting you at all."

"But she was!"

"Now, Dinger, come on, it's just one girl. Besides, you're Mr. Popular. Maybe you'll be able to help her adjust to the school."

"Why is she even here? Did the school need another preppy-rich kid to even out the student socio-economic population?"

Mrs. Smithe narrowed her eyes behind her thick black frames. "That's none of your beeswax, Dinger. You'll get used to her. Now, skedaddle. You've got class."

I fumed as I dejectedly walked out of class.

☼<u>6</u>☼
Swim Team

Central's swim team was more than well-known, all thanks to me. (Of course!) Besides me, there was nothing really worth mentioning. I guess Mikey was mentioned sometimes, but it's almost always in comparison to me. And that was the way I liked it.

Heading off to practice for the last period of the day was a reward in itself. Between getting told I looked like a turtle and having my friends call me "Humdinger," no matter how much I protested, I was ready to throttle someone by the time swim practice rolled around. I had a few choice options there.

Including the one who had just presented herself directly in front of me. "Hi Hammy!"

I groaned to myself as Samantha Carter made it her personal goal to make my day even more terrible than it already was. Samantha had this huge crush on me. (Samantha told Brittany who told Gwen who told me who posted it up on the virtual gossip board and laughed at it along with all of my other cyber friends.) She was apparently desperate, too, because even when I was intentionally mean to her she thinks it's her fault and starts weeping and apologizing. I swear, if the teachers caught her crying in the halls, I was going to wind up in peer mediation or get a bullying stamp on my record. I'd learned it's just best to avoid her.

"Hi Samantha," I muttered.

61

Her gray-blue eyes sparkled. "Hi Hammy! I'm glad I caught up with you. I have a question for you."

"What?" I asked brusquely as I started easing around her, moving towards the pool area.

Samantha giggled. "I was going to ask you for a favor. I need some help bringing my math grade up."

"I can't hack into the school's records," I said as I tried to circle around her as carefully, as nonchalantly, as possible.

Her giggles multiplied. "Oh, I wasn't going to ask for you to do *that*!" She laughed, grating my nerves. "I was going to see if you would be willing to tutor me."

"I don't—"

"I'd be more than happy to pay you, of course," she continued. "I really want to do well in Ms. Darlington's class so I can get into her AP classes next year."

At last! I was on the other side of her, and I hadn't even needed to brush up against her. Relief from perdition was in sight.

"So, what do you think, Hammy?"

"I think I would prefer it if you would call me Dinger like everyone else," I grumbled softly, as I headed into the locker room.

She giggled *again. Again!* "No, I mean about tutoring me, maybe after school a couple days a week?"

"Samantha, I don't have time to help you after school. I've got swimming and now my brother to watch, and my work to take care of, frankly."

"I could come over and help with your brother! I'm great with kids."

Okay, that was my limit. I looked her in the eye so she knew I was deadly serious. "I can't. I'm too busy. And besides, I really don't tutor anyone. Not unless I feel some obligation in the matter. And I don't, because we're not even really friends."

"Sure we are," Samantha insisted. "Gwen's one of my best friends."

"Being friends with Gwen doesn't make you mine," I told her plainly. Remembering the scene from Mrs. Smithe's class this morning, I snorted and added, "Just ask Raiya that." And then I slammed the door in her face just for extra dramatic effect.

Finally I could sigh with relief. I shook my head. *Women!*

Moments later, when the water hit me, I felt better. Cheap therapy, I suppose. But there *is* some therapeutic benefit, or so I've heard.

A few minutes later, Mrs. Uzziah, the head coach of the swim team, and Mr. Collier, the co-coach, walked in and practice started getting underway with laps.

Laps were easy for me, but I knew why the others groaned. A lot of the swim team members were beginners, and they were stupid beginners on top of that. Why did they suffer so much humiliation and meaningless work, you ask? Most joined the swim team in order to get better grades in Mrs. Uzziah's classes since she went easier on grading her team members' work. And besides Martha, she was the hardest teacher in the school.

By the end (and even before that), everyone was exhausted and ready to go home. But Coach Uzzy blew her whistle, and like her personal trained hamsters, we stopped. "Okay, everyone line up!" she called. "Boys first!"

I grinned. *We're going to race!* And I loved to race. I'd won all of them so far, and by a significant lead.

"Hey, Humdinger!" Mikey smiled from the next lane over. "I'm going to beat you this time!"

Cringing at the nickname, I had no choice but to make things more interesting. "Loser buys lunch tomorrow."

"I hope you don't mind eating some humble pie," Mikey remarked, leaning into proper position.

"Who says that anymore? That's lame," I muttered back.

"One hundred freestyle!" Uzzy called out. "Ready! Mark!"

The whistle blew, and we were off. I dived in, arms extended, back straight and body in perfect formation. The second I sliced into the water, I began swimming with all my might as my second wind kicked in, pushing for the lead.

But Mikey wasn't too far behind, I noticed a moment later. Wonder if he'd been practicing more, maybe?

With half of a lap to go, we were neck and neck. Much to my chagrin.

Conjuring up all my teenage angst, I swept for the wall. Between superhero troubles, stupid ex-Rosemont students, and irritating family members, Mikey had nothing on me there.

And as I touched the wall, there was no rage left; it was all happiness and victory, even if I hadn't won by as much as I'd hoped.

"Good race, Mike," I said graciously as we headed for the locker room.

Mikey replied but his response was muffled.

I took it with a smile. "Well, you are getting faster," I told my defeated friend.

Another grumbling, jumbled reply. I frowned; I was *trying* to be nice. And if it was one thing I hated more than anything else, it was to be nice, even when it would've been funnier to be mean, and not getting the same consideration in return.

Plus I'd had a really hard day already.

So it really wasn't my fault when my patience snapped. "It's so nice you're getting better at something, anyway. I still have the better grades and Tetris scores, and the—"

"Bigger mouth, too," Mikey retorted. "I'm sticking around for a while; I'll catch you later, Humdinger."

"Don't call me that," I snarled. "It's not even supposed to be a nickname! Some weird girl said it and Poncey took off with it."

"Sucks to be you," Mikey rolled his eyes.

"Yeah, I guess it does, 'cause I have to leave anyway. I did want to tell you before I left that I got a date with Gwen tomorrow."

At that, Mikey did finally turn and pay full attention to me. "Well, congratulations. I see she finally caved into her parents' wishes and decided to go out with you," he muttered. "Have fun at Rachel's."

The rest of my patience flushed out as blinding fury took over. "What are you talking about?" I growled. "She didn't agree to a date with me because of her parents."

"Really? That's not what I heard." Mikey smirked, obviously glad to see I was getting upset.

"You don't know what really happened," I bit back.

"So her parents weren't actually there when you asked her out?"

My fist clenched of its own accord. "You know what?" I spat. "You're just jealous, because I actually have a real date, with Gwen, who is a real person, instead of some hot-tempered, disagreeable harpy!"

Mikey apparently didn't hear me, or maybe he just didn't know he was supposed to care more, because he walked away, saying nothing else.

I stood there and stewed angrily. *That ungrateful jerk.* I slammed my fist into a nearby locker and grimaced, not just because of the pain (or the general stupidity of the motion) but because I had a sinking feeling Mikey was right about Gwen. Remembering the flare of emotions I'd felt as I squeezed her hand, I burned with renewed vehemence.

Mikey could be troublesome sometimes. I kept him on as a friend for reasons even I didn't fully remember all the time. When I thought about our friendship, only really one memory consistently stuck with me, and that was the day I found out his dad left.

We'd grown up together mostly through school, and a lot more through sports. He was always laughing and smiling when we were younger. And then it just started changing. Not really noticeably at first.

Just small things. Like how he couldn't come over to my house as often because he had to buy groceries. Or clean up the house.

About eight years ago, I remembered asking him to come over to my house because I needed someone to practice football with me. It was my first year on a team, and I'd already known going into it I wanted to win the championship. I could tell from Mikey's voice something was wrong. So I went over to his house to more or less make him go practice with me.

I'd run through the rain, barging into his house. I walked in just as he was cleaning up a pile of vomit. I could his mother screaming from the other room, but Mikey and I just looked

THE STARLIGHT CHRONICLES

at each other for a long moment. And then I went to work helping him. No one said anything until late into the night, when his mom was asleep and everything was taken care of.

Turned out his dad had gotten a new job and, as I understand, it basically tore his family apart. His mom went off on this depressive run after he left. She'd throw up, rant for hours about nonsensical things, and cry into the long hours of the night, weeping for her husband. It took her years to recover, even after she'd gotten the necessary medications and moved her family back in with her mother.

But it was a lot for a second grader to take. How can you explain alcoholism and depression to an eight year old?

It took Mikey a long while to learn how to hide it; longer still to forget about it, and even longer to remember the better things about life. Now he's more or less back to normal, but he doesn't talk about it.

Ever since that day, Mikey's been like my brother. And as my brother, he's in a position to argue with me a lot more than others. He took advantage of that far too often. Sometimes it's cool and a lot of times it's not.

And guess what, this was one of those times when it was *not.*

I barely noticed the sweltering sensation creeping up my arm as I left the pool area.

☼7☼
Adam

"So you really don't mind Adam tagging along with us?"

Gwen laughed charmingly at my question. "I like kids," she assured me. "It's not a chore to be around your little brother."

I looked at her now, her auburn hair streaming in the dull winter sunlight, as she held onto Adam's hand. She was perfect, I decided. She was pretty, smart, and kind-hearted. Everything that would fit into my life perfectly.

"Well, still," I remarked, "There was the matter of his daycare. That place is just scary. Makes me wonder how I survived." I shivered to give the proper effect.

Gwen laughed again. "Nice to know daycares are terrifying to you, Hammy."

"I am more terrified at the thought of you not wanting to go out with me today when I'm stuck with my brother."

The sincerity in my voice seemed to affect her quite nicely. She might have even blushed a bit, but I pretended I didn't notice as I turned to go through Shoreside Park. It was the quickest way to get to Rachel's.

Yes, it was a perfect Tuesday. Nothing, not even arguing with Raiya during history, or my friends constantly calling me "Humdinger," could break me. Gwen had a magical appeal to my day, and getting to talk about our date with my friends and social media only seemed to make it more exciting.

"Adam, come back here!" I called out as my brother suddenly sped off. There's a possibility of ice, and if Adam wasn't careful—

"Waaahh!"

I smacked my hand to my forehead. Adam never listened. One of the reasons I didn't really like being responsible for him.

Gwen and I hurried over, picked Adam up, and began dusting him off while Adam cried his eyes out. His wailing drew the attention of all the people nearby, and of course I probably looked like some creepy teenager to everyone watching, or some incompetent type of parent. I sighed, brushing some more snow out of Adam's hair.

Adam inherited a lot more from Mark than I did. He's got the black hair and brown eyes, and even the facial structure of Mark's side of the family. I suppose I picked up more of Cheryl's side, because of my brown hair, but I had blue eyes and a distinctively straight nose which seemed to have popped up out of nowhere. There was also an age difference of thirteen plus years between Adam and me.

"Come on, come on, don't cry, there's no hole in your jeans," I tried to reassure my brother. "Shush, would you? It's okay now."

It took him a few moments, but he eventually tore his hand away from mine and bustled off again, heading towards the play area. Finally, I thought. Gwen and I could actually *talk*.

"So, uh, I wonder when the snow's going to melt?" I asked, gesturing to the high piles of packed snow lining the ends of the streets.

"Probably not till March or April," Gwen replied. "But it's been a mild year for the weather."

Conversation steadily grew harder. But we settled into silence, and for a few moments, we just enjoyed it. I was just thinking about mentioning something else when my chance was stolen.

"Gwen?"

Ugh. I gritted my perfect teeth together angrily enough to make every dental hygienist in a two-block radius cringe. *Of course Tim Ryder had to show up to ruin my day.*

Gwen and I turned simultaneously to see my favorite spaz boy. Of all the nerve. Who did he think he was? He was Tim, the equivalent of a jester in the court of my own little kingdom. The poster child for future busboys, present acne problems, and past mistakes … that was who he was, and who he would always be.

I put on my fake smile, which only became real when I remembered I was on a date with Gwen. "Hi, Tim," I greeted. It's better to take the initiative with things like this. It would make it easier for me to dismiss him when I got tired of him in about a minute or less.

"Oh, hi, Dinger." He smiled, and then turned to Gwen. "I, uh … wanted to ask you if you had the notes from Spanish last week … when I was out sick."

"Oh. Uh, I think I left them in my locker, actually," Gwen said.

It was so much fun to watch them work at their awkward conversation. When Gwen and Tim finally decided a few broken sentences later to meet at her locker in the morning, I decided it was time for me to step in.

"Well, nice seeing you Tim, but Gwen and I are headed to Rachel's for our date. I'd promised I'd meet up with some of the guys while we're there."

He took the hint, noticeably. Thank goodness Gwen was just staring at the ground, or I think she would have been upset to see the wounded look in Tim's gaze.

"Sure. Uh … yeah, well, have fun. I'll see you tomorrow, Gwen. Bye."

And then Tim waved hesitantly, and hurried off. Not quickly enough for my liking, of course, but still quickly enough when he tripped a few yards away, he landed on his knees. I pretended not to watch as a sense of supreme satisfaction washed over me.

"What are you meeting up with the guys for?" Gwen asked, drawing my attention back to her.

"Oh, Drew, Simon, and Jason just need some help with the biology homework from Elm's class," I said, smiling in a reassuring way. "Poncey might show up too. But don't worry. It's more of a matter of exchanging papers than anything else." Was it my fault if I would also get to flaunt Gwen there in front of my friends?

"Oh. Uh, okay." She then frowned.

"What's wrong?" I asked.

"Adam's run off again," Gwen replied in a worried tone. She scanned across the playground and into the woods nearby. "I didn't even hear him run off."

"Great, just great," I muttered. "Well, he is notoriously quiet for a three-year-old," I surmised, starting to get slightly terrified myself (This was enough to make me *not* want to have children.) "I'll look over here in the woods. Can you check the playground?"

"Sure," Gwen nodded, and hurried off towards the larger gathering of screaming children.

I watched her go long enough to appreciate just once more how pretty she was, rushing through the snowy background, and how grateful I was she was there to help.

"Well, are you going to go look for your brother or not?"

I jerked at the sound of the voice coming from directly behind me. "Elysian! What are you doing here?" I growled, pulling the small form of my changeling dragon out of my hoodie. "Never mind. I can hazard a guess. Hey, help me find my brother, would you? He ran away again."

Elysian groaned. "If you had been paying attention, you wouldn't have lost him!"

"Just stop talking, would you? You're giving me a headache."

"*I'm* giving *you* the headache? You've got to be the most thick-skulled, hard-hearted person I've ever met! And I've been in existence much longer than you!"

"Just hush up and help me find my brother," I spat angrily. "We've got to find Adam before something happens to him."

Or more importantly, me. Cheryl and Mark would kill me if Adam gets hurt or taken or ...

"I'll look from above," Elysian told me, half-reluctant, as he jumped into the air. Seconds later, a huge dragon emerged from the quiet of the wooded area of the park. Several children were heard screaming as I ran down the park walkway, calling for my brother.

Several moments go by, at once both fast and slow. Quickly approaching my death. Slowly drawing out my torture. I was about to give up and call the police when I saw a little shadow tottering into the woods.

"Adam!" I called.

"Did you see him?" Elysian asked, flying overhead.

"I think he just went into that woody area. Go around to the other side and see if he comes out. I'll go in after him."

Elysian didn't question me (for once) and flew off. I hurried through the snow and icy patches toward the trees.

I caught sight of my brother's jacket and exhaled, slowly, abnormally. He's not too far from me; thankfully, he's not running anymore. I had almost rejoiced when a sliver of pain leaked out of my marked wrist again.

My feet stopped. My heart raced. Could we be in danger? I looked at the mark on my wrist, peeking out from underneath my hoodie. It's glowing again.

Oh crap. What if Adam got his soul sucked out? Cheryl would kill me for sure!

That had to be it, too, because I suddenly see him, and he's just standing there, his gaze transfixed. I inched closer, trying not to make a lot of noise. Maybe I could interfere enough without transforming and still get Adam's soul back.

I was three thick trees away when I stopped.

Adam wasn't getting his soul sucked out of him. He was staring at a girl.

A girl, sitting on a blanket on a rock. She had a light jacket on, and her plain, brown hair was pulled back behind a winter headband. Her nose was red, and her eyes were focused on the canvas in front of her.

I could hear Adam whisper. "Pretty," he murmured. I was surprised; he almost never talked outside of the house. It was for this reason I curiously stood to watch him.

Cheryl believed Adam was autistic. She was thinking of getting him into see a few specialists before, as he was three and he didn't really seem to communicate well with a lot of people. I didn't really pay attention, but it was true there were only a few people Adam really warmed up to, and he was usually shy unless he'd known them a long time.

I watched as he leapt out from behind his bush. "Roar!" he called out.

"I heard you coming," the girl said; I could hear the smile in her voice, even as it was muffled. "Sorry to ruin your surprise."

Adam walked up closer. "Pretty," he said, pointing to her.

"I thought you looked familiar," the girl said. "You're that same little boy wandering around the woods last fall. I found you and took you to Gwen Kessler. What are you doing here?"

What? I remembered that day as though it was yesterday. It was the day I accepted my duty as Wingdinger, although the name hadn't yet been given to me. I'd lost Adam while I'd been arguing with Gwen and Tim, and then an *eela*, a shadow demon, had shown up, distracting me. It hadn't been until later Adam had been found … by a girl. Who'd turned him over to Gwen.

A girl who'd looked familiar to me, but I couldn't place her at the time.

Now I watched as she climbed down from her seat, and knelt at eye level with Adam. He pointed at her, touching her nose lightly. "Angel," he said.

"You can call me Raiya," she told him, taking his hand, and I nearly choked.

"Raiya?"

She turned and saw me staring at her. "Oh. It's you. What do you want now?"

"That's my brother."

Raiya stood up and brushed the snow off her knees, still holding onto Adam's hand. "He's *your* brother?" she asked. Her eyes widened in what looked like surprise. Or maybe shock. "You're Cheryl Dinger's son?"

Huh? That was a bit weird. "How do you know my mother?" I asked.

Raiya immediately bristled. "Who *doesn't* know your mother?"

"Hammonton!" Adam called, waving.

"Hey, Adam," I waved back. "You want to go get something to eat? You must be tired after running away from me and Gwen."

Adam giggled.

"Mischievous little fellow, are you?" Raiya smiled down at him, who looked up at her with an expression of wonder and reverence. "Well, it was nice meeting you. But time to say good-bye, Adam."

He let go of her hand quietly, and then stomped over to me, as if it was some kind of chore.

I rolled my eyes on the side. *Of course* my brother had a crush on the girl who was the biggest pain in my life, I thought bitterly to myself. I cleared my throat. "Thank you."

"You're welcome," Raiya replied. She brushed back her bangs and sat back down on her blanket. There was a glint in her dark eyes as she added, "Humdinger."

I said nothing to that. As I made my way back to the play area with Adam in tow, I tried not to curse at my bad luck (I had to clean myself up around Adam—Cheryl would've tanned my hide for teaching Adam any words more offensive than 'butt'.)

"What's wrong?" Elysian asked as he transformed and jumped back into my jacket hood. "Is Adam hurt?"

"No … I just … We're fine. Let's not worry right now," I muttered. I didn't want to think about Raiya anymore. I didn't like her. And I really didn't like the idea of Adam liking her (Was there really any doubt about that?) "Let's get something to eat, Adam. And none of this Russian meat diet junk Cheryl's been making us eat."

Cheryl's latest and greatest inspiration for a diet had been included only sugar-free smoothies and tons of freshly slaughtered organic meat. Her new chef, Helga, was very scary. Like KGB scary. Needless to say I didn't find it an appealing diet.

"So, where are we going?" Elysian asked, clearly too interested for his presence to seem like a coincidence to me any longer.

"What does it matter to you? You don't need food to survive," I reminded him.

"I know." Elysian leered back at me. "However, I do like to occasionally snack on some human treats … things like cookies, cakes, those muffin things, and some pudding—"

"You're pathetic," I cut in. "Come on, we need to go get Gwen. She'll probably be wondering where we are by now."

☼<u>8</u>☼
Date Night

Walking into Rachel's Café was like walking into Florida after being trapped in Canada for the winter; it was warm and welcoming to the point of nearly being overwhelmed. It was a perfect day, I thought, for a hot chocolate and a bowl of soup. And maybe a scone. Or a bagel.

It was easy to see why Rachel's was my favorite place to eat. Or my favorite place period.

Adam hurried to a booth near the main counter and tried to sit down (he needed a booster seat) while Elysian sneaked onto his thick sweatshirt. After promising to secure us a table, Gwen hurried after him, determined not to lose him in the small crowd.

I was just about to head over towards them when I noticed a new painting up by the door.

One of the reasons I like Rachel's Café so much was because of the atmosphere. It was cultured but unique, charming in both demeanor and décor. Her paintings were hung with care and class.

For this new painting, there were birds and other winged creatures in it—including a dragon … one that looked a lot like Elysian.

"That's weird," I muttered to myself. It had the same black wings, and the same long body … the face was slightly different, but not to a very high degree. Someone must've managed to get a good snapshot of Elysian in these past couple of months, I thought, as a small tingle of dread crept through my body.

"Hey, Hamilton!" Rachel called out, waving.

"Hi Rachel," I smiled. "Busy day?"

"You'd better believe it." She hopped around the counter and came over to me. "I must've had close to three hundred people since morning. Let me tell you, there are days that end in 'y' and then there are days that end in '*why!?*' and I think this is one of the latter." She laughed before catching sight of Adam as he made his way back over to me. "Aw, are you babysitting today?" Rachel gushed.

"Er, yeah." I tried not to grimace. I didn't want to think of it as "babysitting." It sounded really girly when someone put it that way. "This is my brother, Adam. He's three years old."

Adam just looked up at Rachel. He didn't say anything.

"He doesn't talk much," I warned her.

"That's all right," Rachel brushed the issue aside. "How about I get you some food?"

"Sounds perfect," I grinned. "I'll have a hot chocolate and the special. What do you have for kids here?"

"I know just what to make him, don't worry. Anything else?" Rachel grinned.

"Some jumbo cookies and a glass of milk," Elysian spoke up, hidden in the folds of Adam's sweater.

"Huh?" Rachel looked down at Adam in wonder as I clenched my fists, hoping I wasn't going to have to explain why my pet lizard-chameleon was talking.

Rachel blinked. "Well, what do you know? He can talk. He sure has a deep voice for his age though."

"Uh, yeah," I laughed, nearly maniacally. "Guess so."

"I'll be right back with your drinks," Rachel promised.

When she left, I looked around nonchalantly. Then I grabbed a hold of Elysian, nearly choking him. "You want to give up your cover for food you don't need to survive on?"

"Well, no, but I can smell the cookies from here. They're fresh." Elysian pouted. "Give me some leeway."

I stuck Elysian on my back and said, "Don't pull that again. Ever."

Elysian rolled his eyes and huffed, irritated.

"As if today could get any worse," I groaned.

"What's wrong?" Rachel asked.

I flinched, unaware Rachel had come back. "Nothing. Hey, Rachel, I forgot to tell you. I'm here with Gwen tonight, so get her whatever she wants and put it on my tab."

Rachel's eyes sparkled. "Oh, on a date, are you?"

"Yep," I grinned proudly as I moved over to the table with Gwen. "Gwen, you remember Rachel, right?"

Gwen smiled up at our pretty hostess. "Yes, I do," she remarked. "You have the best food here. And the music nights are great, too. I came to the last one."

Rachel beamed. "Thanks. We're hoping to get some more of those going this year. It's a nice change. And the new regulars Hamilton's brought in for me seem to like it." She gestured towards the booths, up and down, as many of my friends, followers, and cohorts chattered happily across from each other. Several were even holding conversations over several tables.

I grinned. "Glad to help. Although," I added, "It's more Jason's doing than mine. He raves about this place."

Gwen's smile widened. She seemed to like it when I was nicer to other people, even if it was really unnecessary.

Rachel quickly took our orders and then left us alone. Well, alone with Adam. It was more or less being alone.

"So, how're your classes going?" I asked, trying to jumpstart our conversation.

Gwen shrugged. "I'm really kind of worried about the benchmark for Mrs. Smithe's class coming up," she started, and went on to tell me about how she had a new study schedule, and her parents wanted her to do this, and that, and something about college applications, and … other stuff.

I was just reassuring myself that it was good to be this comfortable, even if it was a bit boring, and Gwen was so pretty, and I was lucky to be here, when the four-point mark on my wrist began to burn, slowly but surely.

THE STARLIGHT CHRONICLES

"Hammy?"

"Huh?" I jolted back to Gwen, shifting in my seat to cover up the discomfort of my arm. "Oh, sorry, I was just thinking about the presentations today."

"In history?"

"Yeah. Some of them were pretty lame."

"Oh." Gwen seemed a bit confused. "I thought it was all pretty interesting."

"Come on, Gwen," I heckled, "Wingdinger and Starry Knight are not topics for history class, even if it's a topic on propaganda and the press making up lies." The pain tingling up my arm did not enhance this conversation.

"They are part of current events," Gwen pointed out.

"So what?"

Gwen shrugged. "If you don't want to talk about it, we can always talk about something else."

I nodded. "Good." At that, the twinging tickle in my right arm decreased. Just a bit.

"So. How was your day?" Gwen asked.

"Well, it would've been better if the new girl would've kept her mouth shut during history," I started. "I don't know why some people insist on being a pain in the neck."

"Whoa, sounds like you've got quite a problem there," Rachel interrupted as she handed us our drinks.

"Yeah. I wish my teacher would move her, but she won't. I've already asked."

"Hammonton!" Adam gurgled up, as I finally realized he was eating his napkin.

Rachel looked at him, confused. "I thought his voice—"

"He can do voices sometimes," I quickly interrupted as I tried to clean out the wet napkin from Adam's mouth. "Anyway, this girl has just been the icing on the cake of death destiny has decided to serve me."

"Oh, I see. Nice imagery," Rachel said with a smile.

"Girl troubles, lad? It must be true love!"

Neither of us had apparently heard Rachel's grandfather come inside. I groaned more loudly this time.

"Who's that?" Gwen asked, leaning forward in interest.

Grandpa Odd was quite a character; I was pretty sure he was senile, but Rachel and her family couldn't keep him in a nursing home anymore (especially since he was a lot of trouble and frequently ran away from them) or under a nurse's careful watch (he was still normal enough to be ineligible for the mental institution and it was very expensive to pay someone qualified enough to watch him, apparently.)

I snorted at the old man's remark. "He's Rachel's crazy grandfather," I replied, not really trying to be quiet about it as the old man came up to our booth.

Grandpa Odd laughed. "That's good, lad, that's good." He pulled a chair up to the table and made himself at home, much to my disgust. "Rachel, get me some coffee, would you?"

Rachel looked at me apologetically as she headed off.

Grandpa Odd grinned his old-folks grin at me. "You might think I'm insane, young man, but you are more out of place than I."

"What?" I asked. What was he talking about? He couldn't possibly know about … all that superhero stuff. "What are you talking about?" As if on a cue, my arm once more sparked with pain. Supernatural calling. And it was getting stronger.

Grandpa Odd, fortunately or unfortunately, demanded more of my attention. He had an innate ability to badger me with babble which didn't make any sense. I always felt like a test I hadn't prepared for was coming on when he was around.

There was a playful twinkle in the old man's eyes. "Oh, you know what I mean … You count it strange, but then, so once did I."

"No I don't," I huffed.

Grandpa Odd grew silent. He sat back in his chair and folded his hands together neatly on his lap. "Behavior is what a man does, not what he thinks, feels, or believes," he said. "Ah … Dickinson was always a favorite of mine."

It *was* a favorite thing of his to quote books or dead people. "So?"

"Do we love people for who they are, or for what they do?" He leaned forward for further emphasis, his eyes bugging out. "If behavior is what a man does, not what he thinks, feels, or believes, do we love people—"

"Grandpa, don't bother him," Rachel admonished as she set down a hot mug on the table. "He's had a hard day and he doesn't need you to try to make him feel better."

Oh thank you, Rachel. Thank you for your wonderful timing!

"I was only asking him a question," Grandpa Odd huffed as he took his drink. A second later he spewed it out, retching. "I asked for coffee, Rachel, not tea!"

"You know the doctor says—"

"I don't care what the doctor says—"

"You need to start caring."

"You need to start *listening.*"

It was entertaining to watch Rachel's patience finally break; so entertaining to me, anyway, I didn't notice Adam had shifted out of his seat until he was halfway across the diner.

I groaned, carelessly pushing my way past Grandpa Odd's chair and carefully excusing myself to Gwen. She just smiled back and nodded, sweet and patient like a saint. Between Grandpa Odd and Adam, I could only hope she wouldn't be turned off from a second date.

THE STARLIGHT CHRONICLES

At least this time Adam was inside, I thought. And it did give me an excuse to leave the fight scene (it was starting to get too personal; Rachel was barking about the rubber sheets messing up the laundry, and Grandpa Odd was combating with the rising bills for her upcoming wedding.)

Adam stopped by the door. Good, I mused, I can just pluck him up and—

Raiya walked in.

"You!" I couldn't stop myself from exclaiming.

What was going on? I wondered. I had *another* stalker to deal with? Wasn't Samantha Carter bad enough?

Raiya hung up her jacket calmly. "What?"

"What are you doing here?"

Raiya smirked as she reached down and picked up Adam, who'd been tugging at her stupid Rosemont skirt. "Why do you need to know? I could've just come in here for a cup of tea."

"I—"

The door creaked open between us. "Hey, Humdinger!"

I looked over to see Jason. "Jase," I greeted, a little surprised (and maybe even a little disappointed) at the sudden interruption.

Jason looked at Raiya. "Hey, Raiya." He smiled. "Is your cousin here? I have an application for her."

Raiya nodded and pointed to where Rachel and Grandpa Odd were still arguing over his dietary requirements.

"Cool, thanks!" Jason said, heading over.

It was a definitely a dumbstruck moment for me. "You're Rachel's cousin?" I asked incredulously.

"Yes." Raiya frowned. "Now, if you'll excuse me, I'll see if I can't drop your brother off so I can get started on my homework." She walked back to the table and put Adam back down in his seat. She casually started chatting with Gwen, who was straining to hear her over Rachel and Grandpa Odd's argument.

I couldn't help but stare. Raiya was … so *annoying*! And now I knew where she got it from, I thought, looking over at Grandpa Odd. The apple didn't fall far from the tree. No wonder I'd hated her on sight, I thought. It was not just the Rosemont uniform. It was her genetics.

Rachel started talking to Jason, and Grandpa Odd began sipping his tea remorsefully, obviously the loser in his battle. I made my way back over to the table and sat down once I was sure it was clear of Raiya.

Adam was cheerfully gobbling down the sandwich Rachel had brought out for him. A plate of jumbo cookies and my own sandwich were waiting for me, and I nearly wept with gratitude I could at last eat.

"Psst, kid … give me a cookie, would you?"

"Elysian, not here," I muttered back harshly.

"All right, thanks, Jason." Rachel smiled. "Grandpa, why don't you leave our customers alone and help me with the front?"

Grandpa Odd grumbled into his mug of tea as he got up and left.

Whew! I was relieved. That old man's name certainly suited him.

Jason sat down next to Adam. "Hey Dinger," he greeted. "Didn't expect to see you here so early. I thought maybe you'd be at the school with swim practice or something. Hey, Gwen." He smiled kindly at her.

Gwen muttered a "hi" into her tea and smiled back.

"Nah, swim practice is only Monday and Thursday," I grinned. "Here, have a cookie."

"Thanks," Jason replied as Elysian "accidentally" gave me a nice scratch with his claws. "These look great."

"I'd eat anything of Rachel's."

"Yeah, me too." Jason swallowed the last of his cookie. "If you guys don't have practice today, how come Mikey went swimming?"

"He's trying to practice more. But I don't want to see him miss tomorrow because he's sick of sucking in the chlorine— although it would be quite amusing," I remarked. "There are some college scouts coming for the meet tomorrow."

"Well, I hope he gets some good brownie points with them," Jason grinned. "My parents told me it was time for me to get a job. That's why I came down here today."

"You thinking of working here?"

"Sure. It's close to my house, you know, just down the block, and Rachel could use someone for the hard labor."

"Hard labor?" I cocked an eyebrow, skeptical. What kind of hard labor was here? Pouring refills?

"Yeah, like unloading her shipments and cleaning up and helping out with repairs and stuff," Jason shrugged. "It's not a glorious job or anything, but it'll be good. Plus I get to hang with Rachel."

"You know she's engaged, right?"

"I know," Jason grinned. "But that doesn't mean I have to accept it."

I stilled. Jason's remark eerily reminded me of my own life. Was this the pathetic kind of picture Elysian saw when he looked at me? Someone who knew something but didn't act like he believed it?

I (wisely) decided to say nothing about it, figuring if Jason didn't mend his thinking and his ways soon, it would eventually resolve itself. Like when Rachel got married.

Oh well. At least someone other than me was looking idiotic—actually, more idiotic. But since it was related to the supernatural side of my life, I decided to overlook it for now. I didn't want to think about it.

A loud *thunk!* caused our attention to be drawn to the door. A smirk wiggled its way onto my mouth; Raiya had appeared again, struggling to juggle all her stuff, and in the process she'd dropped a large wooden case full of her art supplies.

I turned back to Jason. "How did you know Raiya was Rachel's cousin?"

Jason shrugged. "When I heard her last name was Cole I thought there might be some connection. They have the same last name."

"They don't look much alike," I noticed. Rachel was vivacious and gorgeous, with bright red hair and bright golden-speckled eyes, plus she was always smiling brightly. Raiya had dark, golden-brown hair, which was nearly always messy. And even though I'd just met her, I was all too-familiar with her smirk.

"Well, they're cousins, not twins," Gwen pointed out.

"I don't think she's around here a lot; at least, I don't think so. I never really see her," Jason said. "But I've seen her on the music nights and helping out when it gets really crowded."

"You would like their entertainment nights, Hammy," Gwen spoke up. "The last one was on New Year's. It was really fun, like a pajama party."

"Oh? I don't know how I missed it," I lied easily enough. I'd been fighting a monster at the time.

"Hey, speaking of missing stuff," Jason asked, "Do you have the notes for us? Poncey and Drew just walked in."

I looked over to see he was right. "Poncey!" I called out. "Drew!"

I thought I heard Gwen sigh. "What's up?" I asked her.

"Nothing," she shrugged.

"Cool. Just give me a moment and I'll be right back," I told her. "Do you mind watching Adam for me?"

"No, that's fine." She smiled.

"Great. Thanks."

I hurried off and talked with my friends, getting and giving my share of homework, and exchanging stories. Glancing back, I saw Gwen texting as she watched over Adam. Yeah, tonight was going well, I decided.

And that's when my mark went from a dull burn to blazing pain. "Ouch!" I nearly jumped in surprise.

"What's wrong, Humdinger?" Drew asked, not looking up from my copy of the biology homework.

"Um. Nothing."

I ducked into a corner and pulled Elysian out from my hood. "We've got a problem."

"Yes, I was wondering if it was going to get bad," Elysian nodded. "We need to hurry."

"Come on, Ely, Gwen's here," I pouted. "Can't you just go and handle it? This is my first date with her, and it's just been a terribly long day."

He huffed, unleashing little smoke trails through his nose. "You can't just decide to fight when it's convenient, kid," he snarled softly.

I rolled my eyes. "Fine," I bit angrily. "Just go and give me a moment to excuse myself. The last thing I need is for Gwen to think I ducked out early."

"Good. I'll go and get started." Elysian nodded. "Don't forget my cookies as you leave," he reminded me threateningly.

"Yeah, yeah … "

☼9☼
Fear

Raindrops spiked through the skies as Elysian and I hustled towards the downtown city area. While it felt like ice striking at my face and biting at my armor, I was enraged with fury.

"Where's the aura, kid?" Elysian called out.

"Over there, near the city museum." I pointed in the general direction before realizing Elysian couldn't see which way I was indicating. "Head right, towards Central Mall and the marina."

My changeling dragon was a pain sometimes, but he was a good flyer. We headed into the heart of darkness just as the thundering clouds began to bleed a vengeful red. I sighed; I was so tired of this stuff. It was starting to seem a bit cliché, like I'd seen it in a movie or something. "How long do you think we'll have to keep doing this?"

"It's not a question of how long, Hamilton," Elysian remarked, surprising me a bit by using my first name. "It is a question of our choosing to do so."

I nodded glumly. I knew what that meant—I would have to do this until Elysian told me it was okay to quit. Which probably meant never.

A flash of lightning dashed out in front of us; or at least, that's all I thought it was until Starry Knight suddenly appeared in the drizzling sky.

95

Even as we were flying, I could tell her mouth was pursed in displeasure. I smirked and waved hello, taunting her.

Her brow furrowed in frustration, but it did nothing to keep her away. As Elysian descended to the mall's parking lot, Starry Knight came up beside us, landing hard and fast on the pavement.

Her eyes flickered up to mine, wasting no time. "You must leave."

I rolled my eyes. "Well, so very nice to see you too, Starry Knight."

"I am not kidding around here, Wingdinger!" Her voice was harsh and strangely hoarse, catching my attention. I looked over at her and studied her for a long moment, studying the strong glint in her violet eyes, the stubborn angle of her chin, and the graceful waves of her long hair. "I mean it, you must leave. It's too dangerous to be here."

I brushed off the slight touch of hesitation. "Oh, my pleasure," I sarcastically intoned, crossing my arms over my chest. "Let me get right on that."

"Are you that reckless you would risk your life?"

I shrugged, determined not to fall for any ploy of hers. "I've risked it before and nothing bad has happened."

Starry Knight glared at me with sudden, striking hatred, and instantly I have to fight off the memories where she had protected me in the past.

"Anyway," I mutter uncomfortably, "I'm already here, taking time off from 'normal' life. I might as well make it worth the sacrifice." Not that giving up time with Gwen would ever really be able to be compensated.

"Do you ever think of something other than yourself?" Starry Knight pulled out her bow as the miasma of clouds around us grew thicker.

"Why bother with anything else?" I snorted.

"Very mature, kid," Elysian rolled his eyes. He lifted off the cement and began to circle us.

I was just about to get into it with him when the blood-washed clouds around us began to darken to crimson purple. Not good, I thought.

The skin on the back of my neck tingled. We were no longer alone.

"Watch out!" Elysian roared, already moving to a defensive position as a dark beam of light shot out from the corner of my eye.

Elysian jerked to a stop, causing me to go flying off towards the ground. I groaned, preparing to once more be thrown onto the hard ground.

Splat!

My lips pursed fiercely to stop from screaming out in pain. Easing myself up, I rubbed my head. "Ouch," was the only response I allowed myself to muster out.

The shadowy figure suddenly slashed at me once more. I wasn't able to stop the yell of "Augh!" as the sharp claws stun my back. My stubby wings were suddenly warm with the thick redness of my own blood.

"Kid!" Elysian came crashing around me, trying to place a barrier between us.

"Elysian! You never told me that these things can kill me!" I yelled.

If it had been any other time, and there hadn't been this huge threat hanging around us, I'm sure Elysian would've laughed at me.

"What did you think? That this some kind of playtime?!" Elysian looked down at me, incredulous. "Come on! You have to get back up there. Climb on!"

I tried to get up, but I doubled over in pain and collapsed on the ground. I was suddenly overcome by a raging fever, as my heart began to beat faster and faster …

Am I dying? I began to spasm. I couldn't be dying! Surely not … but what else could possibly be happening?

Outside of Elysian's protective barrier, I could hear the demon smacking into the parking deck, knocking over cars, scaring children …

Elysian roared in pain as he was hit with wave after wave of dark energy from the demon.

My eyes were owl-wide as I glimpsed up through Elysian's long, tangled body and saw a beam of light through all the madness.

"Here!" Starry Knight's voice called out, piercing the darkness. "Come get me if you can!"

I didn't know whether to be grateful or to groan for her distraction.

The demon roared with irritation, and I knew she'd just managed to get the demon with one of her arrows. I groaned in stinging pain, but I was glad the fight was sure to be over soon with Starry Knight here.

There was a small flash of light and a whisper of wings, and all of a sudden I found myself face-to-face with Starry Knight. She looked me over and I was half-expecting her to start yelling, much as Elysian had done.

Instead, she snaked her arms around me protectively and said, "You need to get out of here. Elysian needs to move."

"I don't need your help," I grumbled in protest as she tried to pick me up. I thought I heard her sigh.

"Don't be so stubborn!" she hissed sternly as she managed to hoist me up off the ground. She grunted, but she did manage to move me onto Elysian's back. "Tell him to fly," she instructed me as she jumped up behind me.

"Elysian! Let's go!" I called out as the burning sensation engulfing my body increased. I cried out in pain, my limbs twitching as I tried to hang on.

"This demon is especially dangerous!" Starry Knight yelled as we sought refuge up in the sky. "She can see everything!"

She? I knew instantly we were dealing with an *eela*, a shadow demon, one of the harder types to destroy. "How is that terribly different from the other demons?" My vision began to blur; it felt like the stinging was literally climbing around my head and binding itself to my eyes.

"She can see everything, not just physical things! She can see our weaknesses, and use that to her advantage," Starry Knight called back to over the loud wind.

"I don't have any weaknesses," I insisted.

Starry Knight grumbled behind me. "Yeah, that's for sure."

I stuck out my tongue at her, but my head swam as Elysian descended. I could half-hear Elysian and Starry Knight talking, but I couldn't make out all of the words; the sting had curled around my ears and clogged my senses.

A stinging sensation slithered into my skin, raking my mind for information. Was this penetrating gaze of the *eela*, or was it Starry Knight? For some reason, I thought she was talking to me. My eyes opened at her beckoning, catching her eyes with my own. The fire inside of me seemed began to slowly drown in violets, as my world slowly began to take on a new shape.

"What's going on?"

Whispers. That's all I could hear. "The demon can make you see things that aren't real."

The voice was Starry Knight's, no doubt.

Woozy darkness flooded around me, burning my vision, scalding my body, before it cleared. A figure moved in the shadows behind me. "Who's there?"

It was Gwen.

"Gwen?" I asked. "What're you doing here? Get out of here! There's a demon attacking the—"

"Hammy, you're so funny," she giggled in response.

"I am serious—wait, how did you know that I'm … " My voice faltered as she giggled again.

"I would know you anywhere, silly."

"I wanted to tell you," I admitted softly.

"I know," Gwen moved forward, leaning in close, her honey-brown eyes locking into mine. I felt drawn to her, as though there was something inside of her pulling me in. Her body was just inches away, when she whispered, her breath tickling my face, "I know."

My feverish vision returned, and the honey-brown eyes of my love turned to fire, and the world around me was surrounded in it. I saw and watched as all my dreams passed, burned by the fire that consumed me.

I screamed in terror as I watched my life, the very flame of being, flicker out and die, smoldering in a pile of ashes. "No!" I cried out. "I don't want this! I don't want this to happen!"

"Then give up," a new voice in my head insisted. "Stop fighting. It's the only way to save your world."

Small, chilly light illuminated the figure who was busy sifting through my mind. "Who are you?" I demanded to know, unable to do much else.

The figure let out a cold laugh, allowing me to focus on her more. She seemed much larger than her predecessors, but since I was pretty sure I was hallucinating at this point, that didn't seem so strange. Her long, messy hair was pulled back in a messy fashion (she had to be close friends with Maia), and she had nails long enough to keep at least four nail salons busy, if not more. I grimaced as she put her hand on my head.

"Eris!"

The demon, who was apparently named Eris, turned at the sound of her name. "Yes, my lady?" she called out.

Who was she talking to now? I wondered.

"Don't forget the true reason for your assignment," came the stern warning.

"I'm getting to it now," Eris assured her.

"Good. I will be waiting for your report at the haven."

"Yes, my lady." Eris turned her attention back to me. A grin slowly spread out on her face. "You'll have to forgive the interruption. You've caused quite a bit of trouble for Orpheus and the Sinisters, and Lady Alcyonë is eager to discover your weakness."

"I don't have one," I declared defiantly.

Eris smirked. "Please. Of course you do." Her fingers splayed themselves in my wingdings and ruffled through my hair. Eris suddenly began laughing.

"What? What's so funny?" I bellowed up at her, managing to get somewhat away from her.

"That's priceless!" She giggled. "Your greatest weakness is Starry Knight, just as you are hers."

"What?"

The laughter left her eyes quickly. "You're jealous of Starry Knight and her power. Well, I think we can use *that* to our advantage."

"That's not true!" I hollered, desperately trying to figure out how to get her out of my head.

"Let me see if there's anything else useful in your discord," Eris purred, once more reaching out her hand.

A burst of celestial fire flared up, engulfing the vision and leaving me breathless, back on the battlefield.

Elysian was circling overhead, while Eris, with her wild and wicked hair, was retreating into the cover of the clouds.

We were still at the mall, I realized. I was still on the ground. My wounds were gone, but my hands were shaking. Shaking terribly. I was in shock.

"Over here, demon!" Elysian called out as he whipped his tail her across the face.

"Ow!" She began to seethe. "You'll pay for that, you snake!"

"I take offense to that," Elysian called as he ducked out of her reach.

Eris showed no sign of relenting. She swatted her arm out again, this time managing to send Elysian flying into the road hard enough to leave a face-print. "Ugh," he moaned.

Eris laughed before a flash of light blazed through the air.

I was wondering where Starry Knight had gone.

"Elysian!" Starry Knight called. "Alcyonë is here!"

"Switch!" Elysian agreed.

Well, he was certainly right about that, I thought. "Elysian!"

The changeling dragon looked vastly relieved to finally catch sight of me, finally stirring.

"What do we do?" I asked. I looked up at the huge and scary she-monster, slightly faltering. The demons seemed to be getting bigger and smarter.

"I need you to get up and move." Starry Knight came up beside me. "Eris and Alcyonë are both here."

"Who's Alcyonë?" I asked.

"Watch where you're firing that!" Starry Knight called over to Elysian. She had narrowly missed the last burst of flames.

Recalling what Eris had revealed to me, I managed to stand up. "Don't bother to listen to her," I rolled my eyes. "Go ahead and blast her if you need to."

"Kid, as long as she's fighting these guys, it's probably best I don't fry her," Elysian called back as he fended off Eris.

Elysian's warming up to Starry Knight, I supposed. He'd been wary of her at the beginning, and still was, but he was willing to overlook the unknown in favor of her fighting skills. I, of course, hated her for reasons too certain for questioning. But I knew now, along with Elysian, she was at least a Starlight Warrior, like I was.

"I told you not to stay!" Starry Knight yelled at me.

"Hey!" I shouted back. "I'm not the one with the problem! Eris just told me that apparently *I* am your biggest weakness!"

"What?" Starry Knight flung around to face me. Her fists were clenched. "We don't have time to discuss this! There's a Sinister and her minion running around destroying things and looking for Soulfire—"

"Eris was just looking for our weaknesses! She told me so herself!" The wind and the sounds of the battle had faded as I glared at my so-called co-defender. "She said I was your biggest weakness. Is that true?"

Starry Knight left a lot to be desired. "I can't talk about this now," she said. "I … " She opened her fists, palms up. Her eyes met mine tentatively; I wasn't sure but her gaze seemed softened, tired. Worn. "You can at least understand why I didn't want you fighting."

"Yes, Wingdinger, she obviously doesn't think you're good enough for the job."

Glancing around, it wasn't hard for me to spot Alcyonë in her own flesh and blood. Alcyonë was one of the Seven Deadly Sinisters, and from what I'd been able to surmise, one of the more ambitious ones. Her skin was toned with a greenish shine, while her hair was pulled back in several braids.

"Alcyonë." Starry Knight pulled out a fresh arrow. "Stay out of this!"

"Don't worry," Alcyonë remarked. "I'll be leaving shortly. I only wanted to say hello to you again." Her eyes narrowed. "After all, it's been quite a long time, hasn't it, *Sister?*"

Starry Knight released the arrow just as Alcyonë disappeared.

"You're their sister?" I asked. Suddenly my anger was more than ready to boil over. My strength was back, my vision was clear, and my patience was gone. "What's your problem, Starry Knight!? What else have you decided to keep to yourself?"

"It's none of your business," Starry Knight snapped. "It's best if you stay out of it."

"I'm already in it, and I frankly think you wouldn't find me such a weakling if *you* were better about sharing information!"

"You've never listened to me before. What difference would it make if I did tell you the truth?"

"Oh, it would make a difference, and that's what you're so terrified of, isn't it? That I would be a better warrior than you!"

"That! That right there is the reason you do fight so terribly," Starry Knight insisted, pointing her finger in my chest. "You only think about yourself and how good you're going to look."

A loud *thud* interrupted us. Elysian landed on the ground behind us. He straightened up and blew whiffs of smoke from his nostrils. "You both need to stop. Eris is getting away." He nodded to the demonic figure as she began pulling power from her miasmic field.

Starry Knight and I exchanged hard looks. We both narrowed our eyes before leaping into action. I ran up towards Eris while Starry Knight took to the skies, flying towards our foe.

Eris blocked her easily enough, letting Starry Knight's power ricochet off of her clouds. I came at her next, ready to hit her with an energy blast.

Eris ducked under my power, and then slashed back at me, forcing me to fall back as she went after Starry Knight once more.

I was getting ready to try my attack run on the demon again when Starry Knight came crashing through the air and flew into a car parked on the side of the street.

"Ooh, that had to hurt," I tried not to grin. The fall had smashed in the car roof and shattered all the windows. "She's going to have a lot of cuts."

But it didn't seem to even faze her. She jumped right back up and started firing her arrows once more.

While my mouth dropped open in shock (and outrage), one of the arrows struck Eris in the leg. Eris cried out in pain as her leg started to dissipate. Eris continued to shriek in pain as she shrunk in size.

"Elysian, get her from the sky. I'll try to cut her down to size!" I cried.

Eris laughed. "That's hilarious," she sneered at me. "You? You haven't put a nick in me at all yet. It's been just your friends who have managed to do any damage. You're not a threat at all to me. You'd best get out of here before you get hurt … like this!"

A small ball of light began to form in her hand. Before anything could stop her, she tossed it down in my direction.

I moved as fast as I could, but the bomb was getting bigger, coming closer … my legs stopped moving as fear, genuine fear, something which never really bothered me until this point, decided to make itself known …

"Kid!" Elysian shouted.

"No!" I cried as I brought up my arms in defense.

An ocean of warmth surrounded me and cascaded all around. But that was it. It was very anticlimactic as well.

"Huh?" I peeked out through my fingers tentatively.

Starry Knight was standing braced in front of me. She'd shot an arrow straight through the energy bomb, slicing the powerful attack in half and deflecting it around us. When the fog from the attack's damage had cleared, Eris was nowhere in sight.

Elysian flew down and landed softly next to me. "Are you all right?" he asked quietly.

I nodded in reply; I was still looking at Starry Knight as she breathed deeply. I was having trouble thinking clearly, all of a sudden. My emotions were pulsating through me with increasing power and frequency; with every beat of my heart, the feeling grew, and I only felt a confusing mix of fear—but not the fear of death. It was fear infinitely and exponentially more potent.

The fear of losing something. Something … but what?

Eyeing Starry Knight, I suddenly wondered if it had to do with her.

She was standing now, mostly back to normal, although I had to say it was nice to see her sweat a bit. I was just thinking of asking her if she was okay when Elysian did it for me.

She looked wearily back at us. Her hair had been mostly blown free, and there was as much dirt on her clothes as on her body.

Some words finally found their way out of me. "I have connections with a doctor if you need help—" I started to tell her, but she shook her head fiercely.

It was then I realized that she was angry, not hurt. All the weariness disappeared from her face as she stood up.

Uh-oh. Here it comes.

"You should not be fighting." Her words seemed to bite into my very soul. "You should not be fighting if you are just going to get in the way."

"We managed to get rid of the monster—"

"That monster, as you call it, is still running free!" Starry Knight exclaimed, brushing herself off. "Eris has gone into hiding."

"I don't think it will take much to finish her, though," Elysian murmured thoughtfully.

"Now I will have to find her all over again—"

"We, not you," I corrected.

"No, just me. You can't fight with me. You obviously have no real idea of what you're doing out there."

"I would be a better fighter if you didn't insist on doing everything yourself!" I yelled back. "You're just a glory hog!" I stepped closer to her, hoping to intimidate her.

It was a lost cause. She merely arched her eyebrow at me. "You may have your own opinions, of course, but you're just an irresponsible fool!"

"Am not!"

"You are too!"

"Am not!"

"Are too! You almost got all three of us killed because you insisted on fighting! If you'd stayed out of it, Eris wouldn't have tried to kill you!"

"You didn't have to step in!"

"Yes I did!"

"Why?" I staunchly placed myself directly in her gaze; of all my questions, this was the one I wanted to know the most (this time, anyway). "No one was forcing you to protect your *biggest weakness!*"

A flicker of uncertainty flashed across her pretty face for just a split second. I swore I saw it.

"I wouldn't let Eris win just so you'd be out of my way!" Starry Knight finally yelled as she glared back at me. "This is a waste of time. I have better things to do than argue with someone more concerned about his fame than his purpose."

She turned, ready to go, and I was just about to celebrate when she sighed. It was a different sigh than I was used to.

"What?" I huffed.

"Eternity is an important matter," she told me softly, her eyes meeting mine with a steady, sagely gaze. "It is not something to take lightly. It deserves every minute of serious consideration until you make your final decision."

I felt the anger inside of me burn. What was she trying to do? Make me feel guilty or something?

I was even angrier as she took flight; I could barely limp away due to my injuries. And she was as graceful as always, even though she'd taken the blunt of the attack for me.

"Elysian," I said softly. "Follow her. See if you can learn anything else about her."

"Good idea," Elysian agreed, transforming into a smaller version of his dragon self and heading off.

Yes, I thought. It was a good idea. I could keep tabs on Starry Knight *and* get rid of Elysian for the rest of my date with Gwen. If she was still at Rachel's. Time had passed much more quickly than I would've liked. Still, though, it hadn't been *too* long. I assured myself that despite everything, not much harm had come to the city.

It was only a few moments later, as I was heading back to Rachel's, when I realized just how badly I'd blundered in letting Eris get away.

Walking up the streets near Shoreside Park, only a few blocks between the mall and Rachel's, I stopped suddenly when I saw a familiar-looking body lying in the grass.

The mark on my wrist burned in familiar heat at the victim, who had just had her Soulfire stolen.

Staring up at me with blank eyes was none other than Samantha Carter.

☼10☼
More Fear

The walk home from Rachel's was physically uneventful, but my mind was reeling from several blows.

I'd called the ambulance, anonymously, and let them know about Samantha's body. And even though it was just Samantha, it was impossible for me to act like nothing had happened when I got back to Rachel's Café. Gwen was appalled as much as worried after hearing the news of an attack, but when I sat down with her at Rachel's, once more, I found I couldn't pretend nothing had happened, not even for her.

I barely registered walking into my housing development, still stinging from Gwen's reaction to my apparent apathy.

I'd managed to score another date with her, at least. We decided not to count this one. She wasn't very nice about it, though. I knew I had a lot of making up to do with her, but I was just glad she was going to let me. My biggest fear during our conversation was that she wouldn't be interested in pursuing a relationship anymore.

"Adam, watch where you're going," I muttered, reaching for my brother's hand as he scuttled off into the neighbor's yard.

"Hammonton." He pouted and ran off, causing me to curse softly under my breath.

"You know, it's not like I need this right now," I called out to him as I began to follow him.

Despite everything, I felt a small smile creep on my face as I crept around the neighbor's car and Adam scurried around the other way. I jumped out and grabbed him, proclaiming, "Gotcha!"

Adam giggled and twined his arms around my neck.

A rare moment of softness came over me as Adam clung to me. I didn't always like being an older brother. But when I let him, Adam had a way of reminding me I couldn't imagine life without him.

I hugged him back and smiled. "Let's go home, Adam. Come on, we're almost there." I looked pointedly up the block to our house.

"Car."

"Yes, there's Cheryl's car," I agreed. Oh great, that meant she was home. I felt the irritation inside of me prickle once more.

"Car."

"Yes, I know, Adam." I sighed.

"Hey! What are you kids doing in my driveway?" I swung around abruptly at the voice.

A man was standing on the porch, looking at us with a stern expression on his face. For some reason, I thought he looked familiar. He was tall, with brown hair, and the black suit almost made me think we had stumbled onto his property just as he was leaving for a dinner date.

"Sorry, sir," I replied. "I was just getting my brother."

The man frowned, and a nagging memory in the back of my brain began screaming. I looked around and suddenly recalled this property had been up for sale for some time. Between the shiny car in the driveway and the angry man on the porch, I was able to guess someone had moved in.

I swept a more critical gaze over the car. It was a newer model, pristine and shiny in the cold winter atmosphere. Someone rich had moved in. "We're leaving."

The man pulled out a pair of sunglasses and put them on. "All right then."

Sunglasses? I thought. In the middle of winter? "Sure."

I hurried back onto the sidewalk, still carrying Adam. I didn't turn around but I heard the roar of a powerful engine and the squeal of tires, and I knew he was gone. Weird guy, I thought. But then, my family's housing development had been made for the rich, and that usually meant we had to deal with sleazy salesmen as well as a few eccentrics.

Still, something about that guy made me nervous. I felt like I'd seen him before.

I forgot all my apprehension about the new neighborhood quack when we arrived at the house. I was determined to enter in as quietly as possible; Adam was not.

"Mom," Adam called out.

"In here," Cheryl replied semi-automatically from her study. "Hamilton, it's about time you got home. School ended four hours ago."

Well, hello to you too, Cheryl, I thought bitterly. "I was held up for a bit."

Since I was expecting a reprimand, I was surprised when Cheryl said, "I've been waiting for you to get home. How was your day?" Before I could formulate a quick, meaningless reply of, "Fine," to summarize the awful, bitter, loathing resentment I had for my day, she barreled onward. "You'll never guess what assignment the mayor just gave me."

"What?" I asked, putting Adam down behind her office desk.

Cheryl's eyes lit up in excitement. "You're looking at the prosecutor for the city in the case of *Apollo City v. Flying Angels!*"

I stared at her, my mind's cloud of confusion slowly dispersing into pure fear and overwhelming hatred, and not just because she was drinking one of her special sugar-free diet drinks. "Flying Angels?" I repeated slowly, buying time to get my bearings.

"Oh, you know, those silly so-called superheroes running around town. The Wing King and Starlight Knight."

Resentment was suddenly added to the already confusing mix of my emotions. *Couldn't my mother even get the names right?*

She didn't miss a beat, even as I was tongue-tied. "We're going to hold them up on charges of city-wide endangerment and terrorism. Thank goodness for the Patriot Act, right?" Cheryl smiled, picking up Adam and smoothing down his hair. "Not only is this case going to get a lot of exposure for my career, but it'll be good for you, too, Hamilton."

I strongly disagreed with her, especially since she didn't know *I* technically was on the opposing team. But curiosity got the better of me. "Why?" I asked, in what was hopefully an interesting and not weird-sounding voice.

"Stefano—Mayor Mills—mentioned to me today he wanted to have a part-time assistant working on the case with us, and he specifically asked me if you would be interested."

"Me? Work for the mayor?" Funny, how those words, six months ago, would have made my day, even my week. Now they sent my spirits plummeting into a downward spiral.

"Yes. Wouldn't that be great for your college application?" Cheryl beamed and all I felt was an instant sense of displacement.

Who was I, anyway? I was Hamilton Dinger, superstar athlete, genius, and charismatic leader. I succeeded at school, sports, and social niceties. I was on the fast-track to college, law school, and a career.

But then …

I was also Wingdinger, a fallen Star, called to protect my city and save the day from any supernatural villainy. I didn't understand a lot of the whys or the hows, or even the whats, but I knew it was the right thing to do.

All my life, I thought I was supposed to be sitting up at the prosecutor's table with Cheryl, not sitting in the defendant's chair.

I looked at my mother now, as she kept chatting away with some of the details of the case, talking about legal fees, long-term punishment, social work, counseling, prison time, public humiliation, government cooperation, etc.

Fear unexpectedly tore through me. What would my mother think if she found out I was one of her adversaries in court? What would the government do with me? What if I did die, like I'd feared earlier? How would I live, though? How was the battle between Wingdinger and the Sinisters going to end? I didn't know. They sure seemed to have an endless supply of minions for me to fight. And how was I ever going to have my dream life if I was chasing demons?

Bitterness quickly followed. Starry Knight didn't have these kinds of problems, I'll bet, I thought.

And speaking of problems …

Elysian was slithering up the stairs outside Cheryl's office.

"I'll have to think about it," I sputtered out, interrupting Cheryl mid-lecture. "I just don't know."

"Don't be silly," Cheryl snapped, just a bit too forcefully. "This is what you've always wanted."

She's never doubted that I would say no to this, I realized. But then, I wouldn't have, either.

"Well, I still have school, and swim team, and other stuff," I reminded her. "My SATs aren't going to take themselves. Especially with Mrs. Night's class, remember? I'll be lucky if I get a 750 in English at this rate."

"Oh, honey, we'll work that out," Cheryl insisted. "I'm the District Attorney now, and Stefano is an understanding man. I'm sure we'll be able to work out a schedule for you that fits into your life."

"Oh. Well then. I guess I'll have to meet him one day." I didn't really know what else to say.

"You'll like him, Hamilton. He's already impressed with you and your records. Stefano's very concerned with the next generation and he even told me today he thinks you'll be an exemplary role model for his team."

I wish she would've stopped there, but she continued.

"Getting those two nuisances up on trial is a great opportunity to refine your skills and learn the ins and outs of being a lawyer. This is the chance of a lifetime, Ham! It's everything you've ever dreamed."

I nodded, unable to feel my legs anymore. "Okay," I said listlessly. "I gotta go. I have some work to do." Then I hurried off before I had to deal with any of Cheryl's questions.

☼11☼
Break

"So, how did the rest of your date go?" I walked into my room to find Elysian on my bed. He was curled up in a big pile of his snake-like skin, relaxed, like my strife didn't matter at all to him.

"Shut up!" I snapped, surprising myself as much as Elysian. I slammed the door to my room shut and rounded on him. "Just shut up! I'm so tired of you. You've ruined my life!"

"What do you mean by that?" Elysian asked, yawning a second later. "Sorry. It's not you."

"You! You've ruined my life," I accused. "You, with all your talk of destiny and saving the city and working to stop the Sinisters."

"What's wrong?"

"My mother is downstairs working on a case to sue me," I hissed. "The girl of my dreams thinks I'm too busy for her. My dream job of working in the mayor's office was practically handed to me, but I can't bring myself to take it. And you and Starry Knight are the most arrogant, annoying, confusing idiots in the world!"

I shoved him off my bed as I continued. "What's wrong? You want to know what's wrong? I had a perfect life before you came into it. I had plenty of time—"

Elysian snorted, interrupting me. "Which you mostly wasted on yourself."

"I told you to shut up!" I roared. Angrily, I stomped over to my window, yanked back my curtains, and thrust it open. "Just go away! I quit! Get out of my life."

"Quit? You can't just quit," Elysian sputtered back. "Your powers! They'll—"

"Hopefully go away!" I asserted. "I can't handle this anymore, Elysian. I don't want this. I don't like it. I'm not good enough at it anyway. That demon took a soul today. I wasn't able to stop it. I don't really even care that I didn't."

"I think you do," Elysian insisted. "Or you wouldn't be feeling so guilty right now."

"Guilty!?" I swung around and glared at him, eye to eye. "*I'm* not the guilty one. If anything, *you're* the one who let Eris get away, not *me*! You just like to blame everything on me, and it's not all my fault. It's all your fault, both you and Starry Knight! And you know what? Sam Carter was an idiot too. Frankly, I'm surprised she hadn't already *sold* her soul to try to get a date with me."

"That's not—"

"If I do feel 'guilty,' it's just that I bought into this whole mess in the first place," I declared, my voice gradually getting louder of its own accord. "Someone made a mistake. I can't be worried about or involved in all this. I don't care enough to want to try. I have other things to do. I don't want to do it. I'm too busy. I have school, and now I have Gwen, and soon I'll be working for the mayor, and working towards a future I want!" I pointed to the window. "Now, get out, and don't come back!"

"Hamilton—"

"Get out! Get out! Just go!" I screamed.

Elysian frowned, but he listened. He took flight and hurried from my room, just as a knock on the door came.

"Hamilton, what's going on in there?" Cheryl's voice was a mix of concern and confusion, making me hate her too, since she couldn't understand or know why I was really upset, and she didn't seem to care when she could.

"Nothing!" I shouted back. "I'm just … " I lowered my voice. "I'm just playing a video game," I lied.

"You're getting very loud," my mother said, still unconvinced.

"Fine, I'll turn it off." My tone was harsh. *I need to get out of here,* I thought. *I need to get out of here now.*

I pushed open my door, forcefully, surprising Cheryl. She was indignant, but I brushed past her easily enough. "I forgot something at Jason's house," I told her. "I'll be back later." I didn't wait for her response or permission. I left the house and didn't look back.

The far end of Shoreside Park was not my intentioned destination. I don't think I really had a specific place in mind as I stormed outside my house. But when I finally looked up from my fury, I found myself surrounded by the familiar sights of my childhood.

The evening sky had darkened, allowing the planetarium roof of the Lakeview Observatory stand out against the skyline. The observatory, I knew, overlooked the marina on the other side of the hill, while the fields of grass surrounding it provided ample room for playing sports, having picnics, meeting friends. All the things I'd done throughout my adolescence.

All without a thought or even a daydream of my previous life as an *Astroneshama*, a fallen Star.

Out of breath, I stopped and huddled over, placing my hands on my knees. The mark on my wrist glimmered at me, and I suddenly hated it. I gripped my wrist, as though I was trying to strangle the mark, squeezing it off my skin.

I didn't really expect anything to happen. (At that point, I should've been wiser in aligning my expectations to reality.)

Warm heat fluttered off my skin and I was suddenly very keenly aware of my emotional turmoil. A small aura of angry red, glowing orange, and shadowed purple leaped off my skin. Recognition poured through me as I recalled being able to sense Gwen's emotions before, when I held her hand, and feeling Adam's earlier contentment as I'd carried him.

Well, I thought, there you go. Bitterness, anger, jealousy. All working to build up hatred and darkness inside of me.

I suddenly grabbed my marked wrist again. There had to be more to this, I thought.

I was right.

Pushing past the colored fragments, I drove power deep inside of myself. Fueled by my anguish, I wanted nothing more than to go to the heart of the problem. "Augh!" I felt a scream rise up in my throat as my eyes closed and pain lanced through me.

It was over seconds later. As the pain vanished, I opened my eyes.

I gasped.

A world of shining white surrounded me. There were crystalline structures floating all around me. I looked down to see a small ball of energy, not unlike the power I channeled to defeat the Sinisters' demon puppets. It was a burning flame of brilliant light, giving off a warm, yet distinct feeling.

"So," I muttered to myself, "This is my heart." Metaphorically, I assumed.

I looked around at the different, mirrored panels around me. Memories and feelings resided side by side by side (you have to picture *all* the dimensions of a heart to really imagine this), changing and moving. I saw my friends as we grew up together. Played together, worked together, laughed together, talked with each other. I saw Gwen, the first time Mikey had introduced me, the first time I felt attracted to her. I saw my family, too, in smaller surfaces.

And then, there was a bridge in front of me.

Make that a half-bridge. It wasn't completed. Or at least, I didn't think it was. The clouds of white sheltered the other side from me; the fluffy whiteness of it all surrounded it like fog during a snowstorm, and I didn't have the faith—let alone desire—to cross it.

But that didn't mean I wasn't curious about it, of course.

I stepped closer to it, trying to get a glimpse of the other side of the bridge.

There were some holes in the surrounding smog, but not enough for me to see it. I could tell it was above the core of my power as well. As I took a tentative step out on the bridge, I could hear it.

The music. Starry Knight's music.

Shuddering stillness shot through me.

"I've seen this bridge before." I remembered now. Shortly after the acceptance of my power, my destiny, I'd seen a tiny picture of this in my mind's eye.

I glanced around. Where was the Prince? I wondered. He usually shows up at times like these, didn't he? I mean, he should. It was kind of a supernatural moment for me, and I didn't know what to do.

Didn't I? Didn't I have any clue at all about what to do?

I looked at the bridge again and allowed the music to be absorbed into my memory. I wanted to hold onto the music, to the magic, without letting go of anything of my own.

That sharp truth left me breathless.

I believed in the Prince. I knew he was a real person. I knew I had special powers, and with that, a responsibility to protect others.

But …

I sighed. Believing in something was one thing. Having faith was another. And having enough faith to cross over to the other side of my heart—no doubt containing much more of the Immortal Realm, the Celestial Kingdom, and even Starry Knight—that was really asking too much of me. After all, I was a man of fact. Faith is not fact. And fear was too easily a result of anything less than faith.

I stepped off the bridge. The heavenly music dissolved instantly, leaving me feeling darker and more solid than ever, like I was the only real thing in the world, and it was too lonely to bear.

"If I want to stay away from my supernatural self, I have to get rid of this bridge." The moment I said it, I knew it was true. If I wanted to get rid of my problems, my powers, my responsibility, my destiny, then that was it: Destroy the bridge to the other side of myself.

I reached for the power below and called it to me; the blinding, translucent force of my heart's energy came easily, willingly. And then I held it, breathed deeply, and focused in on the bridge.

Closing my eyes, I swung down my power.

I didn't watch as the bridge collapsed, but I heard it, as though every minute detail splintered like an atom, setting off a chain reaction of horrified freedom within me.

I woke up on the ground by the observatory with a jolt, with no clue as to how much time had passed, if any at all. I found myself lying on the grass, sprawled out on my back. I sat up immediately, embarrassed and disoriented, like I had fainted or something.

As I checked to make sure nothing was amiss, I found something was wrong. Or rather, completely right.

My mark was gone.

I pressed into the now-bare skin, and there was nothing. Nothing!

Happiness flooded through me with rolling waves of pleasure. I looked around wildly. There were no auras, no prickles of pain, no tremors pouring out from the dark corners of my mind. Nothing!

"I'm free," I whispered, awed and humbled. I stood up quickly and looked around. The world looked strange, as though all the luminosity of the world had been taken away, leaving the harsher realities of the physical world; as though the universe had been whitewashed in grayscale paint; as though the hidden background of meaning, purpose, and all the little strings of things that matter had vanished, leaving only potential for pleasure and prettiness to abound.

I felt more solid and hollow than ever before as I smiled and headed home.

THE STARLIGHT CHRONICLES

☼12☼
Elysian

Determination set in early the next day as I decided *not* to think about anything having to do with my supernatural self. I gave up, I quit, I was free. End of story.

The problem with the end of story part was just there were some loose ends I had to take care of, because Elysian was too stubborn to take care of himself.

It wasn't long—less than a week—before I found the small dragon pacing on the floor of my bedroom, his eyes narrowed, his brow furrowed, and his arms folded. When I turned on the lights and walked in, Elysian was greeted with my groan.

"What're you doing here?" I scowled.

"You can't just quit, Hamilton!" Elysian practically shouted.

"Shut up, would you? And I sure can quit, just like that. There's no two weeks' notice in this business, Ely! I *can* quit. And I did." I held up my wrist, now blank, as proof. "See?"

"What's wrong with you? You get a little shaken by an attack and run off scared?"

"I did not run away scared," I insisted. "I no longer want to fight. I do not believe any of the bull crap you fed me before about that starry kingdom or whatever it was."

"What about the people who lost their souls?"

"Maybe they deserved it."

"And maybe they didn't. What then?"

"I guess it's their problem now." I shrugged. "I am not fighting anymore, Elysian. Find someone else to play your games and fight your battles or whatever. I have more important things to worry about than the forces of 'good and evil.'"

"But what about the city? The world?"

"Let the FBI or some other government operation handle it, all right? The media wants them to, and no one else wants me or Starry Knight to do anything about it. They want us gone, and I'm just trying to fulfill their wish."

"That has to be the biggest load of baloney your mother ever let into this house!" Elysian yelled. "You're not doing it for them! You're doing it for yourself. Admit it!"

"So what if I am?" I didn't see where Elysian was headed with this. I was my own person. I had an entitlement to make myself happy. This supernatural stuff was messing my life up *hugely*. And if I didn't want to continue it that should be my choice; that goofy lizard should be able to understand that.

"So? What do you mean, 'So what?'" Elysian sputtered, clearly taken aback. "I've never heard of such selfishness in all my existence—and I'm an eternal being!"

"You want a medal for it or something?" I spat back. I moved over to the window and opened it up. "Get out of my room, get out of my house, and get out of my life!"

Elysian just stared at me, his reptilian mouth agape. "I suppose you have a choice in this matter," he finally wheezed out, his anger barely contained. "But you will not escape this. You will lose your powers, and you will suffer the same as the other humans running around. You have just put your family and your friends in danger, all for the sake of yourself."

"Spare me the lecture," I replied in a hard voice. "I've had enough. I don't need you, or my supernatural powers! I was fine long before you came, and I'll be fine long after you're gone."

"So be it." And then Elysian transformed and swooped out the window, his long dragon body disappearing into the city-lit skyline, along with any hesitation I might've admitted to having. His farewell echoed through me like a disembodied voice. "Good-bye … Hamilton."

☼13☼
Emptiness and Anger

It was amazing how quickly and effectively apathy sunk in, following my rejection of all supernatural responsibility. You might think I am a horrible person for this, but I can say with charging clarity indifference is the most pervasive and preferred state of mind of many individuals, and the world has yet to fall apart. Yet.

Apathy is not hard to conjure. But I discovered, relatively quickly, it is hard to maintain. It requires a lot of distraction, pop-psychological platitudes, and pseudo-logical reasoning. You can only go on so long before you run out, or find out you are running in circles. The bad news is that when you don't run around all those circles, pointless as it all becomes, it's much much much harder to fall asleep at night. That's when all the things you've been holding back all day will come creeping into your mind and crush you. Otherwise, sleep is such a good escape.

Fortunately I was well-stocked up on music, texting, social media, Tetris, Gwen, some actual schoolwork, and hating things. I especially liked hating things because it took up a lot of energy to boot. I didn't like hating things because I think it made it harder for me to *like* things though, and I think that made things difficult for some people. Like Martha.

In all fairness, I don't think Raiya was giving her an easy time, either.

"Quiet down back there," Mrs. Smithe barked as she started handing out papers to the class. "You'd think you two would get tired of arguing after last week, but you don't," she sighed exasperatedly. "Stop arguing about the test answers, would you? It's Friday and we're starting a new unit this period."

"I wouldn't have to argue with her, Mrs. Smithe," I insisted, "If she was more willing to act like a human being once in a while."

"Dinger!" Mrs. Smithe glared down at me. "You can't talk about someone like that. Not in today's world. You'd get suspended for bullying."

"I wouldn't argue, Mrs. Smithe," Raiya said calmly. "If he would just admit he's not being objective about it."

"What does that mean?" Poncey asked me in a whisper off to the side.

"It means I'm right," I muttered.

"Raiya, you bring up an excellent point," Mrs. Smith smiled. Then she frowned. "Although not about Dinger, necessarily." She headed back up to her lecture podium and faced the class. "You have finished all the history from the colonies to the beginning of the twentieth century, so we're going to take a bit of a break from information to more practical history.

"Class, today we're going to start talking about judgment on history. I brought up this example for us to give you an example of what I'm talking about."

I nearly groaned when I saw the newspaper article Martha had produced. The *Apollo City Mirror* headline, in big, bold print, was entitled "The Angels and Demons of Apollo City." I wondered what my chances of sneaking out of class undetected were.

Mrs. Smithe continued. "Class, what do you think our society a hundred years from now is going to think of our actions and our decisions?"

When no one answered her, she started to read the article aloud.

"'Valentine's Day is about fun and celebration. However, Apollo City's latest monster sightings in the Central area have dampened the holiday spirt. Numerous eyewitnesses attest yet another attack on the city for the last several months by monstrous beings … '"

I was starting to get angry as Martha continued reading on about the extensive damages the demons had managed to do, and about the people condemning the superheroes for their failure to destroy all of the monsters before they could attack again.

After all the people I'd saved, Wingdinger's integrity was being questioned?

I burned with fury, my veil of apathy precariously burning up. Ungrateful simpletons.

I was just about to tell Mrs. Smithe the media had it all wrong when she finished reading and posed a question to us.

"So, class, what do you think that the people living a hundred years from now will think?"

I think they'd better not blame me for all of this crap, I thought to myself.

"Herbert Butterfield once stated that 'Among historians, as in other disciplines, the blindest of all the blind are those who are unable to examine their own presuppositions, and blithely imagine therefore that they do not possess any.' What do you think that he was saying?"

Who really cared if I judged something with my own perspective? Wasn't that what postmodernism was all about? How could that be wrong? It's not like there's a good and evil in this world. Really—though maybe in the next one.

"Okay, I can see we're not getting anywhere. Let's try it like this." Mrs. Smithe realized she was losing her audience. A shiny dot gleamed in her hand. "Who can tell me what this is?"

"It's a quarter!" Poncey spoke up; clearly I could tell he was glad to finally get a chance to contribute something to a conversation way over his head.

Mrs. Smithe smiled. "Yes, it is. Good answer, Evan." Then she drew a line on the board, and then a circle. "Okay class, make Ms. Darlington proud. Which of these best represent the shape of this quarter?"

We looked at her as though she'd suddenly told us it was nap time. After all, she was asking them a second-grade question. And this was Martha, not our idiot English teacher, Mrs. Night.

Finally, Hoshi Tokugawa, our Japanese exchange student, raised his hand and pointed to the circle. "It's like the circle," he stated very matter-of-factly.

Mrs. Smithe's eyes twinkled with a mischievous glint. "No."

"The line?" Hoshi's Japanese eyes opened wide in surprise.

Mrs. Smithe shook her head, and even I was momentarily confused.

Then I got it—the quarter, on its side, was an unending line, and its face was the circle. So it was both.

"That's right," Martha told the students as she noticed the dawning look of understanding come over our faces. "It's both. This is where the importance of perspectives can be really seen. Sometimes, we forget there might be other sides to a situation because we're too busy looking at what we see first." She put the quarter down and turned back to the article. "Okay, so what do you think of this now?"

Brittany's hand shot up in the air. "They'd probably think we weren't smart in seeing these attacks were part of some kind of ploy or experiment."

While Martha had her develop that, I raised my hand angrily.

As I did so, Raiya snickered behind me. "You don't think that people a hundred years from now will really care, do you?"

I swiveled around to face her. "I don't think that it's an issue," I asserted, probably a bit too angrily, "But I don't think that the presentation of this information has a lot of credibility."

"I don't either," Raiya assured me. She gave me a small smirk as she added, "Propaganda tends to be misleading."

"Huh?" That came out of nowhere. "What do you mean?"

"Look at the title," Raiya murmured as she turned her attention down to her own paper. "Clearly they're trying to incite the public's fear."

"Yes, Hamilton?"

Mrs. Smithe had called on me. She smiled patiently as I turned to face her. "What do you think?"

"It's very hard to consider this a credible source. Journalism prides itself on being unbiased as a profession, but they didn't do a very good job with this article," I replied.

"Do you think that people will think that these incidents were handled in a good or bad way?"

"They will have a bad judgment in determining whether it is good or bad." I briefly recalled what Elysian had once told me: Good judgment required a broad perspective. "It's only one article. They would need to read more to get a better understanding."

"Good reply," Mrs. Smithe beamed at me. "Because that's exactly where we're headed today. What are some of the limitations this article demonstrates in its presentation of events? Is there a special consideration of this article? What do you think as a response to this article? What about your own conception of this is brought into question?"

While students started making responses, I managed to calm down somewhat. At least Mrs. Smithe wasn't agreeing with that ridiculous article's conclusions. I smirked as I thought that Elysian would probably have enjoyed this class. I'd have to remember to tell him about it—

I nearly hit myself at the sudden lapse; I buried my head in my work as I glanced at the clock.

Time had passed so egregiously slowly since I'd given up being Wingdinger. It was just too slow, and then it was gone, and then it was just ... meaningless.

I glanced over and saw Gwen, probably the only thing keeping me from freaking out or losing it completely. I'd had a lot more free time to be with her. And it had been great, I reminded myself, recalling how much fun the last few weeks had been, getting to hang out with her at Rachel's, and getting ice cream at Frosty's, and having her come to my swim meets, and getting her to help me take care of Adam.

Without a doubt, she was the only thing good in my life right now.

The bell rang, and I didn't hesitate. "Gwen."

She didn't seem to hear me, but I caught up with her outside the classroom. "Hey, Gwen."

"What, Ham?" she asked, as she turned to face me. "I've got to get to my next class. I have four minutes to cram for a test."

"I was wondering if you'd like to spend Valentine's Day with me."

"We've already got plans, remember?" Gwen cocked her eyebrow. "You asked me to come to your swim meet last week."

"Oh." I'd forgotten about that.

She sighed. "Are you sure you want to go out again?"

"What? What do you mean?"

Gwen looked away. "It's just that you are always playing with your phone, or you take me to meet with your friends. I mean, do you even want to spend time with me? You spent most of our last date at Rachel's arguing with Raiya about how mocha was better than tea."

It would have been hard to explain to Gwen how paramount it had been for me to win that argument, on a number of levels, so I skipped over that. "Of course I want to be with you, Gwen."

"You have a funny way of showing it."

I cringed. "I'm sorry you haven't been happy, Gwen." I looked up at her meaningfully, waiting for her to deny it. She didn't. I continued. "You were the one who said happiness wasn't everything."

Her mouth dropped open. "Are you blaming me for being unhappy?"

"No, I am asking you to give me another chance to make it up to you. Let me take you out for Valentine's Day after the swim meet is over."

A long moment of silence ensued before Gwen relented. "Okay."

"Geez, don't say it like that. I haven't forgotten anything important," I protested, anger creeping into my voice. "And if I did, it's just because I'm so excited about being with you."

"You don't have to argue with me," Gwen interrupted, suddenly looking hurt. She looked down at her phone. "I've got to go. I'll see you at the swim meet tomorrow."

"I would love nothing more," I declared, taking her hand and squeezing it, despite her phone getting in the way.

She slipped her hand out of mine. "Okay. Bye."

As I watched Gwen head off in the other direction, I felt a lingering shadow of my conscience. A whisper of longing brushed by me as I recalled being able to feel another person's emotions. It would've been helpful here, I thought. I hoped I hadn't hurt her feelings. Even though I probably did.

Ugh. The last thing I needed was more guilt.

I needed distraction, and quick.

I looked up to see Mikey was at his locker just ahead of me. Perfect! "Hey Mike," I called out, hurrying over.

"Hi Dinger," came the stoic and distracted reply.

"Whatcha doing?" I asked.

There was little emotion on Mikey's face. "Going to the pool now," he said. "Uzzy said I could practice for a while after school if I wanted."

"Oh, I see. I heard you were getting extra practice in," I smiled. "Still trying to beat me?"

"I have to impress the scouts coming tomorrow," Mikey said in a hard voice. It wasn't exactly an antagonistic tone of voice, but it wasn't friendly, either. "I have to start thinking about paying for college."

"You have all next year," I reminded him.

"That's easy for you to say, Dinger," Mikey shook his head. "You don't have to work hard like others do. You have connections, money, and talent. Me … Well, I got some athletic ability, but I'll be shuffled to the side like always when it comes to top pick."

"Well, thanks," I grinned. "I know I'm a great all-around kind of guy." Looking at the resentful expression on Mikey's face, I suddenly wished I hadn't said anything. "I'm sure you'll be fine," I said. "There're always government loans, right? And there are a lot of stupid scholarships on the Internet, like having blue eyes or something."

"I have brown eyes," Mikey replied.

"But you get the point, right?"

Mikey shook his head.

"Wow, you are slow," I joked. "No, seriously, I'm saying you'll be fine, even if you aren't the fastest, the smartest, or the best-looking."

"I thought I was the best-looking," Mikey said.

"Really? You think so?"

Mikey frowned. "Bye Dinger."

I bit my lip as Mikey walked away, not just because our conversation did nothing permanent to resolve my pain but because it made me even angrier. I didn't think that went well.

"That didn't go well," a voice from behind me said.

I jumped nearly a foot in the air. Raiya had appeared behind me from out of nowhere. I managed to keep my cool, but I was steadily getting steamed. "Do you mind? I'm trying to stand here."

She tilted her head thoughtfully as she ignored my commentary. "You hurt his feelings."

"That's how guys talk to each other, in case you're wondering. Or eavesdropping."

"I wasn't listening on purpose. But you did hurt his feelings."

"Really? How?" Okay, I was fully irritated now. She had no right to judge me or my friends. If anything, Mikey was the one who could've been a lot nicer about stuff.

"Wow, you *are* slow," she commented, making fun of me as much as making a point. "Isn't it obvious?" Raiya pushed back a strand of gingersnap hair that had fallen over her eyes. "You hurt him with your words."

"Oh, I'll give you a few words," I muttered.

A lot of girls would frown or start crying, or even rightfully apologize for attempting to correct my actions. Raiya just gave me a smirk. "You don't have to be so hostile."

"You don't have to be so annoying."

"I was just making a comment."

"An unnecessary comment."

"A lot of your comments are unnecessary. You can't use that argument without convicting yourself."

"Don't tell me how to argue. My mother's one of the top lawyers in this city. I know how to argue," I frowned.

"I wasn't telling you how to argue, I was pointing out you weren't arguing very well."

"What makes you think I want to argue with you?" I asked. "Just stop bothering me."

Her voice had an impatient edge to it. "You know, your temper is a sign of immaturity and weakness."

I thought about how much fun it would be to push her over the edge, to make her explode with anger. After all the fights we had had in AP History, I knew she was a worthy opponent.

My conscience struck another chord.

Was I really trying to get into a fight? I had to stop this.

"No one asked you," I replied as evenly possible. "And as for my so-called weaknesses, that's not your business, either."

"True enough, but your temper is starting to get on other people's nerves." Raiya rolled her eyes and excused herself.

I stood there watching her leave, trying to prove to myself I could let her have the last word.

"Shut up," I muttered as she turned the corner.

☼14☼
Swim Meet

Valentine's Day was never my favorite holiday. The previous year, I'd been dating Via Delorosa, the head cheerleader at Central, and it had been less than exciting. She'd ended up taking me out to one of her friend's parties, where she alternated between flirting with a bunch of other guys in front me and ignoring me.

But this year, things were looking up. Gwen was going to come to my swim meet, I was going to have a great swim meet, get to show off for the college reps, and then I would take Gwen off for an unforgettable Valentine's Day date.

Which I actually still needed to plan, I reminded myself as I headed towards the pool locker room.

I was greeted by a large, buzzing crowd of people.

There were two reasons for the popularity of the swim meets: Me, and the 'swim-ghetti', a more recent development. (It was just a small bowl of regular spaghetti, I didn't really see what was so special about it.)

But it was enough to get a crowd. While still a far cry from the crowds of a football game, the audience was steadily filling up. Several of my fans waved from the stands conservatively, while a few others were all-out, decked in school colors and face-paint.

Coach Uzziah was all fired up and trying to hand out last-minute reminders and tips. She saw me and literally jumped with happiness. She pointed into the stands at a couple of men wearing suits. "Ham, those are the early arrivals of the college scouts," she explained softly. "I talked with them earlier, and they've heard all about you. If you do well tonight, they'll be back on Friday to see you again."

"Cool." I gingerly stepped to the side and began stretching. I half-wondered if Uzzy was going to point out the scouts to Mikey.

Thinking of that, I looked over in the pool to see Mikey still doing laps in the pool. He'd started practicing since last period had gone out, apparently. He didn't seem to be tired at all. Guess all that practice was paying off.

The races began shortly, and I forgot all my troubles. My attention was captured as I watched and cheered on my teammates as they tried their hardest to win. I also had my side-attention on thinking how much faster I was than every of them.

"All right, Dinger, let's go! You're up," Uzzy called out. She gave me a smile. "Go out and make me proud."

I grinned. I *knew* I would make her proud. Proud enough to make her go easy on me in Health class. Not that I needed it, of course. But every little bit helps.

Once in position, I waited for the buzzer. And when it sounded, we were off. The hundred meter freestyle was easily the easiest event; Stroke, stroke, stroke, turn for air, stroke, stroke, stroke, turn for air … flip-turn, wash, rinse, repeat …

But then something happened I had not anticipated. My arms and legs still moved, but my mind was whisked away. I would've groaned if I wasn't worried about choking on the chlorine water.

All things around me faded into grayish light, with one splotch of black. Mikey. Black haze surrounded Mikey as his brown eyes turned an ominous green.

A jarring pinch shot through my arm as I smacked pain into my head.

I sputtered as my mouth and eyes filled with chlorine water. Looking up, I found my hallucination had gone, and I'd won the race. But I'd managed to swim headfirst into the pool wall.

The crowd, not realizing (thankfully) I'd had an out-of-mind experience, was cheering madly at my 'endearing, showy tactics.'

I found myself grinning, despite the headache suddenly pounding at my forehead.

Any wonder about the vision vanished as Uzzy reached down and pulled me out of the pool. She squeezed my hand. "Congratulations, Dinger!" She squealed excitedly. "You've broken your previous record!"

I looked up at the scoreboard and saw I had indeed lost a whole 1.4 seconds off my previous record time. "Great," I smiled. "I'm going to get some ice for this bump, Uzzy. I'll be back in a moment."

"Serves you right for your showmanship. But hurry up," she said. "You have another race after this next one. The four hundred IM is a big one for you."

"I know," I remarked brusquely.

"Great going, Dinger," one of my teammates, a guy named Matt (I didn't know his last name) called out.

"Nice job," another one said. "I'm going to run into the wall when I swim next time!"

I smiled brightly as I made my way to the locker room for ice. There was no denying I liked the attention. And it was pathetically cute a couple of swimmers were willing to copy me. But my head needed more immediate care than my ego at the moment.

A voice interrupted me. "Did something happen out there?"

I jumped in surprise, dropping the ice pack I'd found. "Elysian?"

"Up here," the small dragon waved down at me from the top of the ceiling rods.

"What're you doing here?" I muttered bitterly. Why hadn't I bought a cage for this thing when I'd had the chance? Do they sell dragon straightjackets?

"It's a good thing I came. Not only have I managed to get a snapshot of one of your klutz-moments—I'll save that for later—but trouble's brewing."

"I don't believe in—"

"In what? The supernatural?" Elysian cocked an eyebrow.

"Shut up." I felt the frustration rise up again. That argument would do me no good, I knew.

"Anyway, I'm wasting time talking to you. Did you see something?"

Mikey's profile flashed through my mind. I bit my lip. I didn't want to go down this road again.

Elysian sighed. "Did you see something or not?"

I suppose I could have imagined it. I wasn't sure. "No." I shrugged, rubbing my head, careful not to touch the tender area I'd hit. "Does my head look okay?"

"Too big."

"What do you mean, 'big?'"

"I mean you have a big head."

"I do not."

"Yes you do." Elysian sneered. "A big head. A big ego."

I frowned as Elysian began to giggle. "That's not what I meant, you—"

"Hey, Dinger, you're up, let's go!" Uzzy called from the doorway. "You have thirty seconds to get up on your racing block."

"Okay!" I called back. When the door shut, I scowled back down at Elysian. "Just stay out of trouble, okay? I've got to go. This is my big race."

"Watch out for trouble."

"I'll be fine. I'll win, too," I assured him easily, giving the small dragon a cocky smirk.

Elysian rolled his eyes as I headed out. "What I wouldn't give to just slap that smile of his off his face for good," I heard him mutter as the door swung shut.

Despite everything, I *almost* laughed.

Mikey was breathing extra-hard as I approached him. I was half-tempted to irritate him, like I normally would have done. Seeing the sincere, focused, and crazed look in Mikey's eye, however, easily convinced me saying *anything* would be harmful.

The hardness in Mikey's expression was so uncharacteristic of him, even for a crazy version of him. I sighed. I *supposed* I should be encouraging.

After all, I'd never known Mikey, in all my years of knowing him, to take something as seriously as he was taking this swim meet. "May the best man win, Mike," I called. Mikey's frown deepened, causing me to edge away, almost afraid.

Was all the pressure and chlorine causing him to act this way? Or was something more wicked at work?

I couldn't worry about it now. This was the last race of the night, and I had to focus. Uzzy was counting on me, after all, and so were all my numerous fans.

The buzzer sounded. We leapt off our blocks and hit the water one after another.

The four hundred IM wasn't a hard race for me; I'd done it maybe a thousand or so times before in practice, and I knew my limits. For someone who had long mastered all four strokes, I almost felt guilty Mikey was trying so hard.

After all, I wasn't working hard at all, in my own opinion. Mikey must've been working ten times as hard as me, and he's—

Huh?

I nearly choked as I saw Mikey in the next lane over. Mikey's splashy freestyle was steadily overtaking mine. When did he start catching me? I began picking up my own pace, not concerned or anything, of course, but just wanting to give everyone a *real* show.

It was somewhat exciting for me to have a real challenge, because there were really so few for me. For Mikey, it looked like it only fueled him with angry jealousy.

By the time the two of us had reached the end of our breaststrokes, we were neck and neck, and held a significant lead over everyone else.

With one more lap, I sneaked another quick look at Mikey. My would-be friend was flailing all about, his body movements lacking the exact form and beauty of the butterfly stroke.

A half lap to go.

I sped up, having saved the last reserves of my energy. Mikey spurred forward.

Then it was over. The large splashes came to a stop as the two of us pulled off our goggles and looked up at the scoreboard. Both Mikey and I frowned at the results.

We'd tied.

"Wow, what a great meet!" Uzzy was all smiles as she called Mikey and I together in order to pose for the newspaper pictures in a way which would make it seem like she hadn't really been trying to pose for the pictures at all. "You guys did great tonight. You know, you managed to break the record Hamilton set last year and finish in first place!"

"Yeah, just great," I muttered, trying to somewhat sound happy with the news. I had one broken record and another record I would have to re-beat next time. Great. Just great.

Mikey didn't even try. He glared at me harshly, occasionally jerking his body like he was going to hit someone.

THE STARLIGHT CHRONICLES

Elysian was nowhere to be seen as I headed out of the locker room with my stuff. I guess he'd been wrong about the trouble, I thought with a smirk. I liked it when Elysian was wrong.

"You cheated!"

"What?" I turned to see Mikey on verge of full-blown madness. My eyebrows arched in surprise at first, because Mikey looked like the human equivalent of a mad dog, minus the foam at the mouth. "Mikey?"

"You cheated!" Mikey shouted. This time it was loud enough that others were looking over at us.

I gritted my teeth, caught between pity and irritation. "Mikey, deal with it. We tied. Big deal."

"You cheated!"

By now, we had a small crowd of witnesses. I didn't want to have to do it, but there was no choice but for me to defend my honor in the way I knew best.

"No, I didn't. Get over yourself. You think practicing all week is going to help you beat me? It takes a lot more than a week or so of hard practice." I smirked. "You're just lucky you managed to keep up with me. We'll see how different things are on Friday."

"You!" Mikey let out a terrifying cry, revealing a frightening power. "I'll destroy you! You'll never swim again when I'm done with you on Friday! I'll beat you, and not just once!

You'll be crushed, humiliated, completely and utterly defeated—"

"Michael Nathan Salyards!"

I was never so relieved to see Mrs. Salyards than I was at that moment. (I'd been shocked speechless at Mikey's threats.) I smiled at her and gave a friendly wave, but she was too distracted with her revenge-set son to really notice.

"I can't believe you're acting like this! Hamilton is your friend, for heaven's sake! I thought I raised you better than this," she declared, grabbing onto his arm, trying to haul him after her as she continued her rant against his unsportsmanlike conduct.

But Mikey was strong enough and enraged enough to slip out of her grasp. He flung himself under her arm and launched himself at me, shoving me into the glass windows near the door.

I grunted in response, and tried to push Mikey off of me. "Mikey, stop!"

"I'll beat you!" Mikey continued to screech as he threw out punches. I managed to lock arms with Mikey, stopping him, and drive him away from the wall and the windows (we were dealing with Apollo Central—I knew firsthand how easily broken their building windows were).

"Stop it! You're just jealous!" I yelled back.

"I'll bury you, you hear me? I'll take you down and slaughter you!"

"Michael!" Mrs. Salyards came and pulled her son's arms, bringing his punching to a halt. "That's enough!"

Mikey whirled around, his eyes narrowed. Hate burned into his mother as he faced her. She stepped back, falling down. "Michael?" she asked, her voice betraying a hint of fear.

Mikey just let out another screech of rage and ran off.

For a moment we said nothing. Then I exchanged glances with Mrs. Salyards. For a long moment, we shared the same expression of shock.

"Are you all right, Hamilton?" Mrs. Salyards finally asked as she shakily got to her feet.

"Yeah, I'm fine." I scratched my head nervously. I'm not good with moms. I looked over just in time to see Elysian slither out the door and head in my direction.

From one crazy to the next, I thought, groaning to myself. I decided I had more important things to worry about. Gwen was waiting for me.

"Where did he go?" Elysian asked me as I headed over towards the stands.

I moaned and slipped behind one of the stands, hoping above all else no one could see me or hear me. "Who?"

"That kid who was punching you."

"Why? You want to congratulate him?" I asked.

"No. I think he might be in danger."

"Mikey's a jerk. He had a bad night and went off into the deep end. He's insane."

Elysian narrowed his eyes. "Do you ever really listen to me?" he asked, clearly frustrated again. He shook his head. "Look, you have a right to be angry at what he did, but I don't think you understand."

"Understand what? That Mikey's gone crazy and he's obsessed beyond all hope?"

"Ah! Stop right there; there's always hope," Elysian smirked. "And furthermore, you have to understand why Mikey's doing this. There's something wrong. Something that could be *your* fault, you know."

"What? Why would you think that?"

"Well, you seem to do a pretty good job irritating me all the time with that fat mouth of yours! I don't think it's a huge assumption to say it happens with everyone else, too," Elysian remarked, waving his arms in exasperation.

"You need to calm down."

"You need to stay on track. What did you say to him?"

"What, you mean just now?"

"Anytime! Anytime at all! Anything you said in the last week that would make him angry with you!"

"Calm down!"

"Tell me what you said!"

"I don't know! Quit it, all right?" I glared down at the small dragon. "Look, I just got attacked. I only told him, after he was practically threatening to kill me, he wasn't ever going to beat me, and he was just jealous, and had to accept he was never going to one-up me."

Elysian's jaw dropped. "What!? Why would you say that? Did you want to make him angrier at you?" He jumped up, beating his wings furiously. Reaching his claws out, he gave me a small smack on the face. "Who was it who just made a vow only *days* ago to watch your words with people!?"

"Get away from me!" I yelled. "You know, for someone who's concerned about my being nice, you're doing a horrible job of it yourself."

Elysian sighed. "It's not about being nice. It's about valuing others. And right now, your choices have crucial and irreversible consequences."

I groaned. Another lecture from the hypocritical dragon. Just what I needed to round off a perfectly horrible evening.

"I'm leaving," I declared, shoving him off my shoulder. "I've got a date. You know I don't want any part of this anymore. Go bother Starry Knight about it."

"Fine." And with that, Elysian slithered out the door, once more out of my life.

Thank goodness he's gone, I thought triumphantly. I craned my neck around the corner, seeing if I could catch a glimpse of Gwen. I saw her sitting a few rows up; she was texting on her phone.

Good, she hadn't seen me. I smiled. I decided I would just forget Elysian had decided to ruin my evening. And Mikey, too.

"Dinger!"

I turned at the sound of my name. "Hey Jason."

Jason came up to me and reached out a high-five. "Great going out there," he said. "You and Mike sure put on a show. You okay?"

"Yeah, but I can't believe Mikey would do something like that," I admitted.

Jason shrugged. "Maybe he's just stressed. I heard his dad was back in town again."

"What?" That was surprising.

"Yeah. It's bound to have him on edge."

"I guess so," I agreed, slowly shaking my head. I didn't have a clear memory of Mikey's dad, but I easily remembered how much Mikey hated him.

Jason shrugged again. "Well, hey, are you coming to the team after party? My parents are cool with me having a few friends over."

"A few friends?" I inquired with a knowing look. "So you didn't tell them it'll be closer to fifty people?"

"Aw, come on. Only half of you guys will show up," Jason assured me. "So, you coming?"

"Sure, sounds great." And it was great. I'd needed a plan for Valentine's Day for Gwen, right? This was perfect. And I really needed a party after Mikey's little episode. "I'll get Gwen and we'll see you there soon."

"Well, hurry. I got some cake from Rachel."

I brightened instantly. "Will do, my friend. Will do."

☼15☼
Whispers

There was no end to the rumors that found their way through the halls of the high school during the course of the next days. The students—well, those who cared about school spirit and stuff like that, anyway—were all abuzz with the gossip of what happened at the swim meet.

All of them *might* have been talking about how I, Hamilton Dinger, had once again broken a swim record or how Gwen and I were a such a cute couple, *if* they weren't so keen on telling about how Mikey had challenged me to a death match, threatened me, and tried to kill me on the spot when I defended myself.

Normally all this overflow of excitement would have ebbed by the end of the day, but what added to the excitement was Mikey had not gone home after the meet, nor had he come to school on Thursday or Friday. Some kids had filled in the blanks much like they filled in the blanks for their tests—with wrong guesses and things that flat out didn't make any sense.

But I was glad for the attention (no surprise there, really), and I was even a little thrilled the gossip had a more dramatic and mysterious tone than the usual news my classmates heard every other day. I jumped right into demonstrating how Mikey held the knife up to my throat, choking me, as he'd laughed cruelly and vowed he would not rest until he had seen the end of me.

However, by the end of Friday, even I was getting tired of hearing all the rumors. I'd heard varying degrees of Mikey's

THE STARLIGHT CHRONICLES

fate, ranging from Mikey being sent to juvenile hall to killing himself by drowning himself in Lake Erie. There were rumors he was hiding out, plotting some outrageous attempt to show up for Friday's meet to get a chance to beat me again, and there were reports he'd been sent away by his mother to one of those behavior modification camps.

I was willing to bet no one actually knew and that was why everyone thought they knew.

"Hey, Hammy," Gwen waved as she started to walk alongside me.

"Hey Gwen. Looking forward to the swim meet today?" I asked with a smile. "I had a really good time after the last one."

"I'm glad you enjoyed the party," she said. "Did I tell you my parents were hoping to have dinner with you this week?"

Yes, she had, but it wasn't like I needed to pay attention to something I'd already heard. I was already thinking about asking her out after the meet, and where we could go, maybe see if the gang wanted to meet somewhere afterwards.

My attention was caught again only when she mentioned Mikey.

"What about Mikey?" I asked, surprised.

Gwen sighed. "I feel so bad for him. He must be so emotionally tangled up inside."

"Yeah. Right."

"I mean, when someone runs away, it has to be because they have no place to go."

"Yeah, sounds right."

"I wonder what happened to set him off like that?"

"I don't know. No clue."

"Laura told me someone said something to him, and that set him off. Do you think that's true?"

"Don't know, don't care."

"Aren't you worried about him at all?"

That was the question that made me look over at her (I could tell it was one of those trick questions females give sometimes). Her honey-brown eyes were filled with concern for our mutual friend, I could tell, but she was clearly starting to be annoyed with the fact I wasn't as worried and fretful as she was.

"Honestly? I think he's fine. He's a big boy, Gwen, and he can take care of himself."

Gwen huffed. "It's nice you're so loyal to him, Dinger." With that, she turned around and stomped off.

Boy, she's mad at me now, I thought glumly. She rarely called me "Dinger," and when she did it was usually because she wasn't happy with me. Well, what was I supposed to do? Make "lost" fliers and post them all around the town? Call the police? Consult my magic crystal ball? Go to grief counseling? I grumbled inaudibly to myself as I shut my locker.

"Feeling sorry? That's not a usual look for you."

I felt like groaning even more as I turned to see Raiya standing behind me. I sighed. "Why would I feel sorry?" I asked, my tone hard and borderline mean, definitely unwelcoming. "I didn't realize I was the one still wearing a Rosemont uniform."

Seriously, why did she keep wearing it? Surely she had enough money for new clothes when she transferred here.

Raiya frowned before apparently letting the insult slide. "I saw him."

"What?"

"I saw Mikey. He's been camping in Shoreside Park these last two nights," she told me.

I looked at her and then rolled my eyes. "Why would I believe you?" I wasn't really interested in her answer, so I started to walk away.

I was surprised when she answered anyway. "I don't know. You're really just like everyone else."

"What?" I turned around and looked back at her. "What do you mean by that?"

Her eyes met mine for the briefest second before she looked away. "The truth is generally something most people don't want to believe," she said, shrugging. With that, she turned on her heel and started walking away. "And even if they accept it, they generally don't want to do anything about it."

I just watched her as she headed off, dumbfounded. Then I clenched my fists and headed toward the swim team locker rooms. Like she would tell me the truth. She didn't care about me, or Mikey … It didn't matter.

I shook my head. No, it didn't matter now. All that mattered was today. The swim meet was on, and I had a date with Gwen. The college scouts were back, and I needed to be at my best.

"All right, Dinger!"

I grinned as the cheering crowd once more sang my praises. I'd finished up the first race, and of course, I'd won. My groupies were just as excited about it as I was.

"That was really great!" Coach Uzzy cheered. "Our school's already ahead of Clearburg!"

All thanks to me, I smiled. Just in time for a photo op from one of the local newspapers, too.

"It's good we're doing okay without Mikey here, too," Uzzy added.

"Yeah, it's too bad he's not here," I agreed.

One of my teammates spoke up. "I thought he might at least come to wish us luck or something like that."

"Ugh, no, I don't think so. I heard he was in some kind of rehabilitation center," Jason replied.

I stood up and left. I didn't want to think about Mikey. I didn't really want to care about him, either.

The next race was the one hundred freestyle. I checked my goggles, my cap, and made sure I looked intense for any possible camera shots coming my way. Briefly, I glanced over at the block next to me, only to see some teammate of mine—not Mikey—climb up.

"Swimmers, to your marks!" the announcer called out as the next race was getting started.

"Ow!" the swimmer next to me suddenly cried out in pain. The Central swimmer next to me was gone, pushed aside.

Mikey had arrived, and he didn't like being replaced.

I, along with half the other swimmers, stood up and looked at the judges, who were apparently in a bit of frenzy. I stole a glance back at Mikey, just in time for the buzzer to go off.

Beep! The buzzer went off, sending Mikey went off along with it.

It took a full two hundredths of a second for me to jump off and follow him; then race was *really* on.

No one in the stands knew what was really going on, but they weren't picky. They just went along with it. I could half-hear cheers for Team Dinger and also some for Mikey as they grew louder while we quickly became the forerunners of the laps.

I glanced over at Mikey, to see him slicing through the water in a clumsy but powerful manner.

Then a stream of power—light and energy—forced itself out of Mikey, propelling him to the wall with supernatural speed.

He won.

It's probably a good thing Mikey won, I comfortingly reasoned, as time returned to normal and I kept moving. I was going to finish in second place for the first time in my life, but it was the first time in my life I didn't mind (that much, anyway—and I figured Mikey would be disqualified).

After grazing the wall with my fingers, I pulled off my goggles and turned to face my friend. "Well, Mike, congratu—"

My nice (though somewhat forced) congratulations cut off when I saw Mikey had disappeared. "Where'd he—?" I sputtered as I was forcefully dragged under the water, choking as the chlorine water filled my nose and burned in my throat.

I kicked hard, and managed to get up for air for a brief second before I was plunged into the depths of the pool.

I squinted into the water, opening my eyes as I struggled to break free. "Mikey!" I gasped, seeing it was my one-time friend forcefully dragging me further underneath the water.

Or was it? I wondered. Mikey didn't look like himself. His eyes were glowing eerie green again, and a cloud of darkness was fluffing around him.

"You've always had it easy, Dinger!" Mikey told me, the water distorting his voice. "Now it's my turn!"

I felt the sudden rise of pressure and panic. Once more, I tried desperately to escape, letting out a stream of bubbles as I gasped in surprise and terror. Flailing my arms and flaying my legs, I struggled desperately to get free.

And while this was happening, Mikey transformed. Octopus-like legs sprouted from his sides, tangling themselves all around me, squeezing out what little air was left in me even more relentlessly.

I looked down at my wrist. Nothing. I reached out for it anyway, hoping against all hope I would be able to transform and get out of the mess I was in.

But the ugly tentacles were too much for me. My arms were spread out, and I could not reach the mark. I closed my eyes as I felt the onset of drowning slowly sinking in. It was hopeless, I realized.

Then all of a sudden, I was free.

I opened my eyes and surged to the surface of the pool, gasping. I hurried to get out of the water. Some teachers and a few of my friends looked relieved to see me and moved to help me. I noticed Gwen was open-mouthed with shock.

"Dinger, are you all right?" Uzzy called.

"Dinger!" Jason grabbed me by the arm. "What happened? Where's Mikey?"

"You okay?"

"You need anything?"

"Can you stand?"

There were a million questions by a million people, and I didn't have the patience or proper courtesy for them. I looked down at the pool, wondering what had happened. The pool water had turned black and murky. Other tentacles reached out from the water, bursting out of the room and curling around people in the stands.

What caused Mikey to let me go?

I got my answer as Jason brought over a towel for me. "Man, first you get tackled by Mikey, and then that crocodile jumping in the water—"

"Crocodile?" I asked. That was not something I was expecting.

Then it dawned on me. Elysian had saved me. I cringed. I was going to owe him one for that.

Before I could ask anything else, the water surged out of the pool. People scrambled to get away and hurried out the nearest exits. A giant tangle of two creatures filled the room.

"Elysian," I muttered.

I started pushing people out toward the door, shuffling around Coach Uzzy and Jason and others. Some were looking to me like they needed direction. So I decided to give it to them. "Let's get out of here!" I cried.

☼16☼
Adversary

Students were screaming, bricks were splaying, and chairs were overturned. Needless to say, it was pandemonium.

Somehow during the chaos, my reflexes took over. I shuffled people out of the pool area, desperately looking for Gwen as the stream of people poured through the doors. *Where was she?* I hoped she hadn't gotten hurt.

My eyes flew to my wrist. I blinked at the blank patch of skin before I remembered I'd quit. I cursed silently to myself.

The roar of the slug-like glob bellowed out behind me, and that was when I decided I'd had enough of doorman duties. Seeing the stream of people headed outside starting to dry up, I dropped the door and headed over to the stands to look for Gwen.

Before I could get too far, the doors burst open to reveal the policemen—or should I say some kind of SWAT force— had arrived.

I'm not sure if the loss of subtlety was helpful.

Mikey's monstrous, octopus-like body was tangled up with Elysian's; a tentacle lashed out and slammed through the school windows, shattering the glass. I ducked behind the stands and finally caught sight of Gwen.

Her legs seemed to be stuck under one of Mikey's tentacles, unable to move.

"Gwen! What's wrong?" I asked, coming up behind her.

171

It was then I saw Tim Ryder on the ground next to her, covered in one of Mikey's many tentacles. He was, fortunately for me, unconscious.

Oh great, I thought. This again?

"Hammy, you've got to help us out of here," Gwen whispered. "Tim just came over to say hi while the race was on and then … "

Her voice trailed off and I assumed she began talking about some heroic-type effort Tim put forth in protecting her. All I could think about what how much I'd seen her texting lately, and about how much I suddenly wanted to look at her phone.

A surge of jealousy ripped through me, burning through my blood. Tim's body twitched on the ground, bringing me back to the moment.

A ragged, out-of-breath Starry Knight suddenly appeared behind us. "Get back!" she gasped in warning. "It's not safe!"

Her bow was out, and she slashed through the pudgy octopus arm in a single swipe, breaking Tim, still comatose, free of its oppressive hold. The part of the tentacle attached to Mikey's body twisted around and swished back to its owner. I watched as it managed to flick Elysian in the face, who, I couldn't help but notice, was having trouble controlling the beast.

As Gwen tried to wake Tim up, Mikey roared and broke free, launching himself through the wall of the building. Out of the corner of my eye, I saw Starry Knight take flight before I could stop her. Starry Knight began unleashing another storm of arrows at Mikey. The arrows ripped through the tentacles, sending several pieces of torn flesh down onto the floor and pool.

Gross.

"After them!" a policeman ordered.

They jogged after the monster. I looked down at Gwen, practically sobbing over Tim. I'd have to deal with this later, I decided. I was just about to follow Starry Knight and Elysian when I heard a very feminine, very evil laugh coming from above him. I looked up and saw a floating woman of some kind.

This Sinister was certainly maleficent in her demeanor. Huh … It's not the bluish one, I noticed. It was the one from before. Alcyonë.

My fists clenched as I recalled her earlier conversation with Orpheus; she'd done something to Mikey, I was sure of it. "What did you do to him?"

Alcyonë looked down at me, surprised to find someone paying attention to her, no doubt. "I didn't do anything to him. He did this to himself. Sure, I prodded him in the right direction, but this is all his doing. There is no rescuing him at this point. His Soulfire is under my control."

I was just calculating my chances of managing to punch her when a familiar-looking arrow of light shot through the room.

Alcyonë flinched to the side, but not enough to escape the arrow entirely. "Augh!" she cried out as the arrow pierced her. She slumped down to the ground, far from defeated but close to a retreat.

I was just about to mock the jolly-green jerk as she curled up on the hard floor when I was struck (hard) from the behind.

The blow from the tentacled monster sent me reeling back into the pool. Starry Knight immediately sent an arrow slashing through Mikey's body, and Elysian let out a strong whiplash, sending Mikey's body careening into the wall of the cafeteria.

"You're next, Alcyonë," Starry Knight announced, turning her attention back to the green-tinted lady.

Alcyonë wrinkled her nose in disdain. "How do you intend to defeat me? You couldn't before."

The violet eyes of the warrior held steady as she drew the bow back. "I have my ways," she spoke softly, letting the arrow fly.

This time, Alcyonë was smart (or lucky) as she ducked. But it was too close for her comfort. "I think I'll leave my minion to deal with you," she said with malice, before disappearing.

Starry Knight frowned before turning her attention to Mikey. That was when I began to panic. Even though I was mad at Mikey, I didn't want Mikey to be destroyed. Or the school, which was also taking quite a beating.

I hurried to the side of the pool and grabbed my sports gear. A policeman held me back as I tried to go out and catch up with them. "Stop! Let me go," I yelled at the policeman.

"Sit tight, kid. Let the adults handle this."

Kid!? Ugh. "Starry Knight!" I called.

Despite the noise, her violet eyes fluttered to mine. Her hair fell gracefully behind her in gentle waves, and her wings fluttered delicately, belying the solid strength held within. I suddenly felt overwhelmed, as though I'd betrayed her—that I too was a monster, overcome by evil and consumed with helplessness.

I'd have to worry about it later.

"That demon is a person!" I called out. "Please don't kill him!"

The elegant warrior looked over at me. "I told you not to get involved," she said, her words cold and sharp.

"You can't kill him."

"He is corrupted. It is my duty to seal away the Sinisters and all their demons."

Really? I thought. It took me to be a civilian before she would tell me the specifics of her job? Ugh, there was no time to call her out on it. I'd get to it later. "He's a human. That lady did something to him to make him this way. We have to turn him back," I argued.

Starry Knight hardened her gaze as she lowered her bow. "That lady, as you call her, is the Sinister of Envy, Alcyonë. If he became this way because of her, he must break through on his own. And at this point, it's not looking good. If envy is the root of the problem, there has be something done to break its power," Starry Knight told me.

That meant about nothing to me. "But there is hope," I insisted. "I'm not going to take the easy way out and say it's useless to try."

She said nothing, but her eyes flickered back over the monster, and a moment later, she had jumped high into the room, and transformed her bow into a harp.

The waves of music overcame me, but instead of feeling soothed, enchanted, or strangely nostalgic as I usually did, I felt as small and ugly as Mikey was starting to look.

Mikey slowly sank down to the floor in a heavy pile of flesh. He did not transform back into his normal self, but remained there, planked on the floor. Elysian looked questioningly up at Starry Knight, and she shook her head as she put down the harp. The two of them came down looked over Mikey, whispering to each other.

I suddenly wished I was over there too, listening to what they were talking about.

The police broke away from where they had been standing and hurried over, cuffing the boy/monster. They began to drag him away as some sense of normalcy returned, and I could hear others in the stands, those who hadn't made it out of the building, crying for help.

THE STARLIGHT CHRONICLES

Starry Knight and Elysian both then turned to go.

"Wait!" I called back, but Elysian only let out a snort, and hurried off faster.

But Starry Knight looked at me; I knew she couldn't stay. And when she left, I felt a strong wave of nausea rise up within me I knew had more to do with my own actions than Mikey's fate.

I glanced down at my wrist again and felt numb.

☼<u>17</u>☼
Hollow

The first bell of the day rang. "If every time a bell rings an angel gets his wings," I muttered darkly, "I'll bet when that bell rings someone dies."

"Entirely possible," Poncey agreed as he slid into his seat near me. "I don't know if it's all one person though. I think just a little bit of *me* dies every time that bell goes off."

"If a bit of you dies, I'll bet it's from your brain." Jason grinned as he too took his seat.

"You don't have any room to talk, Jase," Poncey argued. "I'm the one who got a better grade on my Biology midterm."

I silently groaned some more as I tuned out my friends' arguments. Normally I would have joined them (and made them both out to be sorry figures) but today I just didn't feel like I had any energy to do so. I'd gotten to sleep relatively early (all things considered), but I was just tired.

Or maybe tired of. There was always that to consider.

The whole day of today had to be a big joke, I mused. Everyone in the school, it seemed, had grown tired of last week's news, the weekend managing to divert attention to other matters.

The news was no help, of course. It's a frightening, terrifying world to live in after discovering the news doesn't like to tell the truth oftentimes. There was little to no mention of the demon forces at work in Mikey, and Starry Knight and Elysian were left out of the story as much as possible. Those who were injured in the attack were not named over the news, but I knew there were quite a bit; the rumors were swirling around faster than draining water in a bathtub.

I knew from personally seeing it Tim wasn't the only one who was in the hospital. Mrs. Smithe had also been hit by one of Mikey's many suction-cupped limbs, as well as some other students, teachers, and even the librarian, Trixie Brain. (I wasn't exactly sorry to hear about her.)

I'd rather have liked to forget them as much as I'd have liked to forget Mikey's unnatural form lying crocked on the cafeteria floor, bound in extra-large handcuffs.

But what was even more impossible to forget was the heaviness I was carrying around in my chest today.

What's wrong with me?

I've been like this for a while now, I realized with disgust. I tried to shake it off, but the shadow of my solemnity clung to me worse than static cling.

I definitely felt awkward in class today. No one was really talking. Even Raiya wasn't here to fight with me, making me wonder if she wasn't in the hospital, too. Martha wasn't teaching today, of course; she'd been seriously injured in the attack, according to the grapevine. Even the best-case scenario wasn't comforting.

So our class was watching a movie.

I was determined to focus on the movie, and the movie only. I had to will myself out of this gloomy mood. And I sincerely thought I could.

I sighed, leaning my head on my hand for support. I shouldn't have moved. I caught sight of my wrist.

There was no hint of the Emblem of the Prince. The sight of it (or lack of it, I guess) sickened me; Martha was in the hospital and Mikey was incarcerated as a result of the mark's disappearance.

It wasn't that I'd brought on my own problems or that I could stop them. It was just there were things I couldn't control, and there were some I could, if I would do the right thing to stop it …

But that was just it. I couldn't do the right thing, because there was supposed to be no right or wrong, good or evil, and all that other stuff.

But what if there is? What if I'd been wrong?

Psh. I couldn't be wrong.

If I was wrong about that, about the condition of the world, about how there was no good or bad, or right or wrong, then I would be more than just wrong.

If there was good and bad in the world, I would be among the bad. One act at all would prove something to be bad. I would never be wholly good, just capable of doing good things.

THE STARLIGHT CHRONICLES

Obviously, it was a matter of deep philosophy, and I didn't really want to think about it.

But I took a good look at myself, and for the first time I could remember, I did not like what I saw. I cared too much about myself and my happiness. Martha's life was on the line, Mikey's fate was precariously hanging just above doom, and all I could find the energy to focus on was me.

And most of it was just to pity myself. It wasn't even to plan on doing anything about anything except feel bad about what had happened.

There was no clear way I could live with myself now I had acknowledged my great, imperfect soul—and I didn't see why anyone else would want to live with me, either. There was no atonement I could offer.

My head collapsed into my arms as despair took hold of me.

I glanced over to see Gwen. She wasn't faring any better than I was, by the look of it. I wasn't really that sorry for her, to be honest. I'd been too shocked and depressed after the swim meet trouble to take her out, and she had been more than okay with that. When I'd called her up later, I'd been the patient, understanding, compassionate boyfriend, much to my chagrin.

Hey, I *still* wanted to find out whether or not she'd been cheating on me. I think it was a reasonable desire under the circumstances. Especially since I was pretty sure she'd been pining to go to the hospital to check on Tim. She had asked me whether or not my dad was on-call at the hospital more than once since the swim meet.

It also didn't help the gossip grapevine was in full swing, saying Gwen had been using me for a cover with her parents while she and Tim had afternoons full of good, clean, 1950's romantic bliss.

When the bell finally rang, I put my stuff away, and, like a hollow automaton, headed for my next class. I purposefully avoided Gwen, and subconsciously, my friends. (I didn't need to have them ask about the rumors of me and Gwen any more than anyone else.)

When did the world become so meaningless? I wondered. And when did I begin preferring it the other way?

I thought about fighting with Elysian over destiny, passionately defending myself to Starry Knight, about seeking out the hidden truths in darkness even while I denied their existence during the day.

I automatically chastised myself for even thinking of anything reminding me of those losers, or my so-called supernatural abilities, or how I'd quit without ever really knowing who Starry Knight was …

What did I have to look forward to now? Checking up on social media? Seeing how much I could play Tetris or sleep during class before getting caught? Sort-of talking with Gwen at Rachel's about unimportant stuff? Running away from demons and putting around school like it was a custom-made hamster maze? Pretending like I had it all figured out even though I didn't, just wanting people to believe I did?

"Hammy."

"Huh?" I jerked out of my gloomy, colorless self-resignation letter on life. "Hey, Gwen."

She seemed a bit shy, wringing her hands together. "Hey. I wanted to … Well, I wanted to see if you wanted to hang out later."

"Sure." Even my response is automatic, I thought bitterly. "Sounds good."

"Would you like to go to Rachel's? I know it's your favorite."

"Yeah. Sounds good." Automatic to the point of a broken record.

"Do you want me to see if anyone else wants to go?" Gwen asked.

She was trying too hard to appease me, a suspicious voice murmured in the back of my head.

"Sure." I smiled, but it felt robotic in the end. "I'll see you then. Gotta go."

"Bye," she called out as I made my way out of there. It was sad; even a trip to Rachel's wasn't enough to lift my spirits.

"I can't stand it anymore, Rachel!"

Gwen and I both flinched at the screechy voice as we entered into Rachel's Café later on. Along with the other people who were trying to enjoy their meals, we stopped and stared at the middle-aged woman loudly complaining to Rachel.

"This is the third time this week I've been stood up, and twice by the same guy! Ooh, I'm going to make him suffer for this unforgivable outrage … "

Rachel smiled. "Calm down, Mom, people are staring," she whispered. "You don't want to scare off the people who pay for your nice outfits, do you?"

"Part of the reason they come is to mock me in these drab clothes!" Leticia huffed disdainfully.

"Letty, get a grip on yourself," Grandpa Odd (Ugh! He's here too!?) spoke up from his usual bar stool. "I don't see why your life is in shambles at the mere thought of spending a night at home instead of at some fancy-shmancy restaurant where you can't even pronounce the names of the food right."

Letty scowled. "Let's just say I need it for my health," she retorted. "I fear loneliness has driven you to madness, Old Man."

"Mom, he's got a point—"

"You be quiet. I need to smoke," Letty huffed, pulling out a cigarette. "That nicotine patch isn't working at all!"

"You have to take it out of the box first, Mom." Rachel smirked. "Besides, no smoking in here. It taints the food. The FDA doesn't approve."

"The FDA can kiss my—"

"Hamilton! Gwen! Come in," Rachel called out. "I was wondering if you were coming today. Jason said you didn't have practice today."

"Hey, Rachel … Letty … Grandpa Odd," I greeted them all as politely as I could and still be able to call it polite.

Only Rachel smiled in return. "Hey, I have some chocolate blueberry brownies baking. When they come up, do any of you want to try a sample?" she asked.

"Sure! I was wondering what smelled so good when I came in." Gwen smiled. "I love brownies."

"Great! I'll have Jason bring them out to you once they're ready," Rachel promised. "If you'll have a seat I'll get someone to get your order taken in just a moment." Off to the side, she added, "I have to take care of these two right now, sorry."

Gwen and I found our usual booth and exchanged comments every so often while keeping an eye on the front counter; Letty was in one of her moods and the old man still wasn't taking meds apparently, so it was sure to be a fun show tonight.

The kitchen doors swung open, and I cringed as Raiya came out the door with a tray in her hands. She's working today?

Come on, I thought bitterly. I really hoped she wasn't going to be our waitress today … If she was, though, on second thought, it would be fun to torture her. That would be just *awesome*, especially since she'd been out of school today.

"Hey, Dinger, Gwen," Jason greeted as he too came out from the kitchen with a tray. "I'll take your order today."

"Thanks, that'll save me some worrying," I quickly quipped, nodding in Raiya's direction. "She's working today?"

"Yeah. The other waitress who usually works here now, Holly, is close to six months pregnant, and she's having some problems. So Raiya might step in until Rachel can either find someone else or Holly's babies are born and maternity leave is over."

"Oh, my," Gwen said. "That is horrible."

"Yes, it is," I agreed, although I was pretty sure Gwen was talking about the complicated pregnancy, while I was referring to Raiya working here for another three or four months.

Jason smiled brightly. "I think it's nice. Raiya's … Well, I like working with her. She's interesting to—" Jason broke off as he saw the look on my face. "Well, never mind. What would you like to have, Dinger?"

"I'll have that blueberry brownie Rachel mentioned," I grinned. "And also a mocha."

Jason laughed. "Sure, Dinger. How about you, Gwen?"

"I think I'll have a brownie, too, Jason, and a cream soda."

"Good choice. I'll go check on the brownies and be back with your drinks shortly."

"Thank you," Gwen replied. She watched him walk away and said, "Jason's so nice. I'm glad he likes his job."

I grinned. "Yeah, where else could he get paid to stare at Rachel all day?"

"Does he really like her?"

"Sure does. The first time I came here with him—it was for his party, you know, when the meteor rock came crashing into Apollo City—he was practically drooling over her. It's fitting that he's waiting on tables for her now, if you ask me. Too bad Rachel's getting married."

"Yeah. Poor Jason."

I nearly snorted and then held it in. I didn't really feel sorry for Jason—after all, Jason was fully aware Rachel was getting married. He was just acting like a fool. When he finally realized the truth, that's when he'd straighten up.

"Ouch! Augh!"

Gwen and I nearly jumped out of our seats, along with the rest of the guests in the restaurant, when Jason suddenly let out a loud screech from the kitchen.

"Stop it! Ouch!"

A number of guests were craning their necks to see what was happening.

We were all anxious to see the kitchen door open. But a moment later, it was only Raiya who breezed through the kitchen door with a tray full of drinks in her hands. Talk about a disappointment.

"Raiya," Rachel stepped away from the counter where she had been talking with her mother and grandfather. "What happened?"

I leaned forward, pricking up my ears.

"Jason was checking the brownies and he got hurt," Raiya replied.

"Did he get burned?"

"He says so." Raiya shrugged. "You might want to go look. I didn't see anything."

"You checked it then?"

"I took hold of his hand and looked very closely," Raiya assured Rachel. "I'm sure nothing's wrong."

"Sounds like Jason got burned," I told Gwen, a smirk creeping up on my face. "Ironic that we were just talking about his love life, too."

There was a fleeting smile on Gwen's face before she shook her head. "You're so mean, Hammy."

I shrugged. "Just being myself. I like being honest."

"When it suits you," Raiya spoke up as she set her tray down on our table.

THE STARLIGHT CHRONICLES

All the remains of any desire to be polite deserted me. "For example, Gwen, I think Raiya is very annoying."

"Hammy—"

"It's all right, Gwen," Raiya remarked as she handed us our drinks. "Humdinger here probably just missed me today from school." She smirked and then waltzed back to towards the kitchen.

"Dinger, I swear, sometimes you are so irritating," Gwen muttered through gritted teeth. "You have no consideration for anyone else—"

"Hey guys," Jason broke in. "I have your brownies here; careful, they're still kinda hot."

Gwen, still half-glaring at me, said, "Thank you, Jason."

He grinned. "You're welcome. You guys okay?"

I shrugged. I didn't care that much; I was thinking about trying to get Raiya back so I could return to our fight if I could. "We're fine. How's your burn?"

"Huh? Oh, right," Jason laughed. "I don't actually have one. I thought I did, because my hand really hurt when it touched the side of the oven, but I guess I imagined it." He held up his hand to show us. There was no evidence at all to any burn or bruise. "But it was really hurting, especially when Raiya grabbed it and looked at it—she could've been more careful, I guess."

I stared at Jason's hand in mock amazement. "Wow. You mean she touched your hand and you still didn't get burned? Astounding."

I thought I saw Jason roll his eyes. "You guys have everything you need?"

"Yeah, unless you have a muzzle back there," Gwen spoke up as she sat down. "Dinger here could really use it."

"Hey, Raiya and I fight all the time," I retorted.

"Was she bothering you?" Jason asked.

"Apparently," Gwen huffed.

I sighed. "Gwen, I just don't like her at all. She's … " I shook my head. I didn't know exactly what I hated so much about her, but that just made me even more irritated by her.

Jason snickered. "I think it's funny. Like you didn't have enough girl troubles before, huh?" He stopped laughing when he saw my expression. (It looked like Jason had been taking irritation lessons from Mikey.) "Oh, I gotta go."

"Yeah, see you later," I grumbled.

"Oh, shut up, Dinger," Gwen muttered.

She was still mad at me? Really? Great. Nothing to do about that now. Women.

While I let her stew in her rage, a new painting on the far side of the café caught my attention. A strong hand was holding what looked like dust, but the "dust" was blowing into the sky, becoming the brilliant starlight. I stared at it in wonder, as I mechanically drank my mocha.

"What are you looking about?" Gwen finally asked.

"Huh?" I nearly jumped. I was surprised she was talking to me so soon. (Scientists determined the silent treatment is found to last an average of two days and thirteen hours).

"I asked you what you were looking at," Gwen repeated. "You have a dumb look on your face."

I rolled my eyes. "Just looking at the painting over there. Very creative, don't you think?"

Talking about art must have triggered her happy brain chemicals. "It's beautiful." Gwen smiled. "Rachel always seems to have the best art here, don't you think?"

"She probably pays a bunch of money for them," I surmised.

"I wonder who she gets them from," Gwen remarked.

"Probably from one of the museums closing down because of the current recession."

We settled down into silence. Have you ever seen married people just listlessly eating at the same table, and you have to wonder if they were communicating without words, or if they were just tired of talking to the same person? That's kind of how I felt.

I turned my attention to the television over the bar and watched it for a bit while Gwen picked at her brownie.

I was almost—almost—grateful when Grandpa Odd looked up from his newspaper.

"Alas, it be Hamilton Dinger!" The old odd man saluted me with his cup and said, "You look down today, my lad. What be it that troubles your soul today?"

I said nothing, just looked down in my cup. I peeked over at Gwen, who didn't seem to care I was about to be bothered. I noticed, to my dismay, she was texting again.

As if she'd noticed me paying attention, Gwen stood up. "I have to go to the ladies' room. Excuse me."

The old man laughed as she disappeared. "Ah, the tragedy of youth. Come you hither to seek my counsel, my pupil? It must be true love."

I glared at him. "True hate is more like it," I muttered before I could stop myself.

"Hmm. Disturbing this is."

I was getting irritated by Grandpa Odd. It didn't normally take much, honestly. But between Shakespeare and Yoda, couldn't he just find a dialect and stick with it?

Grandpa Odd's eyes went dark and blank as he said, "You might hate yourself now, but you cannot help but love yourself. You will need to question yourself and your motives over and over again if you are to find the truth in your heart." He sighed, and then wistfully began to recite a lovely poem about flashy rhetoric, about parrots that talked in Greek, and about pains that were more precious than all other gains.

I didn't hear the whole thing because it was probably against the law or something.

Then he looked back at me and said, "Ah, the power of poetry to ignite the soul. Do you know what Lewis is talking about in his poem?"

I was never very good at poetry. But I was curious, to say the least. Something about the poem had resonated within me.

"Lewis is talking an honest look at himself, finding his shortcomings. Those of us who have souls all need to be honest about what condition we are truly in. And we are all selfish. We all talk of love, but how limited we are in comprehending it!"

"But why does he say the pain he gets is precious?" I asked.

Grandpa Odd's eyes glistened. "It is a matter of perspective, young Hamilton. If you are doing something which will end in self-destruction, would you not want someone to stop you? Would you not want a challenge to make you a better person? The child who flinches at the thought of piano practice today might be the accomplished pianist of tomorrow."

People have to choose how their pain will change them, I supposed.

"Here." Grandpa Odd held out his hand and winked. "Take this. A quarter for your thoughts."

Mrs. Smithe's lecture popped into my mind. A different point of view. That's all I need, I thought as I rolled my eyes in disgust.

"I think I'll take my leave," Grandpa Odd said as he yawned. "It's been a long day already. Adieu, young Hamilton." And then the old man bowed and left.

Rachel came back over and said, "I'm sorry that he's such a bother to you. But he means well, I think, in his own way. He's been terribly lonely since Grandma died. Ever since Raiya came to live with us, he's been better."

"He's not that much of a bother, I guess," I shrugged. At least for today. It was possible I even felt a bit better after listening to him. Don't quote me on that, though.

☼

"Hamilton, where have you been?"

"Hi, Cheryl," I muttered more to myself than anyone else as I walked into the house (not *my* house, you'll notice.)

"Come in here. We've gotten some information on those so-called superheroes I think you'll like."

"Now?" I didn't want to deal with it.

"Yes, now." Cheryl laughed. "I could use your help with it, you know. When were you going to come into the mayor's

THE STARLIGHT CHRONICLES

office, by the way? Stefano's been asking about you. Oh, can you bring me my briefcase? It's out there by the door."

There was nothing my mother loved more than a difficult case. I could tell she was enjoying herself by how talkative she was. I knew I wouldn't have to really answer her questions for a while.

I hauled in her briefcase and sighed, mentally preparing myself for a tirade of some kind. I waited until she pulled out a folder from her briefcase before I asked her about her progress.

"It's been hard," she admitted. "There's something unusual about those Angel fighters."

"What is it?" I asked, not really interested. Not that Cheryl would notice.

"There hasn't been any DNA recovered. None at all; not from them, or any from the monsters they fight."

"Huh."

"After all these months, there should have been some. Hmm." Cheryl pursed her lips together. "It's an interesting anomaly."

"What do you mean by that?"

"Nothing special, I guess." But there was something on her face which made me realize she was lying. Cheryl knew something. Her eyes looked up from her paper and landed on the family portrait of all of us on her desk.

I was just about to ask her what she was thinking when she jolted out of her trance and pulled out another paper.

"Did you see this one, Ham?" Cheryl asked. "There was an attack on a girl a few weeks ago. She's from your school, actually."

Dread crippled my stomach. "So?" I asked, trying my hardest not to choke over my words.

"Didn't your other friend get attacked, as well?"

I didn't say anything I looked down at Samantha Carter's profile. Cheryl didn't wait for my answer as she continued on. "The detective force we're working with has asked us to figure out some of the similarities of the victims. Seems like they're from broken homes, tragic childhood backgrounds, low self-esteem ... "

Cheryl rattled off some of the possibilities as I remembered what Elysian had said about Mikey. He'd been jealous of me. Samantha had been jealous for me. And even Starry Knight had warned me about envy...

I cringed. I hoped Cheryl didn't make the connection back to me. I looked at her now, and figured I was pretty safe; Cheryl was more concerned for her case than the actual victims, so she would probably make whatever connection would help her win. A numbing sensation crept through me as I recalled how much Gwen had wanted to go see them; I didn't care too much about the victims, either. Not even to be nice about it.

"I gotta go do some homework," I said gruffly, trying to shake off the momentary guilt.

"Okay," Cheryl said, as she tacked up the pictures and other information to her corkboard and began to study them. "Try to come see me and Stefano soon. I want to get you set up as an aide soon."

"Sure." My automatic reply was back as my voice was trapped behind a wave of nausea.

THE STARLIGHT CHRONICLES

☼18☼
Regret

It wasn't long before I couldn't sleep.

I blamed Cheryl and her stupid quest inside the teenage mind, but there were other complications.

While my dreams of Orpheus and his team of monsters had disappeared, mysteriously (because miraculously was never going to be in my vocabulary), I kept dreaming of Mikey and Gwen, and losing. Losing what, or who, I didn't really know, and that was the worst part. Well, the second to worst part. The worst part was I didn't know if paranoia had caused my insomnia or if it was the other way around. The bright side was I was at Rachel's a lot more for her coffee.

"Back again, Hamilton? Wasn't one trip this morning enough for you?" Rachel asked me as she handed me my order. "I mean no offense, and I like you as much as friend as a customer. But are you feeling all right?"

"Yeah, I'm fine," I assured her as best as I could.

She frowned. "What's wrong? Are you stressed about school or something? I know my cousin's not your favorite person in the world, but she's been out for the last couple of days. Surely she's not that much trouble for you."

"No." I grimaced.

"Is it something else?"

"Nothing much," I lied again. "Cheryl's just trying to get me to help her with some of her casework. It's just so … engrossing."

"Oh, I see. Well, that's good, I guess." Rachel smiled. "You like it?"

"Not really."

"Oh."

"It's hard with all the schoolwork and everything." For some reason, it was just getting easier to keep lying. "I'll get used to it soon."

"If that's what you want, I guess," Rachel agreed. She gave me a small smile. "I'll get some extra cookies for you."

"You're the best," I saluted her with my near-empty cup. At last, I thought. A non-lie.

"Is Gwen coming in today?" she asked as she pulled down her personal cookie jar.

"I texted her earlier. She said she had stay late at school today."

A scoffing noise came out from behind me as the entrance door closed. "Well, she's not at school anymore."

I turned to see Raiya, coming in from the cold weather, her old art box with her. I refrained from making some kind of remark on where she'd been all week to look down my nose at her. "What would you know about it?" I asked with an indignant huff. "I just got the text about an hour ago."

"Well, I just saw her at the hospital an hour ago," Raiya told me. "So there's that."

"What?" Surely she was mistaken. I mean, Gwen had wanted to go to the hospital, and she'd even asked me if I wanted to go with her, but I'd told her flat-out no. I didn't need to be surrounded by all the people in the stuffed quarantine for the "sleeping sickness," nor did I want to visit all the people who had been attacked or injured in some manner by demon activity.

Talk about torture, seeing all the people I'd failed.

"What were you doing at the hospital?" I asked, turning the conversation on her. "Is that where you've been all week?"

"Missed me, have you?" Raiya ducked under the coffee bar and started dishing out ground espresso. She shrugged and pulled the hat off her head, shaking her golden brown hair loose.

She turned around, plopping the hat down next to me. "I just went to visit Mrs. Smithe. She says hello."

I blinked in surprise, as if what she'd just said didn't make any sense. "Martha's awake?"

"Yeah. She's doing well, too. Better than expected, actually." Raiya's mouth quirked at the one side. "She even asked me if I was keeping you in line."

I didn't respond to that. I felt a surge of relief. *Martha's okay.*

My moment of celebration was short-lived as I recalled Martha's recovery was only one of the near hundred people needed yet.

"Don't get too excited," Raiya told me. "She won't be back for a few weeks yet. Or at least, that's what her doctor told her. I doubt he'll be able to keep her on bed rest." She glanced up at me with shadowed eyes. "She asked me to let you know she'd like it if you came to visit with me next time. Apparently, she thinks our arguments are 'endearing.'"

"I'll head over there by myself, thank you very much," I snapped. "In fact, I think I'll go over there now." I began to pack up my things and toss out my trash when she spoke again.

"You're not just going over there to see Gwen, are you?"

"What?" I'd actually forgotten about Gwen. I was too focused on Martha to worry about her. But now that I'd been reminded, I supposed it wouldn't hurt to catch up with Gwen while I was there. I furrowed my brow. "That's none of your business."

Raiya shrugged and picked up her cup on her way out to the kitchen.

I hurriedly paid my bill and was about to head out when I glanced back at the kitchen door. I suppose I should've been nicer to Raiya, I thought. Since she'd let me know about Martha and all.

THE STARLIGHT CHRONICLES

A moment passed, and with no sign of Raiya's return (not that I was going to apologize or anything anyway), I set out for the hospital.

As a rule, I hate hospitals. When the meteor struck Apollo City a few months ago, nothing about my short stay in the hospital had changed my mind about that.

In fact, I am pretty sure it made it worse. What especially made my trip to the hospital even worse than worse this time was seeing Gwen there.

I saw her almost instantly on my way to Martha's room. The hospital, pitifully small as it was, had needed to shove nearly all the sleeping, now-soulless people in one large connecting room, like some kind of deathlike delivery ward. My fists clenched together so hard I could feel my fingernails peeling into my skin as I passed by. There were just so many people there. It was hard for me to process.

Several moments passed as I saw Gwen just standing at Tim's bedside. He was still unconscious, hooked up to a bunch of devices. There were wires and tubes and all sorts of things surrounding his body. From where I was standing, I could tell Gwen had a worried look on her face.

THE STARLIGHT CHRONICLES

Painstakingly, I uncurled my fingers and shoved them through my hair. I didn't know what to do. I'd have to deal with it later.

Checking the charts, I found Martha's room a few floors up.

She wasn't, like Tim, suspected of having her soul stolen, and I had a feeling since she'd been teaching forever, at least one of her former students had recognized her and gotten her a private room.

I think I got there in time to save a nurse from being hospitalized.

"Get that IV away from me," Martha barked from her bed. "I feel fine, I am fine, and I don't need the IV."

"You have only been feeling this well since yesterday," the nurse reminded her, "And that is not enough time for the doctors to agree with you."

Martha rolled her eyes. "Where's my copy of *Time*? I need my magazines if I am going to be stuck here forever."

I chuckled as I came in the door. "You must be feeling better," I said. "Especially if you're ordering other people around."

"Dinger," Martha raised her eyebrows in surprise. "I was wondering if you'd come to visit. Your father was in here earlier saying he thought you'd come around."

"I ran into Raiya and she told me you were here."

203

"I see you're nice and chipper today, despite that."

"It's not every day I get to see you at the mercy of a helpless nurse," I replied, causing the nurse to huff indignantly.

Martha laughed. "Leave us to talk," she instructed the nurse. "And go get my magazine. I need to hear the latest on that new bill going down in Washington from a reliable source. *The View* is not a reliable source."

"How are you feeling, Martha?" I asked as the nurse brushed impolitely past me.

"It's Mrs. Smithe until you graduate, Dinger," Martha replied. "But I am fine. I have been feeling much better lately. They thought I was going to die when I first came in, did you know? And then everything turned all around in less than a night."

"So I guess that makes you a miracle patient," I said kindly.

Martha chuckled. "From the rational Hamilton Dinger, I get the word 'miracle' attached to my name? I *must* be dead. I thought you didn't believe in that stuff, Dinger."

"I … I've begun to change my mind about a few things."

Martha smiled. "Good. I'm glad to hear it."

I looked up at her, slightly surprised. "Why?"

She smiled. "You can't go through your life expecting to know everything or understand everything, Dinger. And I didn't want to see you become a cynical, bitter, and continually frustrated grown up."

I thought about it for a moment and acquiesced, "I guess no one would want that kind of person for president one day."

Martha softened. "Dinger, listen to me. Life will get you down. There is no denying it—look at me, for example. But the important thing is to keep going. Keep going on. Your challenges will make you a better person—not just in politics, but in real life."

"Is that why you don't move Raiya from behind me?" I asked, half-jokingly.

"Yes and no. Yes, because it is good to see someone question you—a lot of other students seem too afraid to— and no, because it's convenient to keep everyone else where they are."

"I suspected as much." I nodded, chuckling a bit.

Mrs. Smith's eyes gleamed. "It's so boring here. I was rather hoping you'd come with Raiya. You guys have some good arguments." She shrugged. "If nothing else, I would've thought you'd come with Gwen, since you're dating her now, aren't you?"

"Something like that."

"What?" Martha rolled her eyes. "Oh, never mind. I'll never understand you kids and your slang." A moment passed before she sighed. "I always hate being in hospitals. I thought for sure I would die in one. This is the same hospital where my son and husband died all those years ago."

"Died?" That was a bit surprising to hear.

"Yes. You remind me a lot of my son. His name was Michael. He and Scott, my husband, died almost sixteen years ago. He would be thirty-two this year, if he had lived."

Martha's eyes went glassy. "The people you love are the hardest to say good-bye to."

I said nothing. There are some times in life when you can't say anything, and there are times when you shouldn't say anything. Although I was thinking of asking if she'd been put on Prozac this week.

Finally, after a long moment, Martha spoke up, thankfully on a different subject. "Thank you for coming to see me today. It's been so nice to see so many of my students."

"I'm sorry you're in here," I told her. "The movies in class are a poor substitute … and . . ." I hesitated briefly before adding, "I'm sorry you are in here in the first place. You know what happened, right?"

Martha nodded. "I know."

"I feel like it's my fault," I told her quietly.

"It's not your fault, Dinger," Martha assured me. It was weak assurance at best. She didn't know the whole story, I knew, and I also knew there was no way I was going to tell her.

Mrs. Smithe continued. "Everything happens for a reason, Dinger. True, bad things happen, but sometimes it ends up helping us even though it hurt us. Your life is not about you; it's about something greater. Think about how you can help others if the attacks around town are bothering you."

It was there that she lost me. I didn't know what she meant at the time, and it would be years later before I would understand. Or even have an idea of what "something greater" could possibly be.

We talked for a while. She laughed the most when I told her about Cheryl's plan to sue Wingdinger and Starry Knight.

"What's so funny about it?" I asked, almost insulted, even though Martha didn't know *I* would be the one facing my mother's condemnation in court.

"Nothing. I doubt she'll get away with it. Even the great Cheryl Thomas-Dinger has a bad case every now and then, and this one sounds like a doozy."

"You don't think Starry Knight and Wingdinger would get called up on charges?" I asked.

"No. From what I've been able to tell, they've mostly been doing defensive work," Martha told me. "And it seems like they are the only ones really capable of handling the monsters. Oh, don't get me wrong, I saw the report about the swim meet," Martha said, figuring I would ask about it. "But they only led the creature away in chains. I wonder what they did with him, anyway? They didn't say much about it."

That was a good question, I thought. I hadn't heard anything about where they might've taken Mikey, either. But then, I was more worried about other things of late, I admitted to myself.

"I'll say this, Dinger. It seems the media needs a scapegoat, and good people—or fighters, I guess in this case—are more easily persuaded to dance to the media's tune on topics like these. To be honest, it sounds more like the mayor is bringing up charges against Starry Knight and Wingdinger to get his approval rating up more than anything. I mean, people want results, and enough where they got the last mayor to resign."

"What do you think is the worst thing that could happen to the superheroes?" I asked. My fingers gripped onto the armrest of my chair as I waited, breathlessly, for her answer.

"Oh, the media would have a field day," Martha snorted disdainfully. "But despite your mother's best argumentation, the truth is that 'supernatural disasters' aren't accounted for in the law. We are left with the results, but I'd bet anything the worst would be a plea bargain, and that would be just to get their case heard before the judge, and it would be a technical loss to them, but a meaningless win to the city."

"Really?" I asked. That didn't sound as bad as Cheryl's intentions. But then, I thought, this was my mother we were talking about. Anything less than ultimate humiliation was hard to excite her.

"Dinger, you're talking to a fifty-plus year old lady with her law degree in addition to her teaching certificate. I know what I'm talking about." Her eyes slipped over the brim of her glasses, giving her that condescending know-it-all look, and if it wouldn't have prompted too many questions, I would've thrown my arms around her and squeezed her.

Instead, I cleared my throat and said, "Well, that's good for them, I suppose."

We sat for a few moments in silence as I realized I'd been so afraid, so uncertain before, about being implicated as Wingdinger, that I'd barely noticed I'd given up more peace in giving up than I'd had in keeping up the fight. I traced the non-existent outline of the Prince's Emblem on my wrist. Was it possible … ?

My voice sounded hollow as I stood up. "I have to go. I have some work to do."

"All right. You just keep doing your best, Dinger," Martha said. "I have faith you'll commit to doing the right thing when it comes down to it."

My heart sank to the bottom of my foot as guilt once more weighed down on me. What if it was too late?

"I think I need a bit of a nap, anyway." Martha yawned. "Thanks for coming to see me again. It's always nice talking with you."

"You know I need you to be my campaign manager one day," I replied jokingly. "I'll see you next Monday then?"

"Oh, yeah. I can't take off any more days. Once you're a teacher, you feel guilty for missing school. It's no longer fun to play hooky."

THE STARLIGHT CHRONICLES

"See you later then." I waved and walked out the door, shutting it behind me.

I walked down towards the waiting room, still unsure of what to do, if anything, about anything. There was a window, and I noticed there were some stars twinkling back at me. It wasn't late out, but it was dark.

I remembered the day Elysian absconded me and flew me up high above the world to the point where I'd had trouble breathing. I thought about the kingdom of stars, how there was a prince up there I couldn't name, and I'd been called to defend the earth … and how I'd rejected it for a life of personal peace, pleasure, and affluence.

There's something out there much bigger than myself, I thought. And then I began to get angry. Angry with myself, this prince person I didn't even know, and Elysian and Starry Knight … . I guess "bigger" didn't mean "easier." But then, maybe it didn't have to mean "harder," either.

"I don't know what to do," I muttered, talking to myself. "I don't know why. I don't know how. I need help, and I need you to help me out with this. I don't want to take a leap of faith. But I don't want to stay on the ground anymore."

The stars just twinkled at me in response. I sighed. It had to be a choice, I suppose, not a sure thing, in order to count.

"Who are you talking to?"

I jumped, turning around. "Oh, hey Gwen." I hadn't been expecting to see her. "I'm just talking to myself, that's all."

Gwen smiled back. "Oh, I see. Here I thought you were making a wish on a star or something like that."

"I don't watch Disney movies anymore," I scoffed.

Gwen shrugged. "Your loss," she said with a small giggle. She then hesitated. "How did you know I was here?"

"I just came here to see Martha." I didn't really need to tell her the truth after she'd lied to me, I figured.

"Oh." She scooched back a bit. "Are you angry with me for being here?"

"No."

"You're lying. Do you just not trust me?"

"No. I mean—" I stopped talking. I hadn't meant to say that. How could I explain I was angry at something that wasn't supposed to exist?

"Are you jealous of Tim?"

I groaned. "Gwen, I'm not angry at you. I'm confused more than anything, if you want the truth. I know a couple of the other students here are your friends. I think it's okay you want to come see them." I mean, that was reasonable. "I know you like Tim, so I am just frustrated over why you even want to go out with me." Other than the fact she couldn't go out with Tim.

Gwen stilled. "I thought you liked me, and I wanted to give you a chance."

"Okay," I said. Not really sure how to handle that.

She frowned. "What do you want from me, Hamilton?"

"I want to be able to trust you, for one thing." That lashed out a bit too harshly, and I knew it immediately. "Sorry." I shrugged and scratched my head. What did I want from her? "I guess I just want you to decide what you want and commit to it. I mean, I don't want to waste my time any more than you want to waste yours."

As soon as I said it, Starry Knight conjured up in my mind. Was that why I was her greatest weakness? She hadn't been able to trust me? Well, she was smart not to, I guess, I thought as I recalled how I'd quit and gotten rid of the mark.

"Well, for the record," Gwen remarked quietly, bringing me back to the present, "I don't consider time with you a 'waste,' boyfriend or not. We've been friends for a while now."

"Sorry." I shook my head. "I've got some other things on my mind tonight, Gwen. I can't process this right now. So just let me know, okay? I frankly hate hospitals and I'm pretty sure that's why I can't really think about this right now." I lie so easily, I realized.

"Okay." Gwen nodded. She gave me a small smile. "Thanks. I'll see you later."

"Sure. I'm going to head home—"

A blaring alarm interrupted me. I could barely register the announcements over the PA system as nurses and aides of all kinds were suddenly running down the hall to the quarantine ward.

"Wonder what's going on?" Gwen asked, just a bit of fear creeping into her tone.

I didn't need a supernatural warning to know nothing good was happening. But I knew for sure when the sky darkened to a bloody color, the stars were swallowed up by shadows, and the air carried the malevolent laughter of an all-too familiar figure.

Eris had come out of hiding at last.

☼19☼
Courage

"Gwen, get out of here as fast as you can," I instructed. "Go home."

"What?" Gwen did a double take. "Surely—"

Her statement was cut short by the power cutting off. I could feel the hush of uncertainty in the other occupants. The emergency lights flickered on a moment later.

There was a resounding clash outside; I headed over to the window to see if I could see what was happening. I never made it.

"What the—" was all I had time to say before somehow managing to duck. The window—along with several others nearby—collapsed at the explosive power. Glass shards went flying throughout the room. Splintering rain came pouring in.

I gritted my teeth with determination as I stood up and (carefully) brushed the broken glass off of my clothes. "Stay here!" I shouted towards Gwen, as I made my way through the mess and out into the awaiting storm. I didn't wait for her objection.

I was just about to glance back and make sure she wasn't trying to follow me when I faltered. The sight before me stunned me into unmoving silence.

The sky had changed abruptly; it was black with thick, ghastly vapors, and lightning danced menacingly from cloud to cloud. The wind was whipping through the town in spurts, almost like it was being tossed around by a very confused blender. Tree limbs were seen rolling down the street, and debris was everywhere. I could make just out shadows of people scurrying into the nearest buildings.

Fear crept up my spine. *Oh crap. This is bad.*

A very depraved laughter rang through the now-empty streets of the city. I looked around to see where it was coming from, but I couldn't pinpoint the source. The wind had picked up again, and I had to put my hands out to protect my face from the leaves and small twigs suddenly attacking me.

"Plew!" I scrunched up my face as I tried to spit out some of the stuff flowing into my mouth. "Yuck!"

As I saw it, I had two choices. I could head back to the hospital, try to lay low, protect Gwen, and keep my nose out of all of this. I could maybe even convince myself it wasn't a supernatural event. I could lie to myself forever.

I could give up on Elysian and Starry Knight and destiny all together. I'm sure the Prince of Stars would understand. He seems pretty capable of handling all this with his power anyway, I reasoned.

But ...

The last time this happened, I met the Prince, I remembered. The last time I faltered, he'd been there for me. I was half-expecting him to show up now and tell me to grow up, get a hold of myself, and go do the right thing. The

THE STARLIGHT CHRONICLES

strangest part of all this was his silence, I thought. If I rejected him, was it possible he'd rejected me too?

I had to find out.

Keeping my face from the direction of the wind, I began to creep towards the end of the street.

The ominous laughter cackled again, and I faltered. Fear had seized me at that particular sound of doom.

I turned and looked back at the deserted streets and a sense of incredibility took over me. What on earth am I thinking? I wondered. I must be crazy. Anyone in the world would tell me this is crazy.

I glanced down at my wrist. There was no trace of any hope.

I was just thinking of turning back when I saw Elysian. The dragon was weaving throughout the tops of the building and along the windy ways, his flight pattern slow and twisted but still steady.

"Elysian!" I called out, waving my arms wildly. He never made the smallest indication he'd heard me. And if he had, he'd ignored me.

I watched him go and felt angry. All of sudden Elysian didn't care about dragging me into danger? When did this happen?

I was quickly jolted out of my thoughts when a lightning bolt flashed to the ground nearby. I jumped and was nearly blown over from the harsh winds. I gritted my teeth again as I (barely) managed to pick myself off the ground.

A large rumble shook the ground, and this time, I actually did fall to the ground. I scraped my hands as I caught myself, but I was too distracted to think about the pain. "No," I whimpered.

It wasn't only Eris who had come out to play.

The Sinisters—all of them, from Asteropy's blazing yellow to Maia's muffled blue—were here.

"I had forgotten the joy that races through my body at the sign of fleeing humans," Elektra spoke up as she used her power to blow up a nearby telephone pole.

"I have to disagree," Maia remarked as she blew her own power onto some humans on the top floor of a building. She laughed as they all fell asleep and collapsed. "They are enjoyable enough when they are helpless."

"Sisters, hush!" Asteropy scolded. "Do not ruin our fun with your bickering."

"Hey! We're not bickering!" Elektra huffed. "As if I would fight with Maia, of all the useless opponents."

"You shut up, Elektra!" Maia shouted back as she heaved a wave of power at her antagonistic sister.

"Watch it, Maia!" Celaena shouted back, her purple skin dulling as Maia's lackadaisical aim managed to half-fall on her. "Ooh, you make me so mad sometimes with your incompetence!"

That was all it took to get them started. The fight turned inward as the sisters all started defending or lashing out against the others.

If we're lucky, they'll destroy themselves, I thought with a bitter grin.

An arrow of light shot out and pierced through the cloudy miasma produced by the Sinisters' quarrel. A howl cried out.

Turning around, I saw her again; Starry Knight was perched behind a balcony. I could almost see her smile of satisfaction.

"You fools!" Asteropy grasped her arm, burning from the arrow's hit. "Stop fighting each other, and get them!" She pointed weakly at their mutual opponents.

Each Sinister turned, only to have Elysian's fire burn into them from behind.

As the battle around me raged, the buildings surrounding me started to crinkle; a few cracked along the top and bricks and siding, metal and glass all started to scatter down to the street.

I raced to get around the corner, but I only ran into a more deadly intersection. I held my arm protectively over my face as I hurried to dodge objects being blown in my direction.

Out of the corner of my eye, I saw a flash of light. For a moment I thought it was just another bolt of lightning. But a second later, I realized it was different.

Starry Knight and the Sinisters were headed towards the center of the city. I shook my bitterness off, and hurried after her on foot, not even really fully understanding why I was running towards the fight instead of away from it (surprise, surprise), or what I was supposed to do when I got there.

I managed miraculously to make it to the heart of the city battle without getting any permanent damage done to my body. My leg was bleeding, and I was pretty sure a rib was broken, but I'd managed to make it to the battle scene alive.

I watched from behind the corner of a building as Starry Knight fought against the Sinisters. All of them seemed to determine her to be the bigger threat, I noticed. Elysian, for all his size and firepower, was outshone by the pretty girl wrapped in light.

A disturbing sense of déjà vu hit me full force. *I had seen this before.*

Starry Knight stumbled, taking a hit in the chest. I cringed. As much as I didn't like her, I felt pity for her; I was pretty sure the blow had fractured a rib or two. Even Starry Knight seemed to feel the pain; her face crinkled as she tried to fly away.

Elysian came to her rescue a moment later, and while her expression cleared, I noticed her ferocity had dimmed ever so slightly.

I was so intent on watching the battle in the sky I didn't noticed someone had appeared behind me.

A moment later I regretted my intense fixation; five sharp claws raked across my back, causing me to scream in pure pain.

Tears flecked across my vision, but I knew who it was. "Get away from me, you monster!" I yelled, trying to scurry back.

Eris laughed. "You foolish boy! You should have run away when you had the chance!" She grabbed me by the neck and held me up to her face.

My vision cleared as I gasped for air. I saw her face and felt all the viciousness inside of me bubble up. A desire to live and to fight (and brutally!) boiled deep within me. "You—"

Her eyes glinted as she smirked. For the first time in my life, I understood why teachers hated it when I smirked. She tightened her grip. "You have such a bright soul," she murmured thoughtfully. "Normally you can't see it in humans, but you must be a rare, luminous one."

My brain was going fuzzy. I grasped weakly at her arm and glanced at my wrist. I suddenly felt like groaning. I was about to be killed and my supernatural mark was *still* not going to show up?!

"Your jealousy and fear sparkle so deliciously," Eris murmured, almost breathlessly.

Before I could curse (silently, of course) I was released. Abruptly.

Not by her choice, I noticed; her short shriek of surprise roared as I fell hard to the ground once more.

I sucked up a large breath of air before looking up to see Starry Knight grasping her bow in front of me.

"Leave him! Your battle is with me!" Starry Knight shouted.

I wouldn't deny I am a skeptical person by nature. But even as I looked up at Starry Knight, I was doubtful she could hold up much longer.

Starry Knight had really taken quite the beating. I almost smiled, seeing she was nowhere near as graceful as she usually was. Her hair was a mess, her feathers were burned and brittle in some areas, and her stance was tense, probably as a result from that blow to the chest area.

Eris unleashed a whirlwind of dark light before anyone could say anything else.

I felt myself moving; I also heard a small choke of pain, and saw a blinding explosion even as I shielded my eyes.

Amidst the twisting strands of pain wrapping around me, I felt a cloak of safety enfold me. I glanced up warily to see Starry Knight had encased me in her bruised wings and was holding me close to her.

I was at first repulsed by this; I didn't like being around Starry Knight, let alone this close to her. She even smelled funny, I thought, as the odd aroma of sweet bitterness tickled my nose.

My knee-jerk reaction was to tell her to go away, but as I looked up at her, to see her in pain, while protecting me, not even knowing I'd betrayed her before ... I suddenly felt like throwing up, disgusted with my own actions.

Before I could hold onto her, the flow of energy stopped. I twisted away and ducked, my head before my lunch made its first reappearance.

Starry Knight wobbled as she awkwardly stood up. "Get out of here," she told me. "You'll be all right. I won't let anything happen to you."

My eyes met hers briefly before she took off again. And then I doubled over and let out the rest of my stomach's half-digested contents. I whimpered softly as I felt my vomit burn into the cuts on my leg. Get out of here? I thought bitterly to myself. How? What a stupid order! I could barely move.

I weakly turned back to the battle. I watched as Starry Knight fought with the Sinisters. It was awful.

Elysian had been blown into the ground so hard, the gutter had collapsed in part of the street. A helicopter in the sky, probably belonging to a news station, was also suffering as another Sinister or two was attacking.

I watched as Starry Knight glanced towards me again. I felt like telling her I was okay where I was (because admitting I was in too much pain to move would have been too painful), but I didn't get the chance to even not to be able to try.

Starry Knight's second of distraction had cost her. She was flung into the ground, close to the middle of the street, as the Sinisters' power managed to strike a hit.

"No!" I strangled, half-gasped cry of despair barely cried out.

There was a moment of standstill. It was as though time had stopped, unable to process what was happening. I just watched, hoping fervently, that she would move.

Her fingers twitched a moment later, and I felt the breath rush out of me. I hadn't noticed I'd stopped breathing.

She straightened a moment later, and something on her cheek sparkled dimly. Teardrops.

The sensation of déjà vu struck me again, as real and as painful as the pain in my own body. I struggled to sit up.

Eris closed in on her, grabbing Starry Knight by her throat, much as she'd done to me earlier. "I see you've disposed of your little sidekick. Was he really your greatest weakness?" Eris laughed.

Starry Knight clenched at Eris' hands. "You leave him out of this."

"That silly boy? Her greatest weakness?" Alcyonë laughed from a short distance away. "You're still not strong enough to fight us, sister dear, even if you are a Guardian Star."

"Once I'm finished with you, I'll have to go see him," Eris murmured playfully. "Don't you agree, Alcyonë?" She giggled.

"Augh!" Starry Knight's hands gripped Eris' even more tightly. Power unleashed from her, trapping Eris. The power forcefully exploded, and I watched, amazed, as Eris imploded; suddenly she was gone, her laughter still hanging in the air. Starry Knight, wide-eyed and breathing heavily, turned to face Alcyonë. "I won't let you hurt him."

I felt all prickly; even as I was glad to know Starry Knight wasn't after harming me, her power was much more intimidating than mine.

"Kid, you need to get out of here." Elysian had gone unnoticed while he had slithered up behind me. But now he was tugging on my leg with his claws, pulling me as much as he could away from the battle.

"Elysian, what's going on?" I felt myself ask, even though I was pretty sure I knew.

Alcyonë appeared unimpressed with Eris' demise. "You'll still have to stop the rest of us," she glowered.

"So be it." Starry Knight began to glow. She whispered something; I wasn't quite sure, but I thought she said, "I have no choice."

That really scared me. I'd never felt this afraid before. "No!"

"Hamilton," Elysian grumbled.

My cry of angry fear and dismay, along with Elysian's reprimand, was drowned out by the eerie silence. All seven Sinisters fell silent as an immense light poured from Starry Knight, and bubbled around her and began to draw them in closer to her.

I could stop it, if I just had my power! I glared angrily at my wrist when I saw it was still not there.

Okay, Wingdinger isn't going to show. No choice, I thought. Hamilton would have to suffice. I prayed it would be enough.

I shoved Elysian off me and crawled as fast as I could (which was not very fast, all things considered) to the edge of the light now swirling around. I looked up but I couldn't see its end; later on, pictures would show it was almost like a star, circular and wide, giving off flares.

Looking deep into the middle of the light, trying not to worry about going blind, I could just barely make out the slim shadow of Starry Knight. I pushed at the resilient force, feeling it repel me. Bearing down, I marched forward into the torrent winds of her energy.

The pressure of Starry Knight's power pushed hard against my advance. It figures she wouldn't cooperate, even now.

After much moaning and silent cursing, I finally made it to Starry Knight. I felt the fear in me rise once more. She was very solid and focused. Her eyes had brightened over with violent energy, and her skin was speckled with power and light.

If she wasn't careful, she was going to use all her power to fight, taking the Sinisters and the earth and everything in it along with her.

Shoot. That's what she is going to do. Exactly what she is going to do!

I reached over and tugged on her hand. "Stop!" I tried to tell her. My mouth wouldn't seem to make any noise. I grabbed her wrist, trying to draw her attention. She didn't move. She seemed lost in the chain reaction of her own power.

With more difficulty than I would've thought possible, I stood up, and grabbed her shoulders. My wounds burned as though the light was full of acid. I tried to shake her, but I couldn't move her. Not even an inch!

"I tried." I flinched at the silent voice. What was that? Was it her? I felt something wet on my hands and looked up. Her tears. What are you crying for? I thought. This is all your fault! I'm the one who should be crying, not you!

"You stupid girl!" I mouthed, still without a voice. Despair took me. I was going to die without finishing high school! Along with all the other important things I wanted to do in life.

A new sense of desperation overwhelmed me as I stood there, in the middle of a star, in a world where time had no measure. And then suddenly there was more. A familiar scent of heavenly fields. The heartbeat of a song. I found every layer of myself chiseled away, the blackened cynicism of my heart breaking open and oozing the kind of fear which only stems from the deepest sort of longing. "Don't leave me."

And then I kissed her.

 ☼20☼
Sparks

I kissed her.

I'd meant only to stop her, or so I told myself.

But the instant her lips met mine, I found stopping was the last thing on my mind. If there was anything on my mind.

Sparks dashed through me as quickly as disbelief, as I finally kissed Starry Knight. Her body stilled under my embrace, leaving me to absorb the full shockwave. A surge of desire like lightning struck me; suddenly I could take on the world, or even a supernova. But I didn't particularly care. I could have cheerfully wished for death at that moment, so long as I was kissing her.

Her lips were as familiar to me as much as they were foreign, like reliving the magic of a first kiss over and over again. The taste of sweet starlight, of spices too rich for this world, swamped through my senses, and I was unable to stop kissing her, to stop the flooding tide of satisfaction and longing as I held onto her.

It was my secret from the world, and I gloried in it. My fingers threaded themselves through her tender tresses, memorizing their softness. My arms tightened around her, drawing her closer to me.

Just as I began to force myself back into my mind, properly chastising myself for enjoying this, she began fiercely kissing me back. Her arms wrapped around me, consigning all my intentions to nonexistence. The rush was like nothing else I'd ever known.

But I had known this feeling before.

The blinding light of the supernova melted, throwing me back into the realm of my heart and my memories. The clouds of light cleared up, and I could almost see her; I could almost remember her name …

Before me, I could see the broken bridge of my heart; I felt myself racing inside, as I leapt off of its ledge, amazingly fearful and free, and then all at once caught up in her arms, safe and secure.

My fear was gone; Starry Knight had conquered it with a single kiss.

A roar began to echo in my ears, and I, reluctantly, opened my eyes. The supernova was receding, and the brightness overshadowing us slowly retreated. The Sinisters were nowhere to be seen.

Wanting to savor the moment even as I knew it had to end, I slowly pulled back from Starry Knight. But she jerked back as if the slight movement had broken some sort of spell, hastily ending it.

I watched her eyelids, heavy with soft passion, as they fluttered open. Her violet eyes were clouded over with sedated ecstasy. I suspected my own face had a similar quality to it, but I wasn't concerned with myself at the time. I took a moment to study her face, to see if I could remember her from the other side of my memory; to see if I could summon her name like a long-forgotten incantation of the deepest magic.

But then her eyes cleared, and her expression became stricken; her arms promptly fell away from my body and began to push me away. "No," she breathed. "Not you."

I frowned and jumped back as if she'd struck me. What was wrong with me? I wondered. I looked down at myself.

That was when I noticed I was Wingdinger again! Joy swelled up within me, and I probably would've shouted excitedly if Starry Knight hadn't decided to collapse just then.

I managed to catch her, of course. In my arms.

And I felt that wonder again, that deep-seeded wonder, of just who she was. I didn't know that maybe, but I did know at that moment she was dangerous.

The huge, globular circle of destruction from her power was evidence enough; the cement streets had been carved out, and buildings on the event horizon of her power had sliced out in a perfect, though now-crumbling curve. Her erratic pulse remained throbbing with the remnants of her recent power surge as I held her.

I looked up at the sky, once more searching for signs of the Sinisters. I saw with no uncertain elation they seemed to have been warded off. It was not the last time I would see them. But for now I was satisfied.

Of course, it didn't last long. Seconds after I breathed a small sigh of relief, I felt an unexpected pain electrify through me. The network of nerves in my body channeled the shock, numbing my skin while stinging at the same time; I tried to call out but the severity of the agony coursing through my veins caused me to pass out in mid-scream.

The first sensation tingling through me I could recognize was the cold dampness associated with dungeons. The second feeling was similar to being tickled—almost as though I was stuck in an overloaded birdcage.

Opening my eyes, I looked up to find my perceptions had both been correct in the most awkward way.

I was curled up on the floor of a small jail-like cell. The ground was made of stone, surrounded by think bars, and there was a leak coming from somewhere. I would have probably figured out where it was coming from if my ears weren't been ringing. I looked down at myself to see I was lying on one of my black wings, which was surprisingly comfortable (the only alternative being the stone floor).

Looking to the left of me, I saw Starry Knight. Her wings and her position on the floor hid most of her face, but I was pretty sure she was still unconscious.

I sat up, my back aching from where I suspected I'd been tasered. I stretched out my arms. Something on my wrist caught my eye.

It was my mark; but it was not quite the same. Rather than being a black star crossed over with a red one, the black star had been replaced with a deep, blood red. Cool.

I glanced over at Starry Knight, and felt my breath catch in my throat until I could see her own shallow breathing. Should I wake her up? I wondered. I scooted over and touched her shoulder. "Hey," I said, shaking her gently. "Hey, wake up."

"She probably won't wake up for a while," a new voice told me.

I jumped slightly and whipped around. Before me was a familiar-looking man, but not the one I was hoping to see.

It was my new neighbor. Standing on the other side of the cell. Wearing a black suit. Checking his watch. All exactly like he wasn't some kind of secret agent in some kind of secret agency secretly letting his bosses know I was awake.

"Hello there," he said, a small smile growing between the lines of his beard.

"Who are you?" I asked, not really sure I would get an answer. Or that I wanted one.

"My name is Dante," he said.

All of a sudden, the pieces came crashing together before they came around and slapped me in the face. I'd thought before, when I'd been walking home with Adam, that our neighbor had seemed familiar. I barely heard him tell me he was the director of the unit division and he had been watching me for quite some time.

THE STARLIGHT CHRONICLES

All I could think of was that *this was Mikey's dad.* About ten years older than the last time I'd seen him, with his voice deeper than I remembered, but it was Mikey's dad. The darkened brown of his eyes and the shape of his face didn't lie.

Mikey's dad had gotten a new job and had been taken away from his family. He'd been required to sever all ties, emotionally and physically, for some kind of secret work. And now I knew what it was, and where I was.

I was in a secret black site probably hundreds of yards away from civilization. I'd seen all the movies. I knew how these things about the FBI worked. I looked around the cell, trying to see if I could find the surveillance cameras. (I wasn't able to; they must have been camouflaged really well.)

"Please, make yourselves at home." Dante indicated the small cell. "Welcome to SWORD."

"What sword?" I asked.

"It stands for Special Worldwide Operations and Research Division."

"Isn't that just a bit cliché?" It was out of my mouth before I could stop it.

I turned slowly to see Dante Salyards staring at me with piercing brown eyes, eerily glimmering in the poor lighting. "Well, we couldn't go with SHIELD, could we?" He smiled at me. "As much derision we've gotten in the last decades, there's something to be said for our name. Swords are thought to be weapons of the past, outdated, even romantic.

Our name, while cliché, as you say, gives the illusion of comfort, of hope, of some meaning in a grand narrative." His smiled dropped and his eyes narrowed. "It's a perfect front for us to use before we take you down."

I gulped as quietly as I could.

As I gazed at him, Dante nodded over to Starry Knight. "She's quite a fighter, your partner. She woke up when we tried to move you. We had to taser her twice as much to get her to stay down."

I hid my fists in my lap as they clenched. Dante continued. "I had a feeling she would have fought with us more, but she used up a lot of power trying to kill everyone."

"She was trying to protect the people," I said evenly. "She managed to ward off the Sinisters at least."

"The Sinisters? You mean that tie-dyed mess of women who were causing all that trouble?"

"Yeah. What do you call them?" I asked arrogantly, even though I *was* somewhat curious and embarrassed. I'd forgotten the FBI—sorry, *SWORD*—didn't know about the monsters the way I did.

Dante smirked. "You certainly have spunk, kid." He stood up straight from where he was leaning against the wall. "So you're just like all the teenagers out there, aren't you? Well, in that case, let me cut to the chase. You're in here until we say you can leave. We want answers."

"We?" I asked. (It was just part of my counter-ploy.)

"SWORD. The FBI. The CIA. The American people. The Global News Network. Anyone else I need to add to the list?" Dante's tone was light, but I knew it was spoken with quite a bit of power behind it.

I turned my attention back to Starry Knight. I was having a hard time not freaking out. If I was found out, I'd never make it into law school! Overwhelming fear bit at my mind, making it hard for all of this to process …

As if he'd been reading my mind (which I could only pray he wasn't), Dante spoke up. "I'll give you some time."

The moment he was gone, I shook Starry Knight harder. "Hey, come on, get up!"

A small moan escaped her and I felt guilty once again. Her skin was cold and limp.

I sighed; she wouldn't have been in this situation if it hadn't been for me. "I'm sorry," I muttered, disgruntled even if I was sincere. I picked her up and moved her onto my lap. I didn't like her much sometimes, but the least I could do to make up for my mistakes was to keep her from getting pneumonia.

Besides, if she did wake up and wanted to kill me, I'd be able to quickly get her into the headlock Poncey had shown me a couple of months ago.

A few minutes passed in silence. I started getting fidgety. What if she didn't wake up for hours? I'd be stuck here until she did. Reaching up, I touched my fingers to her neck, trying to get a pulse reading. Relieved it was normal, I relaxed; it was then my nose tickled with her scent.

Cinnamon and some other kind of warm spiciness clouded my mind's senses. I couldn't decide what it was, but it seemed to fit her spitfire personality.

I wasn't used to seeing Starry Knight up so close. Usually we would just fight the monsters, and then have our own little spat, and then walk away. I sniggered to myself as I recalled some of our fights. They were amusing, if nothing else, I thought. Although I vaguely remembered hating it at the time.

I felt her forehead. No, no, she was fine. I supposed. I didn't really pay attention during health last year (though I'd passed the class with flying colors—thank goodness for being on the swim team).

My fingers brushed against the red feather she always kept in her hair. I wondered where she'd gotten it; the feather didn't really fit with the rest of her outfit. Someone like Via Delorosa would have a heart attack if Starry Knight wasn't famous, I thought with a small smirk. Famous people could get away with anything.

I touched the feather again. This time I was surprised to feel warmth coming from it.

Huh, that's weird.

Noticing Starry Knight was still not waking up, I decided it would be all right if I borrowed it for a moment. I carefully pinched the feather between my fingers, about ready to pluck it from her for just a moment of careful scrutiny, when all of sudden it burst into flames.

"Augh!" I jumped, letting the feather go and letting Starry Knight fly out of my grasp.

A moment later, after I'd calmed down (and had made sure I had no burn marks on my skin), I breathed deeply. "Whew. That was a close one."

"Maybe for you," the grumbled voice muttered from the floor.

I grimaced. "So, you're up, are you?" I asked tentatively. I noticed out of the corner of my eye the feather had turned back to normal.

"Now I am," Starry Knight remarked as she sat up, rubbing her now-sore face and trying to smooth down her hair. She looked over at me and then around at our prison. "What did I miss?"

I snorted. "We were captured by some knock-off version of the FBI. It's this police—kind of service—"

"I know what the FBI is," Starry Knight interrupted smoothly enough.

"I didn't know that," I muttered under my breath before filling her in on the details of SWORD and all I could gather. I didn't tell her my best friend's dad was the one in charge of holding us captive, but I figured I could let that slide.

"And so anyway, we're stuck in this prison. And we're not getting out until they say we can."

"What would they want with you, anyway? I thought you'd quit."

The words were softly spoken, but I still felt the sharp snap behind them. I folded my arms across my chest. "I didn't quit," I asserted.

Starry Knight cocked her eyebrow.

I shrugged. "I just … took a vacation for a while, that's all."

Her response was one of hard silence before she said, "You should have stayed away. You wouldn't be here if you had just given up."

"Why did you want me to quit so bad?"

The words hung in the air for a long moment before Starry Knight responded. "It is not easy, you know."

"The whole saving the world thing? Yeah, I know it's not easy."

She narrowed her eyes. "But you just don't get it."

I frowned. "What exactly am I supposed to get?"

Starry Knight sighed and stood up. She waved around her arm, and a second later, her bow appeared.

That was kinda cool, I admitted reluctantly. So she can pull it out of thin air. I'd been half-wondering where it had gone.

She looked back at me. "This is the Bow of Righteousness. I got it when I accepted my destiny as a Starlight Warrior. It has the power to hit any mark I choose, slice down any foe, and increase my own power a hundredfold."

I looked at the bow. It was a beautifully carved weapon, I had to admit. Not that I would want it for myself or anything.

"It was freely given to me to wield, but it is costly."

"What do you mean by that?" I asked. She'd told me something like that before.

"I mean, that it's not always a convenient thing," Starry Knight said. "I know it's the right thing to do. But it can be very inconvenient to me when they attack. And there are other complications in the matter as well." She looked down at me and I had a feeling she was talking about me.

I was shocked at this, not because it was amazing to me Starry Knight didn't always like fighting the bad guys, but because it made her sound as normal as I was. (Well, about as normal as an average human anyway.)

"Sacrifice is necessary. But it does not come naturally. It is hard to make the right choice to act on what you believe, to suffer for the sake of righteousness. To have faith your pain is not meaningless or ignored." There was a layered look in her eyes as she plucked her bowstring, as though a hundred different moments from her life were being relived.

She glanced over at me and the hardened look returned. "And then you come along, like it's a game or something to you. People's souls are on the line, and you think it's all about you and your image, or competing against me. And then you think you can quit just like that, and nothing bad could possibly happen!"

Ouch. That stung.

But it didn't really slow me down any (of course). "Hey, that's not fair!" I snapped back. "I don't have the luxury you did. I didn't get a chance to choose this. It was thrown on me and I had to just go with it."

"Everyone has a choice," Starry Knight huffed. "You just can't live with some decisions."

"Don't you think I know that?" I asked, incredulously.

"A mistake once made cannot be taken back. There is no free atonement for this."

I figured I'd had a rough enough night that it was okay to not clearly remember what the word "atonement" meant. I was just about to tell her off when I recalled how I'd felt, holding her. Kissing her.

I sighed. "All right. I'm sorry."

From her reaction, I might as well have hit her across the face. She swiveled around and gaped at me with a half-annoyed, half-shocked look on her face. I had to restrain myself from laughing.

Finally, she closed her mouth and straightened up. "You shouldn't apologize to me." And I wondered at that, because all of a sudden, she seemed content. Like that had been what she'd wanted all along. (Women!)

I sighed and stood up, wincing a bit as my back tingled with the memory of being electrocuted like I was a stray cow or something. "Look, Starry Knight," I began, and instantly her eyes filled with wariness. I scratched my head, almost nervously. It had been a long time since I'd tried to explain myself (let alone felt I *should*). To anyone.

What else should I say? I looked back up at her eyes, and while they were still resistant, I could also sense the hesitation in her. And then there was a push of confidence from my heart; suddenly, I needed to say what I'd been thinking, deep in my heart, about this matter.

"I didn't choose this; it was something that chose me. And now I have decided to choose it, too. I didn't like it or want it or believe it at first. But now I do. I thought it was a punishment, but I see now that it was actually a gift." I really did want another chance.

For a long moment, Starry Knight did not say anything, but just looked at me. Finally, she took a deep breath. "You're hurt, aren't you?"

Okay, just completely change the subject now, I thought, irritated. But I was tired of trying to explain myself to her anyway, so I just shrugged. "I just got tasered, that's all. It's nothing like it was last time with all the blood. Hey, what're you doing?"

She'd come up to me while I'd been talking and had placed her hands on my shoulders. I fidgeted a bit, before I asked again, "What are you doing?"

A soft glow began to leak from her hands and flow into my body. A second later, it was gone. Then a moment passed, and Starry Knight looked up at me and shrugged. "I have healing powers," she explained. "All Stars have a special power, even fallen Stars."

Ah, just what I wanted. Another reason to hate you. But I smiled at her regardless, because for some reason I found it funny. No wonder she'd been able to take on a lot. She'd had supernatural help. In an ironic sort of way, anyway, I thought.

She gave me a small smile back; I felt a rush of what felt like surprise.

Something inside me broke. I reached out almost involuntarily and grabbed her by the shoulders. "Who are you?"

"Huh?" Starry Knight was just a bit caught off guard and did not move, as though she was unable to decide what to do.

I felt my fingers tighten against the bare skin of her arm. I had wanted to know this from the first day I'd met her. "Who are you? Who are you really? I feel like I know you, but I just can't … Tell me who you are!"

Boy, hope that didn't sound desperate, my mind briefly thought. But I did want to know. No, I *needed* to know.

I had to know who she was, and what that made me. I stared into her violet eyes hard, as though I was searching for an answer hidden deep down, far beneath the surface of those bewitching eyes. Those eyes so lovely, yet so terrifying to me.

"Yes, that would be the million dollar question," a voice called out from the other side of the cell. Footsteps against the stone floor echoed quietly as the figure came closer. "In fact, there are many people who would like to know just that."

Starry Knight shoved free of my grasp as she turned her full attention on the newcomer.

Frustration ate at me. I really never was going to get any answers out of her, was I? "What do you want now?"

Dante grinned devilishly. "Hey, can't we be friends about this?"

"Sorry. Friends don't let friends be thrown in prison," I muttered back.

"We're not your enemies," Starry Knight spoke up.

"Prove it," Dante challenged. "Are you interested in making a deal?"

"I don't want to make a deal with you. You already haven't kept some promises you've made," I shot back, still angry I'd been interrupted earlier. "Get us out of here."

"Now, now, don't be so uptight," Dante said through gritted teeth. "You can hardly blame us. After all, you've both caused millions of dollars' worth of construction damage."

"So? That's supposed to be good in this economy. Creates jobs, right?" I remarked.

"I was right about you. You are a troublemaker."

"Enough," Starry Knight said. "You are still under the jurisdiction of the United States. You have yet to read us our rights."

"SWORD is not under any jurisdiction. We are not obligated specifically to America, nor any particular government or system. We are a private, international company contracted by countries and businesses of different influences who want to ensure their safety on a more … shall we say, ambiguous level?"

"So you're like a Global Mafia?" I asked. Again, it was more of a knee-jerk reaction.

"I guess you could call it that." Dante lost his smile. "Good guys and bad guys are for political storylines, ad campaigns, fairy tales, and Super Bowl commercials. This is just business, and we are in the business of power. Controlling it, squashing it, redistributing it. Doing whatever needs to be done without the hassle of moral injunctions, patriotic pride, or financial fingerprints."

"If you can't tell the difference between yourself and the bad guys, then you're most likely already one of them." Starry Knight frowned.

"I wouldn't worry about it. Several people want answers, and they are paying me good money to get them out of you."

"No one is going to believe us when we say we are doing this for their protection," I remarked. "Let alone you."

Dante laughed. "True enough. Faith is a silly foundation for any game, and this is far more than a game. Facts are the only thing that will take you where you want to go, and controlling the facts means you control the players."

"What ever happened to doing the right thing?" Starry Knight muttered.

"The right thing is not always the best thing." Dante's eyes glimmered darkly. "You and those monsters have been running—or flying—around this city for too long. You've cost many people their lives or their livelihoods. It's time to give us some answers. You have two choices. You can refuse, and you will be incarcerated, just like your other friend, or you can answer our questions—*all* of our questions—to your full knowledge."

"What other friend?" I asked, suspiciously.

"That monster from that high school," Dante informed him. "He's, or I guess, *it's*, useless."

I felt as though something invisible had struck me. Surely he doesn't mean Mikey.

"How dare you!" Starry Knight lashed out. Her arms reached through the bars and tried to grasp at Dante's trite-looking black jacket. "He was a human being!"

"He was an unearthly creature from Hell," Dante reminded her, "who had managed to put quite a few people in the hospital."

"He was confused! He didn't know what he was doing!" Starry Knight yelled back, anger and sorrow interlaced in the tone of her voice. "You have some nerve calling us monsters!

Who do you think you are, to decide whether or not someone should live?"

"Justice does not look at emotions, girl," Dante spat back at her. "Justice is blind to all but the facts."

"Justice is not blind to the truth, only to the illusions of deceit!" Starry Knight snapped. She was so upset, I wondered why she just didn't pull out her bow and shoot him. I would've.

Dante pulled back from her frantic attacks and shook his head. "Cute, but it does not alter the terms of our commitment to our contractors."

"So you're going to kill your own son?" I said the words out loud and didn't realize it until Starry Knight and Dante both sent me the same confused look.

"I don't have a son," Dante finally spoke up a moment later.

Hesitation overcame me. Dare I play the ace up my sleeve? "You did once," I said. "You're Dante Salyards. You have a son. His name is Mikey, and he was the one who became that monster at Central's swim meet."

Surely I'd rattled him with that. "You don't know what you're saying," Dante insisted.

"Sir."

All three of us were momentarily distracted as a new agent walked into the door.

I hope they're not going to play "good agent, bad agent" with us, I thought almost humorously. I watched as the new agent pulled Dante aside, whispered something in his ear, and then walked away again. Dante sighed before turning back to face us. "You got lucky," he told us. "I have an emergency to deal with. More of your friends."

He headed out of the door, calm as ever. "Don't worry. I'll be back later."

I watched as he left and decided I really didn't like Mikey's dad. Not that he'd been any prize before, but now, for sure, I hated the guy. I turned back to see Starry Knight was clenching her fists in anger. Her eyes snapped open, firm with resolve. "We have to go and save him," she said.

"We?"

"Yes, 'we!'"

"You mean that you want me to fight with you?" I was trying to sound innocent even though I knew I was baiting her on purpose; I wanted her to admit she wanted me to join her.

"If you don't come, you will be fighting with me," she huffed as she held up her bow.

"Come on, that's not what I meant."

Starry Knight sighed. "Now is not the time for this."

"Yes it is!" I insisted. "If we are going to fight together, it's going to be a mutual decision." I held out my hand. "Allies?"

She held her ground, and then looked away.

I could hardly believe she was being this reluctant about it. Wasn't she the one a moment ago who demanded I come along with her to go and see if we could save Mikey? Did she really still doubt me? I held out my hand further and said, "I promise I won't give up again. You have my word. I know this is the right thing to do."

Starry Knight looked back. "Your word will bind you," she warned. "You will not escape such a promise without punishment. And you will only be free if I release you from your promise."

"Well, we both know that you won't have a problem with that," I reminded her.

A fleeting smile appeared on her face. "Yes, I guess that's true," Starry Knight agreed. She reached out and took my hand. "All right. I accept."

I smiled happily. Finally, she had accepted me. *It's about time!*

"But that doesn't mean I have to like you." She dropped my hand and began to contemplate the bars again.

"Oh, believe me, I don't like you either." I agreed. "But I do want to get out of here."

Taking the hint, Starry Knight slashed her bow through the bars, causing a bright light to break free from her weapon and a small explosion to ensue.

I was just about to tell her she might have been a tad excessive when I heard her murmur, "I guess my full power's back."

"What do you mean by that?" I asked.

Her cheeks flushed over red. "Nothing. Let's just go."

I didn't push the issue as we began to jog down the long, seemingly endless hallway. I figured I'd made her annoyed enough because I'd held us up from going to save Mikey.

As I hurried beside Starry Knight, I thought about asking her about what the plan was when we found Mikey. But as I looked over at her, I was overcome with another question. Did she remember our kiss? Unconsciously, I trailed my fingers over my mouth, thinking once more of how she'd tasted.

Get a grip, Dinger, I chastised myself. It's Starry Knight, not Gwen.

Oh, great. Thinking about Gwen was absolutely no help. What was I going to say to her? Was I supposed to say anything to her? How could I even begin to bring this up? *"Sorry, Gwen, I had to kiss another girl in order to prevent the city from being blown to bits by a supernova-type explosion?"* As excuses went, I don't think she would buy it, let alone excuse it.

Fortunately, my unfortunate squabble with myself was postponed at Starry Knight's interruption.

"Look," Starry Knight interrupted. "What is that?"

Following her direction, I looked over to see nothing out of the ordinary. Until I saw a tiny, lizard-like shadow creeping alongside the wall. "Elysian."

The small beady eyes of my changeling dragon squinted and focused on me. Even in his smaller animal phase, I could tell he was frowning. "Kid," Elysian said more out of annoyance than acknowledgement. "I thought you'd quit."

"I've been getting that a lot today." I rolled my eyes.

"So you've decided to come back all of sudden?" Elysian's narrowed eyes remained skeptical as he began to transform to his regular, smaller dragon form.

"Don't start taking bets, Elysian," Starry Knight remarked, her tone sullen. "He promised me he would not quit this time." She glanced back at me. "Come on. We have to get going."

I nodded. "Let's go."

"Where are we headed?" Elysian asked.

As we all started down the next hall, I lagged behind a bit, letting Starry Knight take the lead the way while I kept pace with Elysian. "We're looking for Mikey."

Elysian, staring fixedly straight ahead, nodded. "Yes. The one who likes the math teacher."

"No, that's Simon." I sighed. "Geez, you are just as bad as my parents, getting my friends all mixed up."

"You don't know any of my family or friends, either," Elysian grumbled.

"I wasn't aware you had either," I snapped back. "Ugh, I don't have time to argue with you right now. Do you think you could smell him out or something?"

"I'm a dragon, not a dog!"

"Really? I didn't notice," I bit back. "Isn't there anything that you can do?"

"Nope. We're just going to have to search around," Elysian told me. At his cue, a discordant *crash!* echoed around us. Starry Knight had started the search, breaking and entering into one of the hallway doors.

I was just about to wonder what level her spy skills were at when an alarm started blasting off. Great, they knew we were free and just started worrying about it, I thought.

"Nothing in here," Starry Knight confirmed. "We need to find him, and then we need to find a way out. Quickly."

"I did hear something about a specimen a few floors up," Elysian spoke up. "Could that be Mikey?"

"I don't know," I admitted. "But I do know Dante was headed up to meet the Sinisters. We have to be underground somewhere close by the hospital. I don't think we are far from Apollo City, if we even left it."

"Yes, where are we, Elysian?" Starry Knight asked.

"I followed you here. You're in some kind of warehouse by the marina," Elysian confirmed. "We are about four floors below the surface."

"Good to know this black site is as cliché as I'd expected," I muttered. (Again, I *had* seen all the movies).

"Okay." I looked over to see Starry Knight beginning to pace around, her fingers raking themselves through her hair. She looked up at me, before her eyes darted over to Elysian. "You go and find that boy," she said. "I'll go deal with the Sinisters."

"No." I reached out and grabbed her by the arm. "You can't. What if—"

There were so many things I could have said. What if you die? What if I'm not there with you and you need me? What if you *don't* really need me?

Thank goodness she interrupted me and saved me from embarrassing myself.

"We don't have time," Starry Knight insisted.

"The city can't survive another one of your attempts to 'save' it by destroying it," I argued back. But she was right about time; it was a factor. I turned to Elysian. "Take him with you."

"Me?" Elysian asked. "But what if you need my help?"

"Please, don't get me started," I huffed. "Just go with her. I'm sure I can find Mikey and get him out of here."

Starry Knight pursed her lips as she considered it. After a long, silent moment, she nodded. "All right. I'll take him with me." She looked down at my hand, still clutching her arm. "You can let me go now."

"Huh? Oh, yeah, whatever," I murmured back. "See you in a bit." I took off and headed down the hallway, looking for any doors, secret or otherwise, while Starry Knight and Elysian began to coordinate plans.

"Kid, the stairs are down this hall and around the corner to the right," Elysian called after me. "If you need a quick exit, I recommend making one."

"Allow me to demonstrate," Starry Knight said, drawing out another arrow. "We can get to the Sinisters much more quickly that way ourselves."

I turned around the next corner just in time to hear the successive splintering of old wood and rotten insulation as her arrow shot through the floor like a small, flying bomb.

It was the worst time to feel the pang of jealousy at her skills. So I kept running, keeping a look out for anyone, Mikey especially, and desperately hoping I would know what do if I actually did find Mikey. I had no doubt I would end up beating up any SWORD agents who came my way, but I didn't know what I could possibly do for my best friend.

☼<u>21</u>☼
Regrets

It took a few floors, but I soon managed to find where Mikey was being held.

The first thing I noticed was Mikey was still half-way through transforming. It was gross. There were baggy, flabby flag-like skin appendages coming out of his back, like he had some kind of radioactive back fat in addition to chopped tentacle-arms. His head looked better, only slightly inflated … but still. It was, in true Sinister-evil tradition, disturbing.

I started to grab at the fatty arms(?), thinking I would need to tell Mikey to go on a diet when he woke up. I cursed myself momentarily for sending Elysian out with Starry Knight; he would have made this job much easier, for once.

Mikey's body was very cold. And it was sort of hard to get a good hold onto, almost like silly putty that lost its silliness. Almost like he was …

"Come on. He's not dead. He can't be," I told myself. "Can't you remember the movies? The FBI doesn't tell the truth to its prisoners, and SWORD probably doesn't either. I need to get him out of here so we can get him back to normal."

A few heaves, some inappropriate comments which were just too appropriate at the time, and a second reminder to tell Mikey to go on a diet later, I was ready to give up. The flabby, gushy, goopy body was just too slimy, too inconsistent, and too huge to move.

I flung him on the floor, in half-resentment, half-frustration. I didn't know what to do. What was I going to do? There wasn't much I could do, according to the laws of physics. I need a miracle, I thought.

A miracle.

I looked down at my warrior suit and reached up, tracing the feathers of my wingdings as they curved their way around my ears. Was it possible to get another miracle for today?

"Okay, Prince, man, I need you to change Mikey back. Can you help me out here?" I asked, feeling like an idiot. I don't care if Elysian said he existed outside of time and space, if he wasn't in time or space and I was essentially talking to no one, I felt like an idiot.

I especially felt the humiliation of an idiot when I didn't hear anything back.

Ugh. Really?

I scrapped through every corner of my mind, trying to think of what I knew that could help me. Think, I commanded myself. Think! I knew I couldn't shoot Mikey full of energy beams like any other demon monster; that would probably destroy him, which was bad.

Frustrated, I dropped my head into my hands and fell into a sitting position on the floor. This wasn't working. Anything in the world would have been better than going back to Starry Knight and Elysian and telling them I couldn't do my job. I could hear Elysian's comeback already: *"At least it's not a matter of you refusing to do it this time … "* That smug turd.

My foot toed some of his extra tentacle appendages as I continued to sit there. I was trying not to worry about time.

"Hey, Mikey! I know you're in there! Stop this, and return to your normal self!" I called.

Nothing happened. Maybe I needed to …

Ugh, I needed coffee. I was definitely going to Rachel's after this, I thought. I hoped it wasn't too late.

Oh, great. And then there was Cheryl and Mark to worry about. There was no telling how much later I would be, or even how much time had passed since I'd been transported here.

"Okay, that's enough. Focus." I shook my head. *Think!*

An idea popped into my mind and I stood up. I looked down at the mark on my wrist. The one time, I'd grabbed onto it and used some kind of power inside of me to get inside my heart.

Power. That was it! Starry Knight had told me herself: *"All Stars have a special power, even fallen Stars."* I had a special kind of power, since I was a fallen Star. Recalling the other times I'd felt that particular inkling of power—feeling Gwen's emotions as I held her hand, Adam's feeling of contentment as I'd carried him, even my own tumultuous turmoil—a sense of certainty overtook me. I was able to discern other people's feelings.

255

With a renewed sense of hope, I picked up one of Mikey's many mangled extremities. I closed my eyes and tried, feeling stupid and unsure, to see if I could sense Mikey's emotions.

A whisper of otherness whisked up beside my power. It had to be Mikey! I silently cheered to myself; no matter how much Mikey had changed, he was still my friend, and I was glad he was alive.

Closing in on the flouting foreignness, I pushed through with my power. And then, all of a sudden, I was transported into another world.

Even though I was in a different world of some kind, I could still see into the one I'd left behind. Later I would liken the experience to being inside a negative of a photograph. I could still hear the alarms running through the SWORD black site, and I could feel the chill of the physical world. But for the first time, I noticed the warmth of my spirit, the engulfing waves of contentment. Straining my ears to block out the physical world, I even thought I could hear some kind of symphonic welcome song.

I could see a flaring aura around Mikey's body, which was beckoning my curiosity.

I turned my attention back to the pit of blazing aura before me, where Mikey's mind must be firing. Entering into the green-tinted flames, I gasped.

I looked around at the mess before me. It was a cityscape, covered in greenish goo-looking glop; Apollo City in apocalypse form. There were strands of the ooze all around me, all backdropped by the grayest skies I'd ever seen.

So this was Mikey's heart. I grimaced; I'd never wanted to see inside of anyone's heart, unless I was getting to perform open-heart surgery with Mark. And there were reasons I wanted to be a lawyer more than a doctor. "Mikey?" I called into the unreal city.

I took a few cautious steps and grimaced; trash was everywhere, and I saw no end to the ugliness. And a bunch of slimy stuff, too. *Great,* I thought, *more ooze for me to fall into.* Some things never change.

Walking gingerly through the shadow streets, awed and disgusted by the destruction and garbage everywhere, I continued to look for Mikey. "Mikey, where are you?"

I skidded to a halt when I at last saw my friend.

There he was, bound up in the heart of a spider's web, covered in green threads of ooze. Mikey was asleep—or at least his eyes were closed. His body was also very still, almost like he was dead, or getting there. "Mikey!"

I was about to ask him if he really wanted to miss out on next year's football season when a sparkle caught my eye.

"Huh?" All around me was a glitter-like shimmer, spreading all around. "What is this stuff?"

A shifting sound caused me to jump. *It's poison.*

I looked up to see the same blank expression on Mikey's face. "Was that you?" I asked.

There was no movement, but the words were not to be mistaken. *Yes, it's me.*

"Can you turn back into a normal person?" I need to work on my tact, I decided. Oh well. It would have to wait for now. I had to hurry.

I want to be normal again. But I am afraid.

"Why?"

Because I ruined my life. I made bad choices. I hurt people.

"What?" I was surprised to feel sympathetic towards Mikey. It was true he had committed crimes, and bad ones; I recalled quite clearly how I had burned with rage towards Mikey after getting Martha in dire straits.

But one look at the sad, teary-eyed figure, wrapped up in his own despair, and I couldn't bring myself *not* to care. One glance at the mark on my wrist, and I knew I could appreciate rightfully the value of a second chance.

"Look, it's true that you've done some bad things. But it doesn't have to end with that. You wouldn't want it to. There's still a chance for you to do some good. You can't give up just because it's hard." Or because it's not fun, or because you have a loud-mouthed dragon hounding you day and night, I added to myself.

I yanked at the thread, trying to pull him from the deadly-looking trap. "I'll help you!"

"Leave me alone!" Mikey's eyes now snapped open, glowing green. "This is my home now."

"No!"

"I want to be alone!" Mikey yelled, this time with enough force to send me slipping backwards. Strands of the green thread began to creep toward me, intertwining around my feet and arms.

"Stop this!" I called out, this time a hint of desperation in my voice. "I know you're not like this! You don't want to be alone or hurt anyone!"

The words had no effect.

Maybe there was something I could do as myself. It made sense, after all. Mikey didn't know me as 'Wingdinger,' but he knew me as his best friend. "Mikey, it's me. It's Hamilton. Hamilton Dinger. I'm your best friend. You're like my brother, man."

I untangled some of the spidery thread as more whip-like web strands assaulted me. "I know you've been going through a rough spot, and I haven't made it any easier. But I'm here for you! I am. And I'm sorry, Mikey … *I'm sorry!*"

Mikey stilled. The eyes burned with a fierce green before began to darken to their usual brown.

THE STARLIGHT CHRONICLES

I sighed with relief. *It's working.* I was getting through. "Please, Mike, trust me. Fight this. You can trust me. I'll help you. Just like I did when your dad left."

Suddenly, Mikey struggled as he began to wake up to the world.

A flash of light flickered, bubbling up all around, like a top-rated bathroom cleaner in a gas station restroom. I felt a wave of relief and satisfaction wash over me as the unreal city around slowly started to change and then fade away.

I was returning. No, *we* were returning.

THE STARLIGHT CHRONICLES

☼<u>22</u>☼
Reclamation

The threads of the unreal city pulled, merging with a new reality as I held onto my friend. I fully expected to see the bland, tastelessly decorated holding cell I'd left behind in the physical world.

So much for expectations.

My eyes opened to see a world of light and sunshine, on a road of translucent substance, looking down at more than just the earth, but all the worlds and stars of the universe. Mikey's body, hung over my shoulders, twitched wildly before once more going completely limp. Clouds wafted around me as a bright, shining light bubbled up in midair; the music I'd heard before, trapped between the physical and spiritual worlds, melded from a musical song into a powerful, if soft, fanfare.

I knew at once why I was there, if not where I was.

An invisible presence drifted out from the distance and encircled me. Recognition poured through me like Niagara Falls, fast and strong and shattering everything. My knees suddenly became unsteady as fear broke through my calm.

"Do not be afraid." The voice was a gentle thunder, powerful as it was reassuring.

"I know who you are," I murmured.

"Who am I?" Light manifested itself in the form of a man, and began to walk through the mesh of clouds to where I stood.

"Yes," I remarked. "You're the one who gave me the power to become Wingdinger when I first began to fight."

The man of light stopped and hovered; I could see the outline of his face, and glimpse into the fires of his eyes through a veil of remaining clouds. "You did not become your supernatural self from my power. I gave you the power, and it has been yours, and will remain yours, as long as your soul is alive."

He reached out and gently took me by the wrist; I didn't look up at him, as much as I might have wanted to. "When you did not really want to become Wingdinger, your heart could not find the power to make a choice. The soul can be divided as easily as the mind, and the consequences are no less shattering."

The man wrapped his arm around my shoulders, reminding me of my father briefly. Mark would do this sometimes. That was suddenly probably why I flinched and drew back. Or it was paranoia, shame, or any other of the unidentified feelings which had been swiveling around in my mind of late.

"The time has come for you to decide for yourself who you will be."

I peeked up at him, absolutely sure I heard him but unsure of whether I should answer him.

There was a small smile on his face. I could even see the little smile lines, maybe even a hint of dimple. The white hair of his beard, contrasting with the bronze of his skin, quirked up a bit more as I relaxed and met his gaze. The question had formed inside of me long before I asked it. "Who do you say I am?"

"You are my bright Star of Mercy; a forgiven soul, a treasured light, fallen to Earth, born into human flesh, your heart still burning with true Starfire."

It would have taken me centuries to figure out all of that, but I focused on the most important part. "Forgiven?"

"Yes." There was no tint of uncertainty, no hesitation, no distrust.

Tears speckled my gaze and a swollen mass blocked my throat as a fragrance of peace settled around me, welcoming me home.

"Command me."

My body shuddered with a sudden, alarming amount of fear. My fingers were trembling. "I am not worthy," I stated slowly. "And I can't ask anything of you, sir. I don't even know your name."

A wave of approval and acceptance washed over me as he said, "You may call me Adonaias."

I felt a strangely warm terror in my heart at the sound of the name. "Adonaias," I whispered to myself. It was a name which pulled power inside of me, even as it left me weak.

"Command me, and I will do what you ask."

I felt my inner greed take over at the offer immediately. Love, riches, youth, insight, foresight—all of my options came running out from different corners of my mind, each one hollering out for my selection.

But what did I really want? That was the tricky part: What do I want most? "There are many things I want," I admitted. "I would love to be rich and have a big mansion one day, and be successful at school and my jobs. But … but these are things I want, not things that I necessarily need."

The patient smile remained steady. "What is it that you need, then?"

My memory flashed back to the time I'd seen Adonaias before. My situation hadn't changed much since then. But there were some things that had changed. I was going to be a bit wiser at trusting others—and myself. I knew, looking up at Adonaias, that he could be trusted. He wasn't trying to push something on me, or take advantage of my suffering, he was offering me anything—everything, in fact.

But what hadn't changed was my condition. "I need your help," I admitted at last. "You've helped me before, maybe even in ways that I don't even know about."

Adonaias nodded.

I wanted to believe that; I chose to believe that. "Then give me faith to follow where you lead me, and give me the courage and strength to do whatever it is I need to do."

"What you ask, I will do." He paused. "I work out all things for the good. But you must continue to do what you believe is good, too."

"I will. I promise." As I said it, my head ducked down. My words sounded so weak, coming from someone like me, and all the more because I was saying it to someone like him.

"Why do you ask for this?"

I looked up. "You don't know?"

"Do you know?" Adonaias was smiling, and at that moment, I thought of how much he reminded me of Martha sometimes, or even Raiya. It was like he was making sure I knew what I was doing, even if he already did. I guess he doubled up in his kingdom as a teacher.

"No, I guess I don't. I can't explain why I need this. There is just something inside of me that believes I am doing the right thing." I looked down again. "You don't think I make a wrong choice, did I?"

The man placed his hands on my shoulders. "No. I don't. And neither, I think, does Aletheia."

"What?"

"Go back to your reality, Hamilton. I will do as you ask; but be advised, I will do it in my own way."

"That's okay, it's probably better than what I had in mind." I laughed.

Adonaias laughed along with me; he had a hearty, warm laugh, I noticed. I liked this guy. And then the world before me faded, washed away into blinding light.

☼<u>23</u>☼
Confidence

Reality's return hit me like a punch in the face. I even winced, squeezing my eyes shut, trying to block out the heady mess of humanity. Compared to the celestial realm, the human world was a messy headache.

But as my vision clear a moment later, I looked to see my hand wrapped around Mikey's wrist—his regular, normal, non-octopus wrist. I pushed up from my knees and straightened, watching as the last of the dark power dissipated from his body.

"Thank goodness that's over," I muttered.

"So you were right about him."

I jerked around at the surprise. "You!"

"I'm surprised you were able to change him back." Dante Salyards looked at me, meeting me eye for eye, almost as if he was trying to assert his reality over my person. He gave up a moment later and headed over, handing me a syringe. "Here. This is the antidote for the poison we'd given him, in order to sedate him."

The long needle and the clear liquid, connected by the syringe, made me shrink back for a few seconds. I was no doctor, that was for sure. Still, Mikey needed it. I swallowed hard before injecting the medicine into his body, hoping I didn't seem like some kind of awkward, uncomfortable intern. Relief ushered in as I finished with no apparent negative consequence.

Dante spoke as I handed him back the empty plunger. "You know who I am."

"Yes." What else was I supposed to say to that? For all his knowledge, and from what I knew of his individual training, and what I could guess from his resources, I felt his response was pretty stupid.

"How?"

I snorted. "You don't seem to know a lot about us, or the Sinisters, or anything. Why does it surprise you that we might have a few tricks up our sleeves?"

Dante's gaze drifted over to his son's limp body. "I know more than you think." He glanced back at me. "I know much about the paranormal, for example. I know you are a kind of warrior. An *Astroneshama,* in the language of the stars, if I am not mistaken."

Hearing that made my heart skip a beat. "You know about that?" I asked.

"Yes." He turned around and began to walk out the door. "Which is why, for the moment, I am going to let you go."

"Why?"

"The Sinisters, as you call them, are a new breed of supernatural power. Their patterns do not match our registry of alien anomalies or paranormal outliers. Their arrival is even very different from previous encounters of fallen Stars—"

"You mean there are more of us?" I asked.

Dante glanced back at me. "You have much to learn, it appears."

Anger bubbled up inside of me; I knew it was a cold, calculated assessment of my skills, and he was glad to make me upset. The little smirk on his face said it all.

"As I was saying, the Sinisters are a new and dangerous breed of demons so far as we have recorded. We have reason to believe they are the *Maybasayla,* demons of the highest order, and it is beyond our human power to contain and destroy them."

"So I'm allowed to leave as long as I'm useful?" I asked. It was the familiar chain of logic I'd seen used in FBI and/or CIA movies.

"You could put it like that," Dante agreed. Just before he disappeared out of the door, he stopped. He gripped the door frame before he spoke again. "Take care of my son."

And then he was gone.

I watched him disappear and felt confusion add itself to my frustration. Was I the only person in the world who didn't really know of the Starlight Warriors or anything else which went with it?

I gritted my teeth. I'd have to worry about it later, I decided. Reaching down, I hauled up Mikey's lagging behind and tossed him over my shoulders; I was glad to see my flightless wings at last proved useful, as they provided balance and support for Mikey's body as I carried him. "Come on, Mikey, let's go."

Walking out of the black site and into the night-shrouded marina moments later was of very little comfort; I was glad to be free, but I still faced some trepidation in what was next to come.

To say I was a little disoriented at the time would be an understatement; while I'd been held captive, the city's power had been disrupted. The darkening skies were full of stars and as they cloaked over the shadowed cityscape before me.

Glancing around, I tried to figure out exactly where I was. Elysian had mentioned we were close to the marina, and that was true; looking around, I could see some of Lake Erie's harbor, as well as some of the Lakeview Observatory.

The observatory.

That was all it took for me to know where I was. I was in the Central Northern division of the city. The observatory had been built on the high, mountainous end of Lake County, about the same time as the Apollo City Time Tower.

As I turned to face the tall, white clock tower, a bright burst of energy lit up the night, like a powerful fireworks show.

"Well, I guess we know where everyone is," I muttered. I was surprised when Mikey groaned in response. (Then again, I was used to some kind of commentary from my friends after I made my witty remarks. Was it a real stretch that he was semi-unconscious?)

Judging by the distance, it was about eight blocks away.

"Okay, here we go!" I tried for a moment to get my wings to work, thinking for sure this is when they would start to work. And then I would be able to fly, and life would get much easier.

Only to have the same bitter disappointments eat at me a moment later. Nothing! Nothing? I grumbled a bit and frowned up at the night sky, mentally berating destiny for the cruel trickery. There wasn't even a squad car to try to steal from SWORD nearby.

Another blast of light shot up from the clock tower area. So I decided to grumble about my lack of movie life hacks later, and began running for the Time Tower.

When I finally came upon the battle scene, I was an interesting mix of irritated and scared. Not only was Mikey starting to get unbearably heavy, but there were some idiot people craning their necks from behind dumpsters, around alleyways, and through broken windows. Like civilians had nothing better to do!

But as I shoved through a small crowd of bystanders, I could appreciate their stupidity a bit more.

The battle between guns and science fiction had erupted from the pages of fantasy to the horror of reality. Gunshots and surges of power whipped back and forth between the

THE STARLIGHT CHRONICLES

foes. Several cops were trying to keep the crowd of civilians at bay, while SWORD agents, much like their FBI counterparts, were in suits and even some had their shades on. Which had to be those night vision shades, all things considered.

I watched in disgust and terror as Celaena *licked*—yes, licked!—an agent, causing him to fall over as a cotton-like fluffiness protruding from his torso (his soul) was slicked up by the Sinister. Just like spaghetti, I thought. Gross. I am *never* eating spaghetti again.

Before I could completely formulate a plan to carefully dump Mikey's body somewhere safe (behind the dumpster with some other goofy civilians would have to do for now), I was distracted a moment later when Elysian yelled. "Kid!"

I looked up to see Elysian ducking down towards me. A rusty rush of adrenaline jolted through me. It was time to fly.

"You're just leaving him there?" Elysian asked me.

"What? We don't have time to worry about it," I declared. "Besides, he's still in a coma. The best thing to do would be to beat the Sinister who had him under her power, isn't it?"

"Euh. All right, we can do that."

I could tell from his tone it wasn't what he would've done, but who cared? I mean, really. All seven Sinisters were unleashing their own little corner of the underworld on the SWORD agents and the rest of the city. We had to act fast. "What? We just have to make sure we don't let anything hit the building or anything."

Elysian rolled his eyes. "Okay, okay, we'll do it your way."

"Good." I jumped up and grappled with a pair of his horns, letting a sweet moment of brief nostalgia overtake me as we took flight. It was good to be back, I admitted.

Starry Knight was ahead of us, fighting off a number of them with her bow and her other well-honed fighting skills. She nodded when she saw me, sending a rush of awareness down my spine. She turned her attention to the Sinisters above her. I had no doubt her eyes were searching for the sinister who was pulling the puppet strings. "There!" she cried out, pointing to Alcyonë, the green sinister.

Elysian and I exchanged a quick glance and a silent agreement passed between us. I hurried to climb up Elysian's back and launch myself at the angry-looking Sinister.

Alcyonë was surprised as I tackled her in mid-air; my momentum carried us to a nearby apartment building. I grunted as we smacked into a window. (In movies, the windows usually break, so I was more than a bit upset at this.) We stumbled onto a fire escape and the punches began to fly.

Suddenly, Starry Knight screamed.

That was probably the last thing either Elysian or I had been expecting.

My eyes darted up to find her. I immediately lost focus, and saw two of the other Sinisters, the yellow one—Asteropy— and the orange one—Elektra—had managed to take hold of Starry Knight, one on each side. "Starry Knight!" I called out.

"Don't be a moron! Don't worry about me!" she called back.

As if to prove to her point, Alcyonë cackled and managed to push me from behind, sending me over the fire safety railing.

"Kid!" Elysian was shouting at me, but I knew he would be too late.

I grazed across the sidewalk with a sickening *scrape*. Fortunately I wasn't too scratched up. "I'm okay," I moaned, trying to sound strong even though I knew I sounded more like a nincompoop.

"That boy is a complete idiot." From the tone of his voice, Orpheus had been clearly thinking the same thing.

I flinched. I hadn't even noticed him.

Starry Knight, while she may have agreed with him, glared at him from between her Sinisters captors. "Who are you to call that judgment?"

"Are you bothered more by the fact that I called him an idiot, or that I was judging him at all?" His dark eyes maliciously glittered as they watched her. "Rumors say that the lovely Lady Justice, the Guardian Star, has returned," he told her.

Elysian let out a disbelieving *roar!* at his words, even as he found himself surrounded by four Sinisters who were bent on destroying him. Picking myself up, I stumbled over to him. "What's your problem, Elysian?"

Before he could explain, Starry Knight laughed before straightening up under the hold of Asteropy and Elektra. "Was that all this was about, Orpheus? You wish to see if I was the one that you were looking for?"

Orpheus felt a fury burn within his gut, but he gritted his teeth and muttered, "You dare laugh at me?"

"Oh, I would not dream of doing so," Starry Knight assured him. Even from where I stood, I was able to watch as her eyes went from hard to soft. "It is not funny at all that you are in such a state as you are, considering who you once were."

As Orpheus charged up his own brand of power, his bumbling charges all turned to face him. "What does she mean by that, Orpheus?" Elektra spoke up curiously.

I watched as some of the SWORD agents were using this time to radio in their contacts. Nothing good was coming, that was for sure.

"Yes, I don't even know what she is talking about," Asteropy muttered, displeasure emanating from her very words.

Elysian took the initiative. He let out a fiery blast of celestial fire, breaking through their conversation and driving them back. Seeing this as a chance to escape, Starry Knight took flight. "Thanks, Elysian," she replied as she hovered behind us.

Elysian turned to her. "When this battle is over, Starry Knight, there are questions I would like for you to answer."

She was about to reply (most likely with a rejection of such a request) when a sonic bomb rang out from the street.

"Augh!" My wingdings curled around my ears, saving my eardrums from breaking. I squinted up to see I wasn't the only one who was affected; Elysian snarled and swiped out his claws, and the Sinisters were apparently paralyzed by the piercing noise.

The windows to several surrounding building cracked, and the SWORD agents, who clearly had prepared for this, moved into formation.

Taygetay, a moment later, sliced down from the sky, and swiped at the device, setting it off.

"Now!"

Another *pop!* and an electrified net reached out, covering up her body and sealing it. I barely watched as her reddish arms thrashed helplessly at the mesh.

I released my ears and tried to go and tame Elysian, who was still upset by the echoing attack. "Elysian!" I called, grabbing a hold of his nose and trying to get him to still. "It's all right now."

He roared again, and I felt a tug of sympathy despite myself. Good to know he had his own weaknesses, I thought. "Are you okay now?"

The monstrous body of my changeling dragon visibly relaxed. "Yes. Let's hurry and help Starry Knight," Elysian agreed a moment later.

"Good idea. The SWORD agents seem to be distracted." I nodded to the scene behind me. "Looks like they got Taygetay."

Elysian snorted. "I'll be surprised if they manage to keep her. She's the Sinister of Rage, and there's a reason she is considered one of the more deadly ones."

"At least they seem to know how to fight her," I remarked. "You don't think Starry Knight had the right idea trying to blow up everything, do you?" But even as I said it, I knew I had done the right thing in stopping her. "There must be another way to beat them."

"You're right. There is."

"Huh?" I turned around to see a new face behind me.

In my most honest moments (which were still relatively few), I had never thought I would meet anyone quite as beautiful as Starry Knight. And now, looking up at the strange girl who'd appeared before me for no known reason, I still held to that belief. But the girl in front of me came astonishingly close.

Her green eyes were gentle—something that automatically made me like her. Her hair, a pretty shade of blond, was loose and flowing all around her. She wore a glittering circlet of what looked like stars on her head. And when my gaze met hers, she smiled.

I didn't think it was possible at first (I really should have known better by now) she had come to see me. But she looked at me before anyone else.

"Who are you? Do I know you?"

The crystal green eyes sparkled in confirmation. "Yes, at last we meet again," she said. "My name is Aletheia, the Guardian of Memory."

"I—"

"I know very well who you are," the girl assured me. "Do you want to fight against the evil in this world?"

"Yes." There was no question in my mind about that. It just sounded a bit dumbfounded because of the unexpectedness of the situation.

Aletheia nodded. "Do you trust in the power that has been given to you?"

"Hasn't failed me yet."

The eyes remained bright, but somehow seemed more serious all of a sudden. Aletheia pulled out. "Then it is my privilege to give you your sword."

A stream of lightning slashed out from the space between her hands, and lit up in the shape of a sword. Elysian gaped at the sword. "It can't be!" he exclaimed softly, unbelievably.

I just stared at it. It was unlike any sword I'd ever seen in my life. It was so much *cooler*.

The hilt and blade had a simple design, but an elegant one. The blade was double-edged, very sharp, long and surprisingly thick. There were small, intricate carvings along the blade and down to the hilt; the hilt itself was masterfully created, shaped into a pair of wings.

I reached out and took hold of it. It was light and strong in my hands, perfectly suited to me, almost like it was designed for me (which I remembered, probably was).

"This is the Sealing Sword. It has the power to cut through the darkness, and capture the heart of the Sinisters. You are its master now, a great honor and sacrifice."

"It's mine? No strings attached?" I asked as I lovingly looked over my new sword.

Aletheia frowned. "There are always consequences to our choices, Wingdinger—consequences we cannot always fully see."

I guess that means yes, I thought, slightly aggravated.

Aletheia smiled and looked past me to Starry Knight. I followed her gaze, only to see Starry Knight, broken free from her captors and paused in her fighting, watching us. Starry Knight's gaze slowly shifted to only me, and then looked away, stricken. Her expression was funny and disturbing all the same; her violet eyes were wide and her lips were slightly parted, as though she could not believe what she had just seen.

Yeah, she would be surprised to see me become an actual threat.

Aletheia turned her attention back to me. She held out her hand, like a handshake. "I will see you again shortly."

THE STARLIGHT CHRONICLES

I reached out and took her hand; once I did, a burning sensation tingled up my arm, and a bright light emerged from our joined hands, causing me to look away and cringe.

I peeked at my hand once released from her grip; I was startled to see my glove had been torn right through, and a bright gold inscription had been placed on my palm:

Sailing on the Stars

Meallán

St. Brendan the Navigator

April 23rd, Earth Time 11:00 PM

Dock 42, Apollo City Marina

I glanced back up at Aletheia, only managing to see her smile before she disappeared. I blinked, but there was no mistaking her disappearance.

Weird. So that was the Guardian of Memory, I thought. I glanced back down at my sword and then over to the Sinisters, who were still not really paying attention to me and Elysian. Starry Knight and the SWORD agents were more than able to keep them busy.

I looked down at the sword and held it up, wondering at the glistening of the moonlight on the edge. It was mystical

THE STARLIGHT CHRONICLES

and magical and frightening all at the same time, evidence of the power within. I grinned. *Awesome.*

THE STARLIGHT CHRONICLES

☼24☼
Strength

Elysian moved next to me. "You need to be careful with that," he warned.

"No kidding," I snorted in response. "Come on. I'll go for the Sinisters up there. You make sure the SWORD guys can get Taygetay out of here and won't get hit."

"What about Orpheus?"

I searched the skies for the one-eyed leader of the Sinisters. I saw him a moment later, starting to pick a fight with Starry Knight. "It looks like Starry Knight's going to take the lead on that one."

Elysian sniffled indignantly. "Do not underestimate his power. He is the one who is in control of the Sinisters."

"Really?" I almost doubled over in laughter. "I wouldn't know it. He sure sucks at his job."

Asteropy spoke up first, interrupting us. "Aw, look at that, girls, the little boy has a new toy."

The other Sinisters laughed. The fat one, Celaena, called out, "It'd be perfect for cutting some cake!"

"Yeah, that's probably all it's about good for, too," Elektra spoke up. "I doubt that kid has enough power to wield it anyway."

I was slightly confused at their sudden willingness to not kill each other in an argument, but I held my ground and decided it was time to unleash my most powerful weapon (my mouth). "You ladies sound pretty cocky, if you ask me," I called out. "But I don't see any of you coming over to check my sword out for yourself."

I had them there, that was for sure.

Alcyonë yawned. "We know that you're not as powerful as Starry Knight," she taunted. "We have little reason to fear you."

Ouch, that burned.

"Hop on, kid," Elysian rumbled. He ducked down and I jumped on as he flew up, heading straight for the Sinisters. Elysian was ready with his fire, and I was prepared to strike with my new weapon. The wind whipped against my face, the simultaneous chills of excitement and the onset of rain energizing me, sharpening me, refining me.

I felt a rush of adrenaline as I sliced down on the cloud of Sinisters with the Sealing Sword.

And completely missed.

"Huh?" I blinked. *Did I really just miss? Ugh!*

The Sinisters had taken to laughing.

"You've got a lousy aim," Asteropy called out, her wicked smile making me grit my teeth in anger and embarrassment.

"I can't believe I was worried there for a second," Alcyonë chortled, her voice saturated in sarcasm.

"Even I think I could've done a better job," Celaena agreed with a smile.

"See?" Elektra spoke up.

"Well, *most* of us," Asteropy corrected, glaring at Maia, who had done nothing to try to get away, obviously.

"Uh, kid? Are you sure that you know how to use that thing?" Elysian asked.

What was this? Even Elysian doubted me? I huffed indignantly. I felt the anger boil within me as the Sinisters continued to laugh and/or mock me. Despite the desire to scream with rage at this grave injustice, I took a deep breath.

Okay, where can I do the most damage? Then the idea struck. "Elysian, turn around."

"What? Why?" the dragon asked.

"Just do it!"

As Elysian swooped around and headed forward, he suddenly saw what my goal was. "You're going to try to seal away Orpheus?"

"Yeah, that's right," I confirmed. I smirked when I saw that it was good timing on my part; Starry Knight looked like she could use some help.

Starry Knight had charged right into Orpheus as I approached. As he was flung back in between the layers of a nearby three-story parking garage, I felt a sense of approaching success.

"Ouch!" Orpheus barked loudly, as he skidded across the hard cement structure.

He didn't have much time to pout. An arrow of light was shot at him seconds later. He had just barely managed to move before it whisked past him and shot deep into the concrete behind him. Orpheus huffed in response. "You'll have to do better than that, *Lady Justice*!" he called out mockingly.

Elysian slowed. "Kid, are you sure about this?" he asked me.

"Yes, go!" I insisted.

"She seems pretty determined," Elysian remarked.

I turned to watch an arrow split straight through his right arm. "You'll do well to address me as Starry Knight, and forget my former title!" Starry Knight called out, a new fury to her words as another arrow was released from her bow.

"Okay, Elysian, slow down," I said. I turned to see the Sinisters approaching from behind me, but I returned my focus on Starry Knight. Or Lady Justice? Was that her real name?

Orpheus grinned despite the obvious inflicted pain. "I see. So it is you!" His smile lit up as he added, "Does it bother you to recall your past glory?" he asked.

Starry Knight narrowed her eyes at him. "That could easily be said of you as well," she called back. "A Leader in the Celestial Kingdom, was it?"

Orpheus lost his smile quicker than the pop of a cheap balloon. His voice was a deadly hiss as he muttered, "So, you do remember." He clenched his fists. "Then we must finish it! Let us finish the battle that we started on the other side of Time!"

"It has been finished!" Starry Knight argued. "I told you then that you would never get what you sought; you have already lost. There is just the matter of carrying out the sentence of your rebellion."

I didn't have any idea of what they were talking about.

But I had my own trouble to deal with. A blur of color caught my attention. Spurts of pink, yellow, and green all flashed briefly in my mind as I ducked, squatted, and scooted around on Elysian's back to avoid the Sinisters and what I was pretty sure were their claws.

I was about to try to fight back when I shot forward onto the hard surface of a roof; after I made sure my face was still on my head, I looked up and saw one of the Sinisters had figured out attacking Elysian was more effective than trying to fight me.

"Elysian!"

Elysian roared, giving me enough time to see Starry Knight was exchanging blows with Orpheus on a parking garage just across the street. I hurried to the edge, faltering as I looked down. What are the chances, I wondered, that I'll be able to fly?

Glancing at my leathery black wings, I rolled my eyes. "Why is it always at the most inconvenient time that stuff doesn't work!?" I lamented.

I stopped when I almost pushed off seconds later. "Ouf!" I grunted as I managed to twist myself onto the ledge. I felt vomit threaten me again at the thought of hitting the road from this far up. I wasn't a physicist, but I was pretty sure I would've been splattered onto the ground.

It was Alcyonë again. She sneered at me. "Too bad. You got lucky."

"No, I didn't. You just got weak!" I screamed, as I slashed through the Sinister with the sword, thrusting with my full weight on the blade.

The sword cut all the way through Alcyonë; her body disappeared in a flash of swirling emptiness and whirl-winding green light as Alcyonë cried out, captured in her own black hole of a heart.

And then it was over.

I blinked a few times as the bright array of lights slowly subsided. When my eyes stopped flashing color dots all over my field of vision, I saw the Sinister was gone. All I saw that remained was a small, black chunk of rock.

The rock blazed, gradually fading from sinister green to bland gray to black; and then it lingered before me, as though it were waiting for me to do something. *Am I supposed to take it?*

Taking another leap of faith, I took a hold of it, and felt the odd texture of it against my fingers. Nothing spectacular happened.

I tucked it into my pocket, deciding to ask Elysian about it later. I turned around to see if anyone else had seen my heroic actions. I was extremely disappointed to see Starry Knight was still engaged in her battle for life or death.

Battle, part two. "Elysian!" I called out.

I watch as Orpheus, enraged, unleashed an attack of his own. The dark energy swirled around them as it sought to bring Starry Knight down, but she dodged it easily enough. The wind of the energy flowed passed her as Orpheus continued his assault.

It was a dance of danger and precise movements, as one would attack, and the other would dodge; for several moments this continued, knocking down several support beams in the parking garage and throwing up a bunch of debris and dust.

"Elysian! Come here!" I cried out again, this time more urgently.

"Just a moment," Elysian grumbled up, as Maia and Meropae had tried to take turns riding him. He was bucking and thrashing horribly, trying to dispel himself from their grip.

Starry Knight landed another arrow into Orpheus' left arm. He staggered, and fell back. Starry Knight saw her chance and went in for the kill.

"Elysian, now! Toss me over to the parking garage."

Elysian reared back and flicked his tail in response, managing to kick off Maia at the same time.

Talk about whiplash, I thought as Elysian's tail hit me hard, flinging me into the air. "Thanks!" I called back, half-serious, half-regretful. I rubbed my butt where Elysian's tail had struck.

Seconds later, I found myself thrown (literally) between Orpheus and Starry Knight. Orpheus, aware of the danger, managed to push his body back over mine, just in time to avoid the killing blow of Starry Knight's bow.

"Ouch!" I muttered, falling over.

Starry Knight, angered by his escape, faltered for a split second at my arrival. It was just briefly, in the twinkling of the eye, but Orpheus saw it, and it was enough time to make his move.

As I flouted around on the floor, his wispy hands shot out from his long robes, and grasped at Starry Knight's throat.

"Starry Knight!" I cried, only to have Orpheus send a blast of energy at me. The cackling energy ball hit me square on, sending me tumbling further away.

I grabbed at my ribcage, and turned, watching as Orpheus tightened his grip on my partner. He squirmed at the touch of her skin, as it still carried the remnant of her light, but he frowned wickedly as he held her. Her breathing caught, and she silently began to choke. "Do you think this is some kind of game?" he asked her, his voice deadly cold. "Do you!?"

She shook her head as she coughed. Her bow fell to the ground with a small clatter as she grabbed his hands, seeking relief from his clutch.

"Starry Knight," I muttered, trying to catch my breath.

Orpheus wrapped his hands around her neck tighter, clearly glorying in the feel of her twitching and struggling under his hold. "I'll admit I underestimated you before. But your power can't last forever! The curse that you placed on the girls is breaking. Soon their full power will be released, and then this world will be mine!"

Starry Knight shook her head, and managed to inhale deeply before sputtering, "It's … not … my power."

"What?" Surprised, Orpheus loosened his grip enough for her to wriggle free. She swatted him back with her power, managing to thwart his advance. She slumped to the ground and scooted away quickly, moving towards me. "Are you all right?" she asked me, her hand reaching down to my chest. A trickle of power leaked out of her hand, and I felt the rush of her healing powers settle me.

"Are you okay?" I asked, letting myself reach up and gently touch the marks on her neck. "He hurt you."

"He hurt you, too," she reminded me. She took my hand though, and whispered, "I'm fine. Now, please go." Her insistence pushed me away as forcefully as her arms.

She turned back to Orpheus, and began circling away from me. "It is not my power that seals back the full power of the Sinisters. It is another's." She straightened, shaking off any inkling of weakness. Her violet eyes narrowed. She picked up her bow and drew back her bowstring, prepared to resume the fighting.

Orpheus flexed his hands impatiently, itching to get his fingers wrapped around her throat again. "That's enough!" Orpheus growled, as he began to lunge forward. "This time, you will perish!"

A burst of power shot out from me, and a second later, I opened my eyes to see I'd managed to push myself in between the two foes, forcing them apart from their sparring before landing on my hands and knees right in the "Customer Only" compact car space by the entrance door.

I shook my head to clear my vision. When I looked up, I saw Starry Knight standing over me. "What are you doing?" she asked, her voice tight. "You need to go. Now."

I ignored her. "You're welcome," I muttered, standing up.

"What? What are you talking about?"

"I just saved you from Orpheus!"

"You did not! I was doing perfectly fine on my own."

"You can't defeat him."

"You interrupted the fight; of course I didn't defeat him."

"I said 'can't,' not 'didn't,'" I snapped.

"It doesn't matter! You shouldn't be here," Starry Knight muttered back. Her eyes shifted from me back to Orpheus, who was suddenly watching me with wicked eyes.

Orpheus' inner hatred burned even more brightly at the sight of me and my sword blocking him from his initial prey. "You!"

I wondered why I'd even woken up this morning. Cold, paralyzing fear had overtaken my body at Orpheus' accusatory tone.

"You! I will kill you this time! I will wring the soul from your body and cast it into Hell myself!" Orpheus cried out as he launched himself forward, his power glowing with an ominous void.

I pulled my sword up, intending to use it as a shield. There was no room for hesitation here, I reminded myself, even if my body wasn't as compliant as my mind.

With what I thought was a pretty brave front, I awaited impact of the growing, circular void and its crushing power.

It never came.

"Augh!" A flash spurted out from behind me, hitting Orpheus in the heart, holding him back. His attack crumpled around him, and I allowed myself a (brief) moment of relief.

I glanced at Starry Knight; there were beads of sweat forming on her forehead as she glanced behind Orpheus and his attack.

THE STARLIGHT CHRONICLES

I noticed suddenly the other Sinisters were all heading over; Elysian was laying limp on the roof of the other building. A twinge of fear interlaced with concern shot through me as the stampeding rainbow of Sinisters bore down on us.

I woke up from my fear just in time to hear Orpheus question Starry Knight.

"Why do you protect him?" Orpheus asked Starry Knight scathingly. "Why? Tell me why!"

I recalled how Starry Knight had been accused of having me as her biggest weakness. Before Starry Knight could chide me for being weak, or incompetent, or useless, I decided to answer that question. "Because we're partners!" I shouted as I stood up.

For some reason, this was even more irksome to Orpheus. The Sinisters arrived just as he pointed to me. "Attack him!" he ordered.

But I was ready this time. I swung out my sword, and took aim. "This ends now, Orpheus!" I announced, ready to deliver the defeating blow.

"No!" the strangled, dying-cat cry of a Sinister shot out of the darkness at the last second. I didn't even see the shadow of bright pink as I cut into it; all I knew was a moment later, my brain was able to process Meropae's scream of terror and rage as she was slowly sucked up into a singular point and sealed away.

I had not managed to seal away Orpheus; Meropae was the one I'd managed to capture. I turned to face Maia, wide-eyed,

THE STARLIGHT CHRONICLES

as I realized Meropae had been pushed in front Orpheus. And it had been done by Maia, of all people (using the word "people" lightly here) at the last possible second.

That was the confusing part for many of us. Maia hated Orpheus, and work. I was confounded as to what had caused her to save him. Starry Knight and I exchanged a quick glance, and from her expression, she was just as surprised by this as I was.

In the meantime, Orpheus had averted his attention to a retreat. He flew up into the air, regrouping with his remaining girls.

With his cruel, fuming glance, Orpheus looked down at me, and then to Starry Knight. "This isn't over," he assured us, before taking off like a black shooting star across the night sky, finding a hideout in the sea of colors in the city night life. The leftover four Sinisters quickly followed, already talking about Maia's unbelievable actions and the possibility of getting some food somewhere.

I looked down to see a bright speck glittering on the cement floor. I reached down and picked it up. The stone-like object was cold and surprisingly heavy against my palm. I put it in my other pocket and heaved a sigh of relief. The battle was over.

The lights of the city began twinkling back on.

I could see over the edge of the parking deck as SWORD agents hurried to deliver medical attention to the injured parties. My gaze jerked over to Elysian. "Mikey!"

I didn't even really register until later I could've asked Elysian to carry me down to Mikey's dumpster.

But when I came over to him, I saw him try to sit up and stumble, shaking so badly he couldn't move much.

"Hamilton," Mikey spoke up. So he was awake. And he knew it was me. There was a huge bump on his head, multiple cuts on his arms and legs, and there was a black eye slowly swelling up on his face. "You're Wingdinger."

I nodded. "Er, yeah. I would appreciate it if you didn't mention that to anyone."

"Dude, that's awesome! Don't worry, I won't tell. You can trust me." He glanced away. "I'm sorry I was jealous of you." His voice had a straggling quality to it when he spoke. "It's hard to not be, when I see you with your grades and your abilities. And now I have this superhero business to get used to as well."

"I can't help being who I am," I shrugged.

"You could work on your bragging and attitude about it, though, if you don't mind my saying."

"It's okay, I don't mind. I'd been thinking about working on that anyway," I told him as Elysian finished landing beside me. "I've heard that a lot this week."

"The kid here doesn't make anyone's life easy," Elysian told Mikey. "And jealousy's not an easy emotion to deal with in the first place. But if you trust in each other, it will help you to overcome it."

Mikey gaped at Elysian with an open mouth. "You can *talk*?!"

I laughed heartily. "Hey, Starry Knight's still here."

"You both saved me," Mikey muttered sleepily.

"She's right over—" I looked up, realizing I'd left her alone several stories up. "Well, she was—"

A pair of wings fluttered behind me. I sucked in my breath sharply. I had seen Starry Knight up close in a long time a number of times today, but somehow her beauty always cut right through me.

No wonder Mikey had been obsessed with her, I thought. She was nothing short of beautiful. Up close, I gathered she was around our age. Too bad for her zero personality, I thought, mustering up a grim look.

Mikey straightened wildly, spurring on a dizzy spell. "It's you!"

Starry Knight barely acknowledged him. "He seems all right now," she murmured delicately.

"Yes, I'm fine," Mikey spoke up, nearly falling over as he reached for her. He cleared his throat. "The name's Michael; my friends call me Mikey, but you can call me 'Darling.'"

"He's a big fan," I explained brusquely.

A softened look came over her face. She knelt down next to Mikey. Her eyes met his and held them for a long moment.

THE STARLIGHT CHRONICLES

I rolled my eyes, frankly annoyed. After all, it wasn't fair of her to lead Mikey on like that. Of course she deserved—no, not her, *Mikey*—deserved so much better.

"You are not the one I'm meant for," she told Mikey gently. "I doubt I will call you 'darling,' but Mikey suits you well enough."

Mikey wasn't deferred in the least. "I might not be the one you're looking for, but I'm the one you found."

It was rather tragic to see him trying to flirt with Starry Knight and stay awake, I decided.

"Okay, Mike, that's enough of Lover Boy tonight," I interjected before turning to Starry Knight. "Can you heal him?"

"Sure," she agreed. Her hand went out and took a hold of his. After a moment of consideration, she took off one of her gloves. She held up her right arm and pulled back the bracelet that she wore. I could see her own Emblem of the Prince on her wrist.

Shining in the moonlight, there was a mark very similar to my own; the only difference between the two was the color. Starry Knight's mark was silvery in color, while mine was blood red. "We can't always see everything that is real with our eyes, you know. You have been marked, Wingdinger— the very essence that is you, not the DNA of the body but of the soul, has been marked for a purpose."

She'd obviously caught me staring.

As her power seeped from her palm, I reached out involuntarily, wanting to touch Starry Knight's mark. She moved away before I could. And then I wondered why she had been marked, too, and what her purpose was for being here. Was it different from mine?

I watched as Mikey fell back into a healing slumber, and then turned to her. "Do I know you?" I asked again. "Have I seen you before?"

A small smile flitted to her lips, one of her rare, genuine smiles. "It's doubtless you have *seen* me," she told me. "But I doubt you would *know* me."

Awkwardly, I turned my gaze away from her. "I suppose I shouldn't have expected anything helpful from you." There was long moment of silence before I turned back to face her. "That reminds me, I have another question."

I reached into my pocket and pulled out the black gem-like stone that had appeared with Alcyonë's destruction. "What is this?"

I didn't have long before I got my reply. Starry Knight came over and swiped it right out of my hand.

"Hey!" I objected. "That's mine." I gritted my teeth. My hand instinctively tightened on my sword.

Starry Knight frowned. "You might have sealed them away," she conceded, "But they are still meant to belong to me!"

"I don't see your name on it," I fought back, trying to grab it back from her. I looked over to see Elysian had finally managed to come over to the parking lot. "Elysian, tell her to give me the thing back!"

"Never mind asking me how I am. What are you fighting about?" Elysian asked sleepy-sounding, as he looked back and forth between our two churlish, childish figures.

"See for yourself," I muttered angrily. What good was having Elysian's help if he was going to be such a slowpoke about it?

Elysian squinted down at the object Starry Knight was trying to concealing in her palm. He shrugged. "I have a better idea," he announced.

"What?" The simultaneous reply from Starry Knight and me was the perfect distraction. Seconds later, the intentions of the changeling dragon became clear, and even I was impressed.

Elysian had transfigured himself into a smaller snake-like animal, and had wrapped himself around Starry Knight's body, preventing her from flying, moving away, and to some degree, breathing properly.

I laughed to see the shock on Starry Knight's face.

"Sorry to do this," Elysian told her, "But I was afraid you would leave before we could talk."

"I have no idea why you would ever think such a thing," Starry Knight muttered back, struggling to find some loosen area to get free through.

I was still laughing, and finally Elysian had enough of the apparently awful sound. "Enough!" he nearly shouted. "Can't you see that this is serious?"

"Hey, I have my sword now," I replied back, "And I am not afraid to use it!"

"Or qualified, apparently," Starry Knight replied easily enough.

Elysian had to fight the temptation to laugh on that one, I could tell. But he let it go. There was business to attend to. "All right, that's enough of you, too!" he told her.

"Elysian, let's get the crystal thing and let's go," I spoke up. I looked down at the street to see some of the members of the SWORD had managed to lock away Taygetay and were coming back for more.

"Can't you see this is more important than just a crystal?" Elysian groaned. "She is a threat to us!"

That stopped me there. "No she's not," I said slowly, as my mind tried to find Elysian's line of reasoning. "We agreed that we're going to be allies ... " But she did just take the crystal from me. And it is obvious she doesn't want me to know anything ...

I thought carefully about this.

"It doesn't matter? Don't you remember earlier? She was just about to blow open the space-time continuum earlier tonight!"

"What?" I was confused; I didn't know much about space. I wasn't supposed to take Astronomy until twelfth grade. There was also the matter I was getting tired. I'd been through a lot tonight. There was so much to go over and to do I didn't really want to know where to begin. And it didn't help I was going to have to take Mikey to the hospital and make up some story about how he'd been stuck in a pothole on the other side of town for two weeks.

Elysian gave up. "Talking to you is wasting time, I see," he said through bared fangs. He turned his attention back to Starry Knight. "Who are you? Tell us!"

Okay, I'll listen to this, I thought as my attention was instantly caught. The desire I'd felt earlier, to know who she was, and how I was connected to her—because there was little doubt in my mind that, as the only other defender-type supernatural fighter around, Starry Knight *wasn't* connected to me—came rushing at me, plaguing me anew.

Starry Knight looked hatefully up at Elysian. I thought she was going to spit on him or something, she was so frightfully disgusted. I decided to take a step closer in case Elysian needed him for back-up or something.

That was when she looked at me, and I thought if she could, she would try to send some kind of mental pain package.

After a moment of studying her face, I felt something behind my heart step back.

This was not the right thing to do. I wanted it. But I would have to hold off for now.

I looked up at Elysian. "Let her go, Elysian."

"No!" the fangs flashed and Elysian's temper was up. "Those Sinisters called her their *sister*!" He glared back at Starry Knight. "And the leader, Orpheus, called you the Guardian of Justice. Whether you are or are not, we need to know."

"Sister?" My brow crinkled, trying to remember that one. "She couldn't be their sister, Elysian … " But my voice trailed off as I noticed Starry Knight's eyes had narrowed.

"What they have said was true, once," she spoke, her voice embittered by anger. "But they are not the same anymore. And neither am I."

"But you were a Star!" Elysian exclaimed. "And a Guardian, no less. You have retained your powers."

"Yes, but my purpose has changed," Starry Knight told him.

"Does that make a difference?"

"Yes. All the difference in the world." There was no playing around or joking inflection in her voice.

I suddenly wondered if she was going to be able to keep her promise to be my ally. I had to admit, I wouldn't want to be allies with people who treated me like we were treating her.

"All right, Elysian," I spoke up. "Let her go for now. We are not getting anywhere in questioning her like this." I looked over at her and added, "We will just have to trust her for now."

Elysian stretched out his head, allowing himself to talk into my ear privately. "Uh, kid? Are you crazy?"

"What? It's not like she's going to kill everyone tonight," I objected.

"Don't you remember she tried to supernova the city earlier this evening?" Elysian asked frustratingly. "I just reminded you of that!"

I grabbed him by the horn and lifted myself up next to his ear. Or where I assumed his ears were (Come on, dragon anatomy is hard.) "Come on, I've got my sword now, and I'm not really hurt anymore, and you're fine. We can take her if need be. Besides, why don't we just wait until that other girl comes back? She should be able to tell us more. And she seems like she's capable of being nice about it, too."

"You don't know how important this information is!" Elysian scolded. But I had to smile; Elysian was losing his resolve to argue.

"We need her trust more than we need her information," I reminded him.

And that was the deal breaker. Elysian sighed, and released her. "You do realize you're not getting your crystal back, right?"

"What?" I'd forgotten about that. I turned only to see her kick the ground and fly off before I could say anything else. I cursed.

"It's your own fault," Elysian taunted. We watched her fly off; as she disappeared into the midst of the city's lights, Elysian whistled. "She sure can fly fast. She looked really sick earlier. Wonder where she gets all that power?"

That triggered something in my mind. "Elysian, is there something about her power that I should know about?"

"I don't know, remember? If you'd wanted to know you should've asked her before making me let her go."

"Stop it, I'm serious here. She mentioned, when we were breaking out of prison, that her full power had returned. Where had it gone? Is it dependent on something?"

Elysian thought about it. "She was tired before, and weaker, when you weren't around," Elysian recalled. "If I had a guess, I would say that her power is dependent on you."

"What?" I cocked my eyebrow. "I doubt that. She's stronger than me." That was a rare admission I didn't like to make. "And I'm her biggest weakness, according to Alcyonë." Thinking about her, I reached into my pocket and felt the other crystal. At least Starry Knight didn't get a hold of this one, I thought.

"That makes more sense, actually," Elysian said. "She began to be less powerful when you went away, and stronger when you came back. If she loses you, I wonder what happens to her?"

"Do you really think so?" It didn't sound quite right to me.

"Well, it's still a guess. But a pretty good one, I'd say. If it is true, we will definitely find out." Elysian's eyes glared at me. "I guess we'll just have to *trust her.*"

I decided that my own words tasted too sour for my liking. "Ugh, let's go," I muttered. I watched as the SWORD agents began tending to the wounded. I was glad to see a medical squad was coming around the corner, and while I didn't see Dante's face, I imagined I could see him glowering at me. "Come on, Elysian. We have to take Mikey to the hospital."

☼<u>25</u>☼
Aftermath

"Hey, Dinger, you'll never guess what! I've got tickets to the space pirates movie that just came out—I got them on the way to school … " Poncey was telling me as we walked into first period.

I sat down, barely listening to Poncey go on and on (and on and on and on) about the new sci-fi flick at the cinema.

When you are in the middle of a battle, and then you hear about it later, there's a jarring discordance ringing in your head while it happens. It's almost as if some kind of surrealist or expressionist decided to paint a memory in your head, and then the news came along and tried to dissect all the shapes and blotches, classifying them somewhere between 'houses' and 'rocks.' I don't know; my paint metaphors are a bit messy.

That's more or less how I felt about most of mind and body though. It was messy. Too messy to deal with at the moment. I settled into my seat in the back of Mrs. Smithe's class, and pulled out my Game Pac.

City power had been restored to normal within the hour of the Sinisters' defeat and SWORD's departure. The Time Tower and its surrounding area had been closed until proper maintenance could be finished. Several streets needed repairs and a lot of windows had to be put in.

Mikey had been admitted into the hospital upon his arrival; they didn't ask me about the dumpster odor. He was there for a couple of days, in a coma, before he began waking up. It was a good sign, the doctor said. I envied him for it.

While the days following the attack were blurry, my nights were full of stark clarity.

I would dream of that moment where I had kissed Starry Knight, only to be full of longing and confusion as my eyes opened up. Talk about reality's brutality. I would hate the thought of going to bed, but then once I was asleep, I dreaded the thought of waking up.

Needless to say, I did not exactly sleep well.

And Gwen did not help, either, what with her finally deciding to be my girlfriend and all.

I looked over at her as she sat down in her seat. She glanced over at me and waved shyly, before she blushed and looked down at her notebook. I didn't have to wonder what she was thinking about.

With Mikey in the hospital over the weekend, I'd gone to see him. He was still sleeping a good portion of the day, but on Sunday afternoon I checked in on him.

After a rousing discussion of what had happened at the swim meet, his likeliness of getting back into school without some kind of juvenile record, and the chances of Starry Knight changing her mind about dating him, I'd left him to continue on with his rest and recovery. Conveniently forgetting to tell him his dad was back in town.

That was when I passed by the delivery room quarantine, only to see Gwen mooning over Tim again.

As I watched her, I decided something. It was okay if she didn't want to commit to a relationship with me. Even with the swim season winding down, I had school to worry about, Cheryl had finally harangued me enough to schedule an appointment with the mayor's office this week, and there were my now-normal scheduling conflicts with Elysian, Starry Knight, and demons of a Sinister nature. All which were largely impromptu, and could not be ignored due to potential disasters of epic proportion.

I thought about all the dangerous adventures which awaited me, and I realized I couldn't really share those with her. I leaned against the wall outside the quarantine, and decided to tell her that.

That's when I heard her.

"Tim, you're such a wonderful guy, and I did really love hanging out with you while we were working on *Romeo and Juliet* together."

Tim, weak but awake, nodded. I could see that much from where I stood.

I peeked in, hoping none of the nurses around would call me out on what I was doing.

Gwen had her hand in Tim's as she spoke to him. "I hope you don't mind, but I'm going to be dating Hamilton now."

THE STARLIGHT CHRONICLES

Shock hit me like a bumper car. I think I even physically stumbled. I heard some noise from inside the room. When I regained my balance, I saw Tim had jerked away so quickly his heart monitor had fallen off of him.

It would have been comical if I hadn't witnessed it. Some things are just funnier when you hear them secondhand.

"What? Gwen, come on." Tim sat up as the nurse came over and patched him up. "I mean, I know your parents don't like me, but still—"

"I know. I've thought about it a lot too, I promise you. But my parents are right, as horrible as it sounds. I need someone who wants the same things I do, and that's worth giving Hamilton a chance. Besides, he needs me, you know."

"What do you mean?" Tim asked, his tone beginning to sound more and more accusatory.

"Hamilton's not like you. You have such a good, loving heart and you're ready for true love," Gwen told him.

"With you!"

"No." It sounded weak though. "Hamilton needs a special kind of love. In fact, I think on some level he is afraid of love. And I want to be the one to be there for him. To help him."

"No," Tim echoed. "Gwen. Please. I'm sorry if I did something—"

"No, it's not you. It's my decision. And I'm sorry if it hurts you—"

"Of course it hurts me!"

As I was hearing this, I was secretly relieved; Gwen hadn't been using me as some kind of distraction to society and her parents while we were going out on dates. But I even began to feel bad for Tim, and after all the trouble he'd caused me, that was a miracle. I didn't hear the rest of the conversation as I headed down the hall and sat down in the waiting room; the same one I'd been in, just moments before kissing Starry Knight and rekindling my Wingdinger routine.

I probably sat there for ages, thinking about that.

"Hammy."

I jumped as I realized I'd fallen into a daze. "Hey, Gwen. Didn't know you were coming in today." I stood up and gave her an easy smile. "I was just here to see Mikey."

"Yeah, I actually thought about going up to see him too, while I was here," Gwen agreed. "Is he awake still?"

"No, he just fell asleep actually. Maybe you can come visit tomorrow. I'm sure he'll need you to help him through math homework."

Gwen laughed. "I'm sure."

"How's Tim doing?" I asked, nodding over to the door she'd just come out of.

"He's sleeping a lot, I guess." She smiled back at me and laughed. "Although, to be fair, it's easier than taking one of Mrs. Smithe's tests. She was discharged and I hear we're going to have a test on all the movies the subs made us watch while she was out."

"Oh, great. I didn't pay attention to any of them." I laughed.

And then a moment of awkward silence passed; it was like we telepathically agreed on it, as though we were mourning the loss of our dignity.

I was grateful Gwen was the one to speak up first. "Hammy." She blushed and cleared her throat. "I thought about what you'd said before. And after seeing all this stuff on the news, and everything, I realized something."

"What's that?" I asked, my mouth drying out. *Why is she making me nervous?*

"Life is unexpected and just, I don't know, full of second chances." Her hands waved around in a jittery pattern as she explained. "Sorry, that's so … cliché but I thought about what you'd said and I remembered how last year, I'd watched you date Via—"

"Please, keep going with the cliché if you're going to move onto horror stories," I interrupted, feeling more like my old self.

"Sure," Gwen agreed, before continuing. "I had a big crush on you then, and then with everything that happened this year, I wanted to grow up and grow away from what I thought were childish things. And I grouped you in with those things, even though that's not true at all." She glanced up at me, as though she was expecting me to say something. And I didn't have a clue what I would say.

Again, I was relieved when she spoke up. "So, yes, I'd like to be your girlfriend. It's what I want." Then she laughed. "Gosh, isn't that just the most awkward way to say that? Sorry about that. I guess I'm just nervous."

Oh, Gwen, you don't know how awkward it really is, I thought.

Before I could say anything, she came up to me and kissed me.

It was a light brush of her mouth against mine. Like a butterfly landing, it was soft and swift, pressing into me the tenderness of springtime, and it was over before I really even began to decide how much I liked it.

Gwen pulled back from me and smiled. "That's how they're doing it in all the movies these days," she said with a giggle.

"Well, uh, thanks, Gwen," I started, but I wasn't sure what to say.

"Did you like it?" she asked.

"It was definitely a surprise," I told her with a smile.

"Great. Let's try to hang out soon, okay?" Gwen held up her phone. "My mom's here. She just texted me."

"Oh, ok. Well. Uh, bye. Bye then. See you tomorrow in class." That was it. That was all I could get out. It was fortunate that by the time Monday did come, all the girls who had heard about it had mistaken my stammering for some kind of true love rather than uncertainty. (Women!)

I'll never understand women. But at least there are some I can understand, I thought, as I glanced up and saw Raiya walking back to her desk behind me.

"Hey there, Humdinger," she smirked as she passed me. "You must have had a busy weekend; you're too tired to even try to trip me today."

I gritted my teeth. "No, I didn't have a busy weekend," I told her simply, almost grudgingly.

"Really? You don't look like your normal self. Usually you're telling people all about how you think the world should be bowing down to you by now."

The wave of irritation hit me hard. She was sure pushing it. "Why don't you just—"

"Time to start class," Mrs. Smithe called out, waltzing into the room. "Dinger, Raiya, get out your pencils!"

It was so nice to hear Martha's voice, authoritative and commanding as ever. I glanced up and smiled before reeling with shock.

Martha was *glowing*. Not just because she'd been released from the hospital, or that she had a test for us to take, but *glowing, as in supernatural healing*. Starry Knight must have stopped by her room, I realized. But why? Did she know Martha too?

I thought about what Starry Knight had told me before. I'd seen her, but I'd never know her.

Ugh, more problems to settle. But at least I would get to them; this kind of stuff was a priority now. So Elysian should be happy, I thought wryly.

There had been other changes, I knew, from the events of this weekend. There had been something in me which had awakened—much more subtle than power, but infinitely more important.

I could tell it was just a small change; so, I grimaced, it was probably one of the most significant ones I would ever make. And while I couldn't exactly explain what it was, I knew I was more aware—and somehow, more alive—because of it.

C. S. Johnson is the author of several young adult novels, including sci-fi and fantasy adventures such as *The Starlight Chronicles* series, the *Once Upon a Princess* saga, and the *Divine Space Pirates* trilogy. With a gift for sarcasm and an apologetic heart, she currently lives in Atlanta with her family.

THANK YOU FOR PICKING UP THIS BOOK!

To Get *Awakening* (A Special Christmas Episode of The *Starlight Chronicles*) for Free,

Download It At:

https://www.csjohnson.me/awakening

THE STARLIGHT CHRONICLES

AUTHOR'S NOTE

Dear Reader,

There is something terribly seductive about a good story.

After Book 1 finished, I was more than ready to work on what would eventually be *Calling*. But much like the storyline of *Calling*, my intention was muddled down with other pressing matters … most of which justified or demanded my endless coffee runs.

Appropriately, and coincidentally, this book, *Calling*, focuses on the idea of commitment. While *Slumbering* introduced the idea of belief, the fearsome question after acceptance remains yet to be answered, and sometimes even asked: What's next?

A lot of people have this terrible habit of believing stuff, and saying they belief this stuff, but not really changing how they live to reflect it. It is irritating, and I can't blame people for hating hypocrites—but I have been on both sides enough to know there is pain on both ends of belief or failing to act like I believe: Sacrifice on one end, and condemnation on the other.

That is more or less the issue Hamilton faces now. In my interim short story, the "Christmas episode," entitled "Awakening," Hamilton is given some hope despite his troubles that everything will work out. But now, after all his time and experiences, pain and suffering and loss, it is time to commit, or to reject, his power and his identity.

Commitment is hard. I know it is hard. To commit to anything is to lose free will in some other area. Commitment means an intense, incisive, goal-orientated approach to something. Whether it is your spouse, your faith, or your duty as a fallen Star to fight evil, it is hard not to sit back and think: "Why did I decide to do this again?" And then there is the added pressure we face from others: Bad mentors, like Elysian; the discouragers, like Starry Knight; and the idealistic pursuits of everyday life, such as the perfect date, social acceptance, familial duty, jobs/school, and the deep yearning, the desire to make a difference in the world.

What is the best way to commit? Learn more, spend time on it, interact with it, and practice. These are things which I am laughing at while I write this, because I am terrible at taking my own advice. So Hamilton and myself are good company for those who try, or even want to try, but feel overworked, under motivated, and need coffee way too often.

Yet we are both keeping on. We will see you again in Book 3!

Until We Meet Again,

C. S. Johnson

AUTHOR'S ACKNOWLEDGEMENTS

EDITOR

Jennifer C. Sell

Jennifer Clark Sell is a professional book editor and proofreader. She works from her home in Southern California. With her years of professional and personal experience, she offers several quality packages for authors. Find her at https://www.facebook.com/JenniferSellEditingService.

Photo Credit: Savannah Sell

AUTHOR'S ACKNOWLEDGEMENTS

COVER ILLUSTRATOR

Amalia Chitulescu

Amalia Iuliana Chitulescu is a digital artist from Campina, Romania. Raised in a small town, this self-taught artist has a technique which is delineated by the contrast between obscurity and enlightenment, using dark elements in a dreamy world. Her areas of expertise include the use of theatrical concepts to create a macabre and surrealistic world that still maintains a highly recognizable attachment to reality. Bridging a diaphanous environment with light elements, an eerie view, she creates a dream world of dark beauty, done with a blend of photography and digital painting. Find her at
https://www.facebook.com/Amalia.Chitulescu.Digital.Art

Photo Credit: Amalia Chitulescu

SAMPLE READING

Chapter 1 *from*

SUBMERGING

BOOK THREE of *THE STARLIGHT CHRONICLES*

C. S. Johnson

322

☼<u>1</u>☼
Expectancy

The smile flew up onto my face the moment I woke up. It was a good day to be me.

Psh. *Every day* is a good day to be me, I thought with a grin.

"Ah." I sighed happily as I sat up in my bed and stretched. I felt happy as a teenager could be. (It was very temporary, I assure you.)

"Ugh … is it morning already?" The changeling dragon on my bed, Elysian—my self-proclaimed supernatural mentor—rolled over onto his scaly back, shielding his eyes from the brightness of the springtime sunlight peeking through my bedroom window. He groaned groggily, and I stifled back a laugh.

"Come on, Ely," I quipped, shooting myself out of bed as I pushed down my brown hair from its bed-head form. "Today's a good day."

"Whoa. Who are you, and what have you done with the real Hamilton Dinger?" Elysian asked, using his bat-like wings to prop himself up.

I glanced over at the scaly dragon on my bed. I knew what he was thinking. Me? In a good mood? It was as rare as petroleum companies going green (meaning it was only done when enough people were ticked off). But there was a good reason I was happy.

The month of April had arrived, and while it came with scholarly benchmarks and horrendous amounts of rain, it also brought a special gift: My birthday.

"My seventeenth birthday is almost here." I grinned as I started getting ready for the day. "That means I get to start harassing my friends for presents, and my parents for money and a party, and maybe a car this year."

"And you'll pester me to start considering you mature, I'll bet." Elysian groaned again, this time with annoyance rather than lethargy. "Ugh, this is terrible."

"Just let it go, would you?"

I lost my grin momentarily as I caught sight of the mess on my desk; I hadn't had a chance to finish my homework from English. *Oh well.*

The homework didn't matter to me anyway. It's not like it was an important class. Really everyone (important) knows English today. Who really cares about books when you have the Internet? And who really cares about school when Mrs. Night is teaching? Her class must've been set up as a charity for capacity-challenged teachers. (I have to stop myself here; if there is one thing that makes me angry, it is incompetency).

There were many, many more important things to think about anyway. I was two years away from graduating high school. I had a great girlfriend, a good, *paid* internship at the Mayor's office, and a college scholarship or two lined up, with at least one full-ride. And even with all of that, there was nothing I wanted more than just *more*.

And I was going to get it. After all, I was also something of a superhero, a Starlight Warrior known to the public as "Wingdinger," and every day I was growing more in strength, power, and speed. A slight bubble of happiness swelled within my heart at the sight of the blood red, four-point star on my wrist—the mark that branded me as a defender of Earth and solidified my calling.

Yes, I thought. Change was coming, and along with it, growth, respect, and understanding.

There was nothing I wanted more, and I was finally okay with admitting it to myself.

"Birthdays don't strike me as happy, so much as depressing or pointless," Elysian remarked, drawing me out of my thoughts.

"I'm not surprised you hate birthdays," I replied, wrinkling my nose. "You seem to dislike anything of supreme importance."

"Birthdays are not that important to me," Elysian explained, "because I don't have one. But even a lot of humans don't seem to like birthdays that much. Some people even find them depressing."

"Just the women, I think," I replied. "Either that or the unimportant people."

Elysian rolled his eyes. "What's the point of celebrating the anniversary of your birth? It's not like you did anything to deserve a party. Mothers do all the work."

"It's just a day that celebrates the awesomeness of a person—and since I'm so awesome, my party's going to be awesome. And I want a car, too."

"Yes, how wonderfully mature and humble you are," Elysian muttered sarcastically. "Why do you even want a car, anyway? If you really need to go somewhere, you can ride on my back."

"I can't just ride you to school or take Gwen out on a date on your back," I retorted. I hoped he wouldn't push anymore on the subject. People don't make careers out of being superheroes—not really. What was I going to do when Elysian and I were no longer needed to take down the bad guys in Apollo City?

For good measure, I pretended to ignore the rest of my thoughts on the matter and focused on preparing for the day. "I'm supposed to meet Mikey and Gwen after work today, so I won't be home for a while."

"You have work? It's the weekend."

I rolled my eyes, irritated at Elysian. *He's supposed to be my mentor, but he doesn't even remember my schedule half the time. He's worse than my parents.*

While I'm not one for giving credit, I could at least admit my parents had proper excuses for not paying attention to me, much as it was still inexcusable. My parents, Mark and Cheryl, had their own jobs and my three-year-old brother, Adam, to look after. From what I could tell, Elysian only had to watch the news, slink around the city looking for our enemies, and … Well, that was about it, actually. And apparently even some of that was not necessary, since more often than not the monsters managed to find me anyway.

"Yes, I have work now. Remember, Cheryl got me that part-time job at the Mayor's office?"

Some part of me figured Elysian just didn't like to recall it. My job with the Mayor's office did not impress him in the slightest; I still got ticked off with him as I thought about his reaction. He was upset that it could interfere with my so-called superhero duties.

I was, even though I'd never admit it to Elysian's face, starting to understand where he was coming from on the issue.

Last fall, a meteorite landed in the middle of my home, Apollo City, smashing up a bunch of buildings and leaving a massive hole in the ground. I considered this an excellent symbol for what its arrival meant for my life.

It wasn't long after the meteorite struck that things started happening. Elysian had shown up, along with my previously-unknown superpowers. Elysian tried to convince me of my destiny to be a fallen Star, something he called an

Astroneshama (in "Star language," no less), and to use my abilities to fight off the other new arrivals to the city, the villainous Seven Deadly Sinisters, and their leader, Orpheus.

Somehow, I'd gone from all-around all-star high school student, top athlete, and class genius (not to mention charmingly irresistible and good-looking), Hamilton Dinger, to Wingdinger, the superhero of Apollo City, who was half-loved, half-hated, fully determined, and slightly irritated—a fallen Star on a mission to destroy evil and save the world (also still charmingly irresistible and good-looking).

It was a classic case of boy meets destiny. Or something like that, anyway.

Elysian rolled over and nuzzled into my now-empty bed, looking like a scaly dog of sorts as he wriggled around. I was half-tempted to rub his belly as a joke, but before I could, he snarled, "Oh, is that the job where you more or less file stuff for three to four hours a couple of times a week?"

"Shut up." I swatted at him. He dodged my blow and catapulted himself to the window, where he settled down like a huge lizard-cat.

"It's raining today," Elysian murmured as he glanced out the window to see the thunderclouds.

"It'll stop by the time I'm out of work." I shrugged it off easily enough.

"Would be a good day for our enemies to attack, too," Elysian observed.

"Seriously? What stops them from attacking any other day?" *What did rain have to do with anything?* "Wasn't it just once? I could think of tons of different attacks that didn't affect the weather."

"I guess you're right."

Of course I'm right.

"You might as well stop worrying about it." I grabbed the last of my English homework and stuffed it into the small briefcase I used for work. Glorified file boy or not, I was still getting paid good money and gaining good experience in the government sector; I was also largely unsupervised, so getting the rest of my English homework done wouldn't be a problem. "You might jinx us or something."

"I don't believe in jinxes."

"Good for you."

"I believe in being prepared–"

"Yeah, sure. You know, you worry too much."

"I wouldn't worry so much if you were more serious about this."

"I don't have to be serious about this," I argued, pulling on my shoes. "The bad guys have been really slacking off in the last couple of months. Ever since that sword was given to me—"

"Even though you haven't learned to use it properly—"

"—there haven't been that many attacks. Maybe they've given up—"

"Or maybe they're just biding their time—"

"—and have realized that they can't beat us—"

"Us? You mean you're sharing the credit all of a sudden?"

"Huh?" I looked up, a bit surprised. I'd gotten used to the broken, fragmented arguments between Elysian and myself, but it was always jarring to hear a completely different subject thrown into my train of thought (not to mention one I didn't particularly appreciate).

Elysian smirked. "You mean that you did that unintentionally? Goodness, what is the world coming to?" He giggled into his claws.

I frowned. I hated to be mocked—particularly by someone who wasn't supposed to be real. I was just about to say something (something especially vile, no doubt) when Elysian sighed, quickly losing the joking demeanor.

"I suppose," he said, "Starry Knight and SWORD have both helped us quite a bit lately."

Heat flushed through my face and I turned to the side, hiding my gaze at the mention of Starry Knight, my mysterious, most-of-the-time ally. "I don't think it matters that much," I muttered.

I knew I was lying, but there was nothing else I could do. Why Starry Knight was helping us, who she really was, and why did it matter at all were questions I desperately wanted to know the answers to myself; I could empathize with Elysian in this matter. But unlike him, from the small conversations and the time I'd spent with her, I knew it was going to take a lot of work and patience before she trusted me enough to give me answers.

"You never seem to think much at all where Starry Knight is concerned," Elysian huffed. "Why do you think SWORD is helping us?"

SWORD, the Special World Operations and Research Division, was a secret agency, from what I could tell, investigating the world of the paranormal and supernatural, and possibly the extraterrestrial. The reality that such a task force existed would not have bothered me at all if my best friend's estranged, runaway dad didn't happen to be in charge of the case file with my name on it.

"Well, Mikey's dad told us that SWORD came in to more or less gain control of the situation," I recalled, thinking of the one time they had captured me and Starry Knight. "And they've been doing a lot of clean-up work." I wrinkled my nose. "Chatty Patty, that obsessive anchorwoman for the city's cable news network, has less to report lately than I know she'd like."

Patricia Rookwood had her spies popping up closer to the battlefields lately, but SWORD agents had been getting good at turning several away. Ratings for her show have been down lately, too, I recalled. Ever since my last big standoff with Orpheus and the Sinisters, actually. The event had been hailed from the press as a severe "gas leak" that caused "hallucinations" in the central northern district of the city.

Thinking of that battle in particular, I glanced at the small, crystalline orb on my desk. I'd told my parents, and the maids as needed, that it was a paperweight. But that wasn't the full truth; it was actually the remnant of a Sinister, Meropae, I'd sealed away with my own sword a few months ago. (I did use it as a paperweight sometimes, though.)

It was almost proof I was capable of holding off the Sinisters on my own, without anyone else's help.

It was also an irritating memory, because the other Sinister I'd managed to seal away, Alcyonë, had been taken from me. Starry Knight laid claim to it the moment I showed it to her.

Irritation briefly shot through me. While I did want to work with Starry Knight, I was also upset with her on a regular basis. And it was mostly her fault.

"Why is Starry Knight helping us?" Elysian muttered. "That's the question that's been bothering me for a while now."

"What about Starry Knight?" I asked, trying my best to keep my tone neutral.

"I've heard of fallen Stars coming down to Earth before," Elysian said. When he saw the surprised look on my face, he snarled. "What? You didn't think you were the first, did you?"

I frowned. "Dante mentioned it," I admitted, "when I was in the SWORD's black site. But you've never mentioned it."

"It's not supposed to happen very often." Elysian shrugged. "Anyway," he continued, "I'm not surprised SWORD is well-versed in their situations. There are many things in this world not everyone is willing to accept. You can be the prime example in that one, kid."

"Shut up." I threw a pillow at him as he laughed. "Just stop," I muttered. "That's not who I am anymore."

"Definitely," Elysian agreed. There was enough of a pause in his words where solemnity had sneaked in, so I forgave him for his previous slight.

"Why are you so fixated on Starry Knight?" I asked again.

"I'm not the only one," Elysian said defensively. "You've always seemed to have a soft spot for her. I just realized too late that it was a soft skull."

"Are you really still angry I made you let her go at the end of that big battle with Orpheus?" I bristled. "Get over it. I told you I talked with her quite a bit in the prison at the black site, and … we came to an agreement, and that's really all there is to it."

"I doubt that." Elysian snorted, letting out a small stream of smoke through his dragon nose.

Part of me cringed; he was right. There *was* much more to it, but I couldn't even admit a lot of it to myself. I still hadn't told him about how I kissed her.

Memories of kissing her rushed through me, as if I'd suddenly crossed paths with a waterfall of warmth. My lips tinged with the sudden sensations of spices, prickly and perfect all at once.

I shook my head, trying to clear it. But I knew it was futile on some level, and reluctant on others.

"She's hiding something," Elysian declared.

I snorted, glad he'd been so caught up in his own thoughts that he didn't seen mine had been derailed. "That's pretty obvious. Congratulations on your stunning logic."

Elysian narrowed his yellowish-green eyes at me and flicked his tail. "*You* were the one I was meant to find," he said. "So why is she so intent on doing the job you were meant to do?"

"I don't see the big deal about that. I mean, you just said SWORD had helped us, too."

"What's her motivation, though?" He began to pace, which, considering he was a small dragon, was pretty hilarious to watch in my bedroom, but the sense of seriousness involved was unnerving. "It can't be to protect this world. After all, she'd just tried to destroy it to get them captured in her power that time … "

"My duty was to capture the Sinisters and protect the other people," I asserted. "Maybe hers was just to destroy the Sinisters. That's enough of a difference to make a difference, right?"

"Your mother would congratulate you on your lawyerspeak," Elysian muttered.

It was at that moment my mother, Cheryl, as though she knew we'd mentioned her, called up from downstairs.

"Hamilton! It's time for breakfast. Your turkey dumplings are going to get cold if you don't hurry."

"Ugh, not breakfast."

"What's wrong this time?" Elysian asked, more out of duty than desire to know.

"Cheryl's still on her meat-heavy, sugar-less diet," I explained. "I don't think I've actually eaten anything in this house since Helga came to cook for us." A mental image of

THE STARLIGHT CHRONICLES

my mother's heavyset Russian cook flashed across my mind, and I felt scars form instantly at its graze.

I might have liked her better if she didn't remind me so much of Mr. Lockard, my old, idiotic drama teacher. Helga was Lockard's unibrow twin, and that was no simple matter to just overlook. It was enough that it made me wonder if they were related, but I doubted it.

After getting his soul stolen and eaten last semester—the thought of which earned my mind another couple of scars—Lockard had been moved to hospice care, according to the gossip grapevine at the school. Helga, on my mother's pay, could afford better care than that. Some of the Sinisters' other victims had recovered quickly enough, after all.

Personally, I would think all the bloody, fresh meat of my mother's diet would be enough to disgust anyone out of a coma.

Cheryl called out again. "We have to get going soon. Stefano's expecting us at nine."

My stomach grumbled, angry it would be missing another meal. It was distracted along with me, however, when Elysian said, "Ugh, I still can't believe you took that stupid job. It's already getting in the way of our mission."

I gritted my teeth. There was just no end to the parade of irritation and idiots in my life. Between Elysian, the parentals, my brother, or the many minions of evil who want me dead or worse, I was beginning to think life was *supposed* to be hard.

But Cheryl was also right; the mayor, Stefano Mills, was nothing short of inspiring, and I hated the thought of letting him down or looking bad in front of him. And the sooner I got through work, the sooner I could meet with Gwen and Mikey to plan my birthday party. What could be better than getting a few hours in on the government's dollar, and then getting coffee with my girlfriend and my best friend, discussing my upcoming birthday party?

I'd have to argue with Elysian another time; it was no doubt likely to happen anyway. "You're one lucky dragon, Elysian, or I'd make your species extinct. I've got to go." With that remark, I hurried out the door and down the stairs.

"I don't believe in luck either!" Elysian called after me. "Besides," he added, no doubt more for his measure than mine, "there's still my brother that you would have to contend with."

Even though I was briefly intrigued, I shook my head. I let it go. After all, I had more important things to worry about and more interesting things to look forward to.

READY FOR BOOK 3?

Thank you for reading! Please leave a review for this book and check for other books and updates!